Stand Still Like the Hummingbird

Stand Still Like the Hummingbird

by Henry Miller

A New Directions Book

Manufactured in the United States of America
New Directions Books are published for James Laughlin
by New Directions Publishing Corporation
80 Eighth Avenue, New York 10011

TWENTIETH PRINTING

Contents

Preface

In reading this collection of essays, prefaces, reviews and what not the reader should bear in mind that these texts cover a span of twenty-five years or more and that they are not arranged in chronological order.* The wonder is that they hold together. It is apparent, nevertheless, that though one may shed his skin again and again one never loses his identity.

Rereading these texts, the thing which hits me in the eye is that if my view of life—my philosophy, if you will—has altered somewhat since *Tropic of Cancer* days, my views about society have not. I suspect that those who cannot stomach *Tropic of Cancer* will not be able to take this book either. The ideas herein presented should prove as unpalatable to the squeamish as the account of my seamy adventures in the early days in Paris.

In this instance, however, new epithets will have to be coined to describe my bad taste. There is nothing obscene about any of the material presented. *And,* there is a beginning and end to each piece, whether obvious or not. I might even say that there is a thread which runs throughout and which holds these pieces together, loosely strung though they be.

The tenor of most of them, though strongly critical of our way of life, is nevertheless strictly kosher. America is seen through the eyes of an American, not a Hottentot. And Europe, which is often favorably contrasted with America, is a Europe which only an American might have eyes for.

* See *Bibliography of Henry Miller,* by Thomas H. Moore, published by the Henry Miller Literary Society, 121 North 7th Street, Minneapolis, Minnesota; or *Henry Miller: An Informal Bibliography,* by Esta Lou Riley, Forsyth Library, Fort Hays Kansas State College, Hays, Kansas. Both 1961.

So what, my dear compatriots? How will you label me now? Un-American? It won't fit, I'm afraid. I'm even more American than you, only against the grain. Which, if you will think a moment, serves to put me in the tradition. Nothing I have said against our way of life, our institutions, our failings, but what you will find even more forcibly expressed in Thoreau, Whitman, Emerson. Even before the turn of the century Whitman had addressed his fellow Americans thus: "You are in a fair way to create a whole nation of lunatics."

It is true, of course, that today the whole world seems to have gone mad. But, like it or not, we are in the van, we are leading the procession. Always first and foremost, what!

The dominant theme throughout this book is the plight of the individual, which of course means the plight of society, since society is meaningless unless composed of individuals. Two of the individuals I have profiled in this book symbolize the nature of the dilemma referred to. I mean Kenneth Patchen, our own American poet, and George Dibbern, the first and only "citizen of the world." The piece on Patchen was written back in 1947; his situation hasn't altered a whit since, unless for the worse. He has been suffering from one serious ailment after another ever since I first met him, in 1940. Today, after several major operations, he is in constant pain, unable because of his allergy to drugs to take anything stronger than aspirin. And, though he has written many more books of poetry and prose since I first wrote about him, though he has painted hundreds more covers for his books, he still remains unrecognized by the public at large. As for George Dibbern, he is exactly where he was when he started; at the age of seventy-one he is working as a stevedore somewhere in New Zealand. That is what happens when one refuses to compromise. We know the fate of Melville, of Poe, of Hart Crane, to mention only the most familiar names. The list is long, and the accounts of the tribulations which our men of genius have endured are shameful to read. Like the Indians whom we pushed to the wall, the true individuals, the creative spirits in our midst, are condemned from the start. Meanwhile there flourishes a flock of foundations whose directors have a genius for aiding mediocrities.

No, things have not changed a whit since *Tropic of Cancer* days, unless for the worse. *La vie en rose* is definitely not for the artist. The artist—I employ the term only for the genuine ones—is still suspect, still regarded as a menace to society. Those who conform, who play the game, are petted and pampered. Nowhere else in the world, unless it be in Soviet Russia, do these conformists receive such huge rewards, such wide recognition for their efforts.

So much for the dominant note. As for the subdominant, the thought is—don't wait for things to change, the hour of man is now and, whether you are working at the bottom of the pile or on top, if you are a creative individual you will go on producing, come hell or high water. And this is the most you can hope to do. One has to go on believing in himself, whether recognized or not, whether heeded or not. The world may seem like hell on wheels—and we are doing our best, are we not, to make it so?—but there is always room, if only in one's own soul, to create a spot of Paradise, crazy though it may sound.

When you find you can go neither backward nor forward, when you discover that you are no longer able to stand, sit or lie down, when your children have died of malnutrition and your aged parents have been sent to the poorhouse or the gas chamber, when you realize that you can neither write nor not write, when you are convinced that all the exits are blocked, either you take to believing in miracles or you stand still like the hummingbird. The miracle is that the honey is always there, right under your nose, only you were too busy searching elsewhere to realize it. The worst is not death but being blind, blind to the fact that everything about life is in the nature of the miraculous.

The language of society is conformity; the language of the creative individual is freedom. Life will continue to be a hell as long as the people who make up the world shut their eyes to reality. Switching from one ideology to another is a useless game. Each and every one of us is unique, and must be recognized as such. The least we can say about ourselves is that we are American, or French, or whatever the case may be. We are first of all human beings, different one from another, and obliged to live together, to stew in the same pot. The creative spirits are the fecundators: they are the *lamed vov* who keep the world from falling apart. Ignore them, suppress them, and society becomes a collection of automatons.

What we don't want to face, what we don't want to hear or listen to, whether it be nonsense, treason or sacrilege, are precisely the things we must give heed to. Even the idiot may have a message for us. Maybe I am one of those idiots. But I will have my say.

It's a long, long way to Tipperary, and as Fritz von Unruh has it, "the end is not yet."

HENRY MILLER
February 16, 1962
California

Stand Still Like the Hummingbird

The Hour of Man

Walking the highway with Walker Winslow, after we had finished
our work for the day, we often found ourselves returning to the
same subject—the miraculous simplicity and effectiveness of mutual aid. As a one-time member of Alcoholics Anonymous,
Walker had had ample opportunity to observe the startling results which a mere sense of solidarity could produce. If the alco-
holic who regarded himself as helpless and hopeless could find
comfort and sustenance through mere association with others
similarly afflicted, what about other sufferers, other addicts, other
victims of society? (Which is to say, the great majority of mankind.) Are we not all virtually in the same boat? How many of us
are masters of our fate? How many of our friends or acquaint-
ances can we point to and say: "There is a liberated individual!"
Or even: "There is a self-sufficient individual!"

The substance of our thoughts I might summarize thus: Supposing that we all considered ourselves members of, not an organization, but an ancient, durable order, the only one we can
truly give allegiance to—humanity. Supposing that, instead of
blame and censure, or judgment and punishment, we met deviations and aberrations of the norm with sympathy and understanding, with a desire to aid rather than a desire to protect ourselves.
Supposing we based our security solely upon the certitude of mutual aid. Supposing we scrapped the web of complicated laws in
which we are now hopelessly enmeshed and substituted the un-
written law that no cry of distress, no appeal for help, should go
unnoticed. Is not the instinct to aid one another just as strong,
stronger indeed, than the impulse to condemn? Do we not suffer
from the disuse of this instinct, from its usurpation by the state
and charitable organizations of every kind? If we knew, in brief,

1

that whatever our plight, whatever the cause of it, we had but to announce it and we would be succored, would not most of the ills which now plague us fall away of themselves? Are we not all victims of fear and anxiety precisely because we lack faith and trust in one another? And more so because we lack the intelligence to recognize a power and a wisdom greater than our own?

There is a short prayer which is often employed by members of Alcoholics Anonymous. It goes thus: "God grant us the serenity to accept the things we cannot change, courage to change the things we can, and wisdom to know the difference."

To get to the crux of the problem, which had become almost obsessive, here is what we asked each other: "Can one really aid another individual, and if so, how?"

The question was answered, of course, long ago by Jesus in a simple, direct way, one which today we are prone to call a Zen-like way. Jesus made a number of explicit statements, injunctions really. All to the effect that one was to take no thought but to respond immediately to any appeal for aid. And to respond in large measure. To give your cloak as well as your coat, to walk two miles and not one. And as we know well, with these injunctions went another, more important one—to return good for evil. "Resist not evil!"

Throughout the parables of Jesus there is implicit another most wholesome idea, that we are not to seek trouble, not to go about trying to patch things up, not to endeavor to convert others to our way of thinking, but to demonstrate the truth which is in us by acting instinctively and spontaneously when confronted with an issue. To do our part and trust in the Lord, in other words.

By responding with a full spirit to any demand which is made upon us we aid our fellow man to help himself. For Jesus there was no problem involved. It was simple. By giving the full measure of oneself—more, in other words, than was demanded—you restored to the one in need his human dignity. You gave from the cup that was overflowing. The need of the other instantly vanished. Because it was met by the inexhaustible reservoir of spirit. And spirit answers to spirit.

The answer, then, is to be ever in readiness, to do the immediate, and to give without stint. Not to examine the other's motives, or one's own, not to debate, not to procrastinate, not to wonder about the result of one's action—and certainly not to look for approval, approbation or reward. If it works for the individual, it will work for society as a whole. One is not responsible to society but to God.

To work a radical transformation all that was required, as we saw it, was to put into practice the simple injunction: "Do unto others as you would have others do unto you." No beliefs, no worship, no ten commandments, no ceremonials, no churches, no organization of any kind. No waiting for a better government, better laws, better working conditions, better this, better that. Begin this moment, wherever you find yourself, and take no thought of the morrow. Look not to Russia, China, India, not to Washington, not to the adjoining county, city or state, but to your immediate surroundings. Forget Buddha, Jesus, Mohammed and all the others. Do your part to the best of your ability, regardless of the consequences. Above all, do not wait for the next man to follow suit.

It seemed so absolutely clear and simple to us. Too clear, too simple, perhaps. Whoever endeavors to act upon this truth has to have the courage of the lion, the tenacity of the bull, the wiliness of the serpent, and the innocence of the dove. It nevertheless remains an illuminating fact that it is only the presence of a handful of men, in every age, that keeps society from degenerating utterly. Tradition has it that these few remain ever anonymous, and that it is they who inspire the illustrious ones.

In a short article called "The Hour of Man,"* Walker attempted to set forth his views. The article begins thus:

> Recently, in a great mental hospital, I sat with a team of scientists who were selecting patients for lobotomy—a drastic surgical procedure that sometimes desensitizes the afflicted to his affliction by damaging the brain tissue. Before each patient appeared, his or her case history was read. Here were stories of broken homes, of jealousy, of natural fear of an economic or social consequence, of people kept in ignorance of sex, and, finally, of people subjected to the terror of

* See *Manas,* January 31, 1951 issue: Los Angeles, California.

war. None of these people had organically damaged brains, none was suffering from physical illness. The cleavage between the life their birth had promised them and the life we as society had inflicted upon them had been too great for their emotional resources.

Oddly enough, one of the criterions of selection for lobotomy was that the patient be able to return to a better environment than the one he or she had come from. Only when this was assured would the surgeon ply the knife. That night I saw one man plead with tears in his eyes for an operation that would leave him forever somewhat dulled. He wanted his sensitivity diminished until he could stand the world in which he had to live. Better environment indeed!

After citing some phenomenal statistics relative to the yearly consumption of alcohol and drugs of every description in "this land of opportunity," he states:

I have wandered in and out of the mental hospitals of the land, studied the mental hygiene movements, and looked to many organizations for a solution to my own problems and the prevention of an occurrence of those problems in others. In one year I interviewed 1,400 alcoholics. I found many noble and dedicated men and women and a legion of sufferers but among them I have found no ready answer.

He then goes on to say:

I want to see the radio or television turned off for an hour a week, the paper or magazine laid aside, the car locked safely in the garage, the bridge table folded, the liquor bottle corked, and the sedatives kept tightly in their packages. I want to see production and consumption forgotten for this hour. Politics must be forgotten, national or international. The hour that I propose could be called *The Hour of Man*. During this hour man could ask himself and his neighbor just what purpose they are serving on earth, what life is, what a man or woman can rightly ask of life as well as what they must give in return. If that man is working and struggling for what he really wants, is it worth the price he pays in personal suffering? Neighbors should learn to listen intently to neighbors. In only that way will the eye turn inward. In other people's souls they could see the undistorted image of their own souls. As they helped others they would help themselves.

I must confess that this idea of getting a whole nation to come to a full stop, if only for an hour once a week, in order to think and meditate, has great appeal for me. I believe the results would be fantastic. And it *could* be done, though it sounds chimerical now. The Moslem world unites in prayer daily when the muezzin calls from his minaret. But when has any community knocked off in order to devote a few minutes to the problems which beset the community? Thinking and meditating, in unison, about a given problem—what possibilities it offers! I venture to say that, given such a procedure, we would receive from the mouths of our *children* the most sagacious, practicable and fecund observations and suggestions. As things stand today, even the intelligent man is ruled out of the councils of our leaders. Despite all the talk about freedom of speech, freedom of the press, electoral freedom, and so on, I dare say it would be a shock to know what the common man thinks about the problems which confront the world. The common man is always cleverly set off one against the other, children are always ruled out, young people are ordered to conform and obey, and the views of the wise, the saintly, the true servers of mankind, are forever scorned as impractical.

No, it would be a grand thing for any community, large or small, to set aside even five minutes of the day for serious contemplation. If nothing more were to result than the recognition of such a feeling as "community" it would be a great step forward. If it be true that we have not yet accepted the fact that we are members of "one world," or even of one nation, how much more true it is that we are not even members of the little communities to which we belong. We become more and more atomized, more and more separate and isolate. We hand our problems over to our respective governments, absolving ourselves of duty, conscience and initiative. We do *not* believe in personal example, though we profess to worship that great exemplar Jesus the Christ. We hide from the face of reality: it is too terrible, we think. Yet it is *we,* we, only we, who have created this hideous world. And it is *we* who will change it—by changing our own inner vision.

The truly lamentable thing about *la condition humaine* is that nine-tenths of the problems which overwhelm us could be solved overnight. They are by no means insuperable problems. All the energies now harnessed to inconsequential, idiotic, degrading and destructive ends could be converted to useful and ennobling ends by a mere shift of position, or attitude. Only a very few souls, at any time in man's history, have been privileged to battle with the great problems, the problems worthy of man. Whenever my mind runs in this channel I think of the English novelist Claude Houghton, the only writer I know of to do it, who invariably frees his protagonist early in the book of the usual mundane problems which ordinary people spend their lives vainly wrestling with. No wonder he is styled a "metaphysical" novelist! And yet it is only by freeing a "character" from the usual everyday problems, that the author may hope to present him as unique and worthy of attention. Arm a man with his God-given powers, set him face to face with reality, then let us see what shape and substance *human* problems may really assume! Sometimes it seems to me that the only heroes are the saintly ones. Doing good, battling for the right, giving to the needy, succoring the weak, preaching, converting, educating the young, what does all this amount to except to remind us that we are only partly developed, partly realized, partly living! The blind lead the blind, the sick minister unto the sick, the strong rule the weak.

The purpose of life! Aye, what is it if not to enjoy life? How can one begin to enjoy life if he is half-dead?

Let me quote a paragraph from Eric Gutkind's little-known book:*

The "pious" attitude, asceticism, spirituality, contrition —these turn the white heat of God into a comfortable household fire. Religion makes God harmless. Our earthly existence unrolls itself before the countenance of Him Whom no man may look upon and live. And this ineffable

* *The Absolute Collective:* published by C. W. Daniel Co., Ltd., London, 1937.

paradox is whittled down to the dimensions of a vision which will conveniently fit to our everyday requirements. Our glorious inescapeable feeling for *this* world was thus made ready to open a hundred ways of escape. But turning our gaze inwards we mistook spirituality for reality. The joy of meeting with God withered before a hateful theology. Religion has betrayed us. It has tricked us out of that miracle of miracles which enables us, when our last hope of escape has died, to rise and attain to absolute reality, to eternal meaning, where, not consumed but tempered in the white heat of God we can proclaim that "all the ways of the earth are ways to heaven" and that the "other world," however distant and remote, is nothing but this created world made manifest. Under the constraint of religion life has never been complete and untroubled. Neither world nor man has as yet truly been.

There speaks a man of God.

And now let us make an imaginary jump for a moment. Let us suppose that man, having grown weary of his ineffectual achievements—miracle drugs, lobotomy performances, atomic bugaboos—suddenly begins to develop his psychic powers. Let us suppose that, through concentrating his whole attention upon the acquisition of such powers, he succeeds in eliminating disease altogether, restoring the dead to life, and even more astounding miracles. Let us grant him that dominion over nature and over the creature world which he has ever craved. Then what? By way of answer I give a story which Ramakrishna once related to his listeners.

There was another Siddha, who was very proud of his psychic powers. He was a good man and an ascetic. One day the Lord came to him in the form of a saint and said: "Revered sir, I have heard that thou possessest wonderful powers." The good man received him kindly and gave him a seat. At this moment an elephant passed by. The saint asked him: "Sir, if thou desirest, canst thou kill this elephant?" The Siddha replied: "Yes, it is possible," and taking a handful of dust, he repeated some *mantram* over it, and threw it on the elephant. Immediately the animal roared, fell on the ground in agony and died. Seeing this,

the saint exclaimed: "What wonderful power thou possessest! Thou hast killed such a huge creature in a moment!"
The saint then entreated him, saying: "Thou must also possess the power to bring him back to life." The Siddha replied: "Yes, that is also possible." Again he took a handful
of dust, chanted a *mantram,* threw it on the elephant, and
lo! the elephant revived and came back to life. The saint
was amazed at the sight and again exclaimed: "How wonderful indeed are thy powers! But let me ask thee one question. Thou hast killed the elephant and brought him back to
life; what hast thou gained? Hast thou realized God?" Thus
saying, the saint disappeared.*

"To speak ever anew of God, this should be our central task,"
said Eric Gutkind.

Let me quote him more fully since his words are a sublime
summation of and an answer to all that has been touched upon in
the foregoing pages.

> God, world, and man. What is, what may be, what should
> be. God, the one and only reality. World, the completely
> relative and insubstantial scene. Man, spoken to and an-
> swering, summoned to come to reality. God, who does not
> wish to be alone. World, which cannot be alone. Man, who
> should not be alone. These three, united in "The People,"
> which is the "Absolute Collective. . . ."
> The completed unity of the three in "The People" has
> nothing that savors of escape, nothing national or earth-
> born, nothing ideological. It is concrete through and
> through. In the blind alley we find subjective man. He is
> shut up within himself; autistic, inwardly broken, though
> outwardly secure—the burgher. Nothing is alive in his
> world. Everything is closed, everything dead. He denies
> God. The one supreme and transcendent idea which alone
> gives meaning to man is to him an object of derision. No—
> we must venture again and again upon that highest union,
> that source of all other unions, that meeting of God, man,
> and the world. No one of the three must be tampered with.

* *The Gospel of Ramakrishna;* published by The Vedanta Society, New
York, 1947.

To speak ever anew of God, this should be our central task. But only he will have the strength to do this who does not only talk *about* God, but is able to speak *to* God Himself. Not for a moment must this discourse be interpreted in a theological sense, though we may hear it in the ring of ancient words charged with the human fervor of bygone ages. And he is best fitted to speak with God who knows how to speak with man and who can proclaim the fullness of the glory of the world. The absolute unity of all beings which is reached in the gathering together of men who have become completed in their humanity, free from fear, nature and ideology—this is the true "Tabernacle of the meeting with God," the tabernacle of the present. The present is free both from the passage of time and from "the world beyond." The world is there. Man is raised up. Whoever is aware of Him possesses the present.*

To come back to Walker and the "hour of man." Was anything gained by these talks? Yes and no. Certainly the hour has not yet struck for such an idea to be taken seriously. Man is still shaping the destiny of the world in negative fashion. He has not yet come to the last impasse. He is not desperate enough yet to join the A.A. or its more universal equivalent. He looks forward to having one more bout, possibly two or three, before showing the white flag. He is still satisfied with explanations which explain nothing, with experiments which he knows in his heart are only halfway measures and consequently more productive of evil than of good. He is still willing to make room for new gods, new religions—more from unbelief than belief. He adamantly refuses to acknowledge that within the immediate focus of vision is the source of revelation. In a rock he sees nothing more than a rock, in a flower nothing more than a flower, and in man nothing more than man. Yet the truth is that in the most insignificant object of creation the secret of all creation lies hidden.

Though it seems at times as if nothing could rout him out of the inertia in which he is entrenched, it is quite possible that he may one day be *shocked* into a greater state of awareness. Precept and example seem to have had little effect: basically the civ-

* *The Absolute Collective, op. cit.*

ilized man is little different from primitive man. He has not
accepted the world, neither has he shown any desire to partake
of the reality which invests it. He is still bound to myth and taboo,
still the slave of the victim of history, still the enemy of his own
brother. The simple, obvious truth, that to accept the world is to
transform it, seems utterly beyond his powers of comprehension.

If the gate will not give way it must be forced. Nothing can
dam the rising tide. And all the evidence points to the fact that
the tide *is* rising. Let man make himself as secure as he imagines,
the gate will give way.

Children of the Earth

After an absence of thirteen years certain aspects of France stand out like fragments of a forgotten dream. It is particularly refreshing to observe the remarkable behavior and apparent contentment, often with little, of French children. Wise beyond their years, they seem no less joyous on that account.

In France one realizes immediately that one is living in a world of adults; the children take second place. With us, as everyone knows, the children seem to come first. As a result we have men and women who have never matured, who are eternally dissatisfied, and who have no real respect for anything, least of all for one another. Is not much of the morbid, frenetic activity of the American traceable to the restlessness and discontent of childhood? The needless destruction and reconstruction which is constantly going on, presumably in the name of progress, is of a pattern with the behavior of the spoiled child who, weary of his building blocks, destroys with a sweep of the hand what he has struggled for hours to create. The only valid reality with us seems to be that of the kindergarten.

We bewail the role of the mother in America, her domination in all spheres of activity, but is it not the result of the abdication of the male? If the man is nothing but a worker and provider is it not inevitable that the woman take over the reins? To the American woman the male, whether husband, son or lover, is a creature to be bullied, exploited and traduced.

The visitor to France cannot help but be impressed by the smiling look of the land. Love of the soil is an expression which still has meaning here. Everywhere there is evident the touch of the human hand; it is a constant, patient, loving attention which the French give to their soil. Indeed, one is almost tempted to

11

say that it is love of soil rather than love of country or love for one's neighbor which dominates.

Chez nous the hand is almost defunct. Wherever it is possible to use the machine the hand is replaced by this monster which performs the most prodigious labours, miracles often, but at what a cost! The ruthless exploitation of the soil, in America, is now a familiar story everywhere, but the tragedy of it has not fully penetrated the consciousness of the European. He too would like to use the machine to the fullest—but without paying the price exacted of us. He would like to reap the benefits of the machine age without sacrificing his traditional mode of life, which of course is an utter impossibility.

As one who has enjoyed the benefits of two utterly different worlds, what never ceases to cause me bewilderment is the seeming impossibility of one country to bestow its virtues upon another—or to exchange them, were better said. At a time when communication is no longer a problem, when it takes only a matter of hours to travel from one end of the world to another, the barriers between peoples, between so-called "free peoples," are stronger than ever. Despite the Marshall Plan, despite the steady invasion of hordes of tourists, despite the existence of radio and television, despite the perpetual threat of war, it seems to me that the French and Americans have less in common today than prior to 1914. What, to be honest, have we imbibed of French culture, or the art of living? Almost nothing, I would say. Whatever seeps through is arrested on the intellectual plane; the populace remains immune.

As for France, what has she in the way of comforts—which is about all we have to offer of value? To me it is as if nothing had changed since I left in 1939. I see no radical change in the French way of life. All the so-called comforts and improvements which Americans are endlessly striving to create—and in the process making themselves wretched and uncomfortable—are missing here. Everything is still antiquated and complicated. Nothing gets done with dispatch and efficiency.

It must seem strange that one who so heartily despises the American way of life should remark on the un-American aspects of French life, but what I deplore are half measures. The

French do not despise comfort, they envy us for it; they admire
efficiency but are temperamentally unsuited, it would seem, to
practice it. An inexplicable inertia seems to hold them in its
grip. *"Français, encore un tout petit effort!"* I sometimes say to
my intimate French friends. It is what the divine Marquis urged
after the fall of the Bastille.

Every time I venture out into the world I find myself asking if
people really want to change. It is so very rare to find an individual who is content with his mode of life. Even the great souls
appear to be disturbed, if not by reason of their own shortcomings then because of humanity's sad lot. Those who have sur-
mounted these problems, or transcended them, are virtually unknown to us; they are already living in the world of the future.
It is interesting to reflect that, could one question these isolated
spirits, these mages, sages or saints, the answer would probably
be: "Accept the world as it is!" Only through complete acceptance, they would insist, does one arrive at emancipation.
    But it is not emancipation that the great majority seeks. When
pressed, most men will admit that it takes but little to be happy.
(Not that they practice this wisdom!) Man craves happiness
here on earth, not fulfillment, not emancipation. Are they utterly deluded, then, in seeking happiness? No, happiness *is* de-
sirable, but it is a by-product, the result of a way of life, not a
goal which is forever beyond one's grasp. Happiness is achieved
en route. And if it be ephemeral, as most men believe, it can
also give way, not to anxiety or despair, but to a joyousness
which is serene and lasting. To make happiness the goal is to kill
it in advance. If one must have a goal, which is questionable, why
not self-realization? The unique and healing quality in this attitude toward life is that in the process goal and seeker become
one.
    Reflections of this order are most frequently dismissed as being
mystical. They are not, of course. They are of the very essence of
reality. Nor are there a dozen different kinds of reality. There is
but one, the reality of life, a reality which is shot through with
truth. It is not to drown myself in the bogs of mysticism or meta-
physics that I make use of such moot terms as reality and truth.

There is something which endures, something which underlies and gives meaning to daily life, and it is in connection with this ever-present fund of creation that such terms have significance. That we have made of them empty symbols to be juggled by theologians and metaphysicians is to acknowledge that we have bled life of all meaning.

There are moments in human history when, through lack of faith, lack of vision, man becomes identified with the frightening forces of chaos. Identified, let me add, not in a grandiose way but pitiably, like a vain sacrifice. Faced as we are today with possible annihilation, where is the ark, and with whom can a covenant be made? The catastrophe which menaces us, moreover, comes not from on high, but from man's own thoughts and deeds. He is begging for destruction at his own hands.

Either we are at this awesome point in time or the destruction which threatens has been grossly exaggerated. In any case the decision which each one now makes for himself will determine the swing of the pendulum.

I have often been criticized and ridiculed as a prophet of doom. It is true that hope is not a word to which I attach great importance. Nor even faith, in the sense of belief. Now and then, like the prophets of old, I have gone so far as to exult over the approaching doom. It was not man I condemned, however, but his way of life. For if there is one power which man indubitably possesses—have we not had proof of it again and again?—it is the power to alter one's way of life. It is perhaps man's only power.

To condemn the whole structure of society does have a ring of madness. More particularly when nothing tangible, nothing specific, nothing remotely resembling a panacea, is proffered. To urge, like the men of old, "Look to thyself!" is to invite ridicule. One can understand why five-year, ten-year, twenty-year programs are more palatable. One can also understand why it is easier to accept the theory of man's snail-like development than to invoke the advent of the miraculous. But which is more life-like, more fecundating—to regard oneself as the sport of an evolutionary hypothesis, and resign oneself to the march of time, or act as a responsible, creative being who, whatever the risk, is willing to assume the consequences of his acts?

The old man, ancestral man, is on his way out. Man has no age, except in the eyes of anthropologists. There is the man of yesterday and the man of tomorrow. Time plays no part in the quickening of the spirit. The gate is ever open. Today is like all other days. There is only today.

The impasse in which we now find ourselves is the result of looking two ways simultaneously. Perhaps there is no way out. But there may be a way in, a way back to the source of life. Of what use to raise the question of security, or even of survival? Who would want to live amid the ruins of his world?

In penning these last words a hideous truth suddenly assaults me. Has man not been living amid the ruins of this world for millennia? Go back as far as you will, you will meet only with the evidences of his abortive efforts. Man, as man, has never realized himself. The greater part of him, his potential being, has always been submerged. What is history if not the endless story of his repeated failures?

Man has his being not in a vacuum of historical facts but in a realm of magic and mystery. Only in the myth does he have the courage to acknowledge the glory of his origin, the power of his spirit.

Again and again it has been pointed out that there is no issue on the historical level. No genuine solutions are possible through political, social or economic changes, or even through moral transformations. The only level on which a vital, meaningful change may take place is the level of spirit. To be regenerate means that one may travel back to the source, recover the creative powers with which to meet all problems. In the eternal trigon—God, Man, World—we have the three fundamental aspects of creation. Man is the measure of all three. He *is* that which he has named God and put beyond him. He *is* the world in all its multifarious aspects. But he is not yet *man* in that he refuses to accept the conditions of his sovereignty. By his refusal to live to the fullest he brings about the death of God and the utter meaninglessness of the world in which he finds himself.

After all that man has suffered and endured throughout the ages it seems scarcely possible to believe that any fresh catastrophe, however terrible, however widespread, will cause him to alter his ways. His proclivity to submit, to bend the back—a proneness to abdicate, one might call it—seems inexhaustible. A thoroughly crucified being, he chooses to revolve on the wheel of hope and longing. The astounding variety of disorders—physical, mental and social—which now ravage humankind would indicate that it is the soul of man which is in revolt. For all his ills the only counsel that is offered him is: "Dog, return to your vomit!"

Of one thing he is now certain, that hell is not in some hereafter but here on earth, and that it is he, and he alone, who has made it such.

The whole activity of the race now seems to have but one end —to make life more and more the agony which it has become. Whether one functions separately or collectively, harmoniously or otherwise, the end points to disaster. Revolt has become meaningless. Man is in revolt against himself. How can he overthrow himself?

Life is not the tool of death. Life seeks ever to manifest itself more abundantly. It is not death, moreover, that man fears; it is the thought that he may cease to be. It is only when we give up that death takes over. Death is not the end of life, much less the goal. It is but another aspect of life. There is nothing but life, even among the dead.

I come back to the children, the children of the world who have done nothing to bring about the present gruesome condition of things. As a father or mother one must hang one's head in shame. Even the best of parents are condemned to look on helplessly. What about the fate of our children . . . is there nothing to be done for them? If there were still a spark of mercy, still a grain of intelligence left in the human race, would it not be possible, even at this late hour, to do something about the plight of our progeny? Is there not a domain, a haven of safety, somewhere in this wide, wide world where the children of all the peoples of the earth could be gathered and protected against the folly and stupidity of their elders?

To rouse the sluggish minds of adults to such a point of awareness is in itself an almost insuperable task. But even more difficult, assuming that this might be accomplished, would be the
task of getting them to agree as to how their young should be
reared and by whom. In their present state of madness one is
inclined to suspect that they would rather the young perished
with them than risk the possibility of seeing them grow up into
fearless, independent-minded, peace-loving individuals. Any solution, indeed, which envisages a separate fate for our children
must seem, at the moment, utterly chimerical. That children
have a special claim to life, a life uncontaminated by the vicious
influence of their elders, is still unthinkable. A simple peasant,
threatened with calamity, has sense enough to make provision
for his seed, but the race as a whole, faced with its own imminent destruction, lacks the will and the wisdom to provide
against the day of destruction. To die in root, seed and flower—
that is man's seeming purpose.

Confronted with the naked horror of the world as one knows it
today, I relive the anguish, the melancholy, the despair which I
knew as a young man. The vacation which I had hoped to enjoy
by going abroad has become an ordeal of a strange, intangible
sort. Viewing the world as would a visitor from another planet,
I have become involved once again in the throes of universal
torment. As a young man, brash, impulsive, ridden with ideals,
I came close to being annihilated by the sorrow and misery which
surrounded me on all sides. To do something for my fellow man,
to help deliver him, became my personal affair. Like every fanatical idealist, I ended by making my own life so miserable and
complicated that soon all my time, all my efforts, all my in-
genuity, were consumed in the mere struggle to survive. Though
speedily disillusioned as to my own powers, I never became indifferent to the plight of those about me. It did appear to me,
however, that something like a stubborn refusal to be aided was
inherent in man's nature. In the process of saving my own skin
I gained a little wisdom, a greater sense of reality, and a compas-
sion which stilled the senseless conflicts that had ravaged me.
     Years later, many years later, in a manner altogether providen-
tial, I found myself living the life I had always desired to live, as

a member of a small community, seemingly isolated and apart from the world. In these last years at Big Sur I have tasted to the full the bitterness of Hell and the delights of Paradise. Above all, I found a place in my own native land which I could call "home."

Living in this remote corner of the world, I came to discover that one can be "out of the world," as they say, yet closer to the earth and to all creation. It never occurred to me that I had deserted the ranks. On the contrary, I had the impression that for the first time in my life I was giving myself the chance to live the life which every sincere, sensitive, well-meaning individual desires to live.

Living apart and at peace with myself, I came to realize more vividly the meaning of the doctrine of acceptance. To refrain from giving advice, to refrain from meddling in the affairs of others, to refrain, even though the motives be the highest, from tampering with another's way of life—so simple, yet so difficult for an active spirit! Hands off! Yet not to grow indifferent, or refuse aid when it is sincerely demanded. Living thus, practicing this simple way of life, strange things occurred; some might call them miraculous. And from the most unexpected quarters astonishing, most instructive lessons. . . .

And all the while an obsessive desire was shaping itself, namely, to lead the anonymous life. The significance of this urge I can explain simply—to eradicate the zealot and the preacher in myself. "Kill the Buddha!" the Zen master is known to say occasionally. Kill the futile striving, is the thought. Do not put the Buddha (or the Christ) beyond, outside yourself. Recognize him in yourself. Be that which you are, completely.

Naturally, when one attains to this state of awareness, there is no need, no urge, to convert the other to one's way of thinking. It is not even necessary, as Vivekananda once phrased it, to go about doing good. The unknown Buddhas, those who preceded Gautama, he asserted, made no stir in the world. They were content to shed the light which was in them. Their sole purpose in living was to live, to live each day as if life were a blessing and not an ordeal or a curse.

To such emancipated souls what difference could it make in what circumstances they found themselves? To them Paradise was not associated with a remote and isolated corner of the earth, any more than in a beyond, nor was it to be attained, as a state of mind, through an austere and singular manner of living. They were free in every sense of the word. It mattered not what role they adopted or were obliged to live out. Even to live the life of a slave could hold no terror for them. They were in the world and of it, utterly. They renounced nothing; they made no distinctions; they counseled nothing. They *were,* and that was sufficient.

It was the example of these blessed ones which undoubtedly inspired the "saviors." For these active spirits, however, the light of truth proved not only blinding but shattering. In ways unpremeditated and unforeseen they activated the soul of man. And in their wake strife and conflict multiplied. Man was not regenerated, not made over: he became the battleground of darker, more disturbing forces.

And so, regardless of their heroic behavior, regardless of their sublime motives, I have come to regard such activity as indefensible. Even from the purest of motives one has not the right to "molest" another. The effort to bring a man to God, or to bring him enlightenment, is an act of violation. It is even more reprehensible than to subjugate him bodily. Does not the whole art of living center about the practice of tolerance, of noninterference? Before it is possible to love one another, as we are so often enjoined, it is necessary to respect one another, respect the privacy of the soul.

To come back to Big Sur, to my new-found freedom, my inner peace, my sense of at-homeness and at-oneness. . . . Is it selfish of me to try to preserve it? Is it anything which can be preserved, indeed? Can it be shared? And to whom would it have meaning, the meaning which it has assumed for me?

When all is said, I nevertheless concede that as long as I continue to write I remain perforce a propagandist. Only one kind of writing have I ever found which is devoid of this lamentable element, and that is the Japanese haiku. It is a form of poetry limited to so many syllables wherein the poet expresses his love, usually of nature, without making comparisons, without the use of superlatives. He tells only what is, or how it is. The effect, upon the Western reader at least, is usually one of jubilation. It is as if a weight had been taken from his shoulders. He feels absolved. "Amen!" is all he can exclaim.

To live one's life in this spirit which informs the haiku strikes me as an ultimate. Even to voice the thought is to negate all I have written. Perhaps I am approaching that point of illumination which made Thomas Aquinas exclaim upon his deathbed: "All I have written now seems to me like so much straw."

A new heaven and a new earth! Can they not be ushered in without slaughter and destruction? Can we not bring the sense-less machine to a halt, declare a moral holiday, as it were, and with a fresh new vision establish order, harmony, justice, peace? How much that is rotten and useless can be done away with by merely letting go! The greatest revolutions known to man had their inception in moments of silence. The inventions and dis-coveries, the visions and prophecies, all had their birth in mo-ments of quiet. What was it that spoke? Whence these thoughts which again and again change the face of the earth? Travail there must be, assuredly, but a travail of the womb, in darkness and certitude.

Let us voice the thought openly: man will not perish from the earth! At the darkest hour his eyes will be opened. The earth and the fullness thereof are his, but not to destroy. Jehovah made that forever clear in answering Job.

But how much farther into the darkness must we descend?

In no celestial register is it written how far we must go or how much we must endure. It is we, we ourselves, who decide. For some the darkest hour is already past; for others it may still be far off. We are all in the one pot, yet it is not the same pot for all. Our fate lies precisely in the ability to distinguish the endless transformations which this vessel of life—*la condition humaine* —is capable of undergoing. They who speak of it as one and the same speak the language of doom. Creator and creation are one and indivisible.

Whoever has experienced the oneness of life and the joy of life knows that to be is the all. "Ripeness is all," said Shake-speare. It is the same thing.

Open Sesame!

In every period of despair, such as the present, attention is focused upon the young, as if in them lay our last hope. To set about re-educating the world is, however, an almost hopeless task. To give it real meaning, the execution of such a program would entail the aid of exceptional minds, the very ones whose counsel the world has ever refused to follow. Every great sage has maintained that it is impossible to impart wisdom. And it is wisdom we need, not more knowledge or even "better" knowledge. We need wisdom of life, which is a kind of knowledge that only initiates have thus far been known to possess.

In the opening pages of *Walden,* Thoreau writes: "The greater part of what my neighbors call good I believe in my soul to be bad, and if I repent of anything, it is very likely to be my good behavior. What demon possessed me that I obeyed so well? You may say the wisest thing you can, old man,—you who have lived seventy years, not without honor of a kind,—I hear an irresistible voice which invites me away from all that. . . ."

Rimbaud, with all the fire and genius of youth, said: "Everything we are taught is false." Jesus set about to destroy the old way of life, reminding us that the only true guide is the Spirit within us. And does not the Zen master, in his endeavor to free the mind of its trammels, employ any and every means to shatter our way of thinking?

In the book called *Siddhartha,* Hermann Hesse makes it clear repeatedly that to cope with the world his enlightened one relied only upon three "noble and invincible arts"—how to think, how to wait, and how to fast." Is it necessary to remark how altogether lacking is modern man with respect to these? What is worse, he is not even aware of the lack.

What is the great problem? Is it to develop beings who will be different in spirit from those who begat them? If so, how does one go about undoing the damage of the centuries? Can we raise children who will undo the evil we have done? How do we bring about a "brave, new world"? By education, by moral and religious instruction, by eugenics, by revolution? Is it possible to bring about a new order of men, to make a new heaven and a new earth? Or is it an age-old delusion?

The great exemplars all led simple lives. Inspiring though they be, no one follows in their footsteps. Only a rare few have even attempted to do so. Yet now and then, even today, a unique individual does break away, breaks free of the treadmill, as it were, and demonstrates that it is possible, even in this sad world, to lead one's own life. We know very little about the secret springs which enable such individuals to lift themselves above the great mass of mankind. All we know is that each one found the way for himself, and of himself. We suspect that the chosen path was never an easy one, never one that the man of common sense would elect to follow. "The Way is not difficult; but you must avoid choosing." There lies the great difficulty.

The men I speak of—gods in the eyes of most men—were all revolutionaries in the deepest sense of the word. The great thing about them, that which they had in common, was the ability to revolutionize themselves. In the process society itself was leveled from top to bottom. What they urged upon us, what they demonstrated first in their own person, was to think afresh, to look upon the world with new eyes. They did not address themselves exclusively to youth, but to one and all, regardless of age, sex, condition, belief, pursuit or education. They spoke not of gradual amelioration, not of ten- or twenty-year programs, but of instantaneous conversion. They were possessed of certitude and authority, inner authority, and they worked miracles.

Men still continue to worship and adore these shining figures. And in doing so they reject them. As for the pillars of society who exploit their names, they have long inoculated us with the very opposite of all these superior beings represented. This strange and contradictory behavior, which seems ingrained in men, has led to an impasse which can only be described as a kind of "cosmic schizophrenia."

Meanwhile "the Way" is always open for any and every one to follow. But who dares any longer to point the way?

The very first line of the booklet called "Open Sesame—Books Are Keys," reads thus: "The masses of the world are mentally starved." One could put it much stronger. Not only are the masses mentally starved, they are emotionally and spiritually crippled. And it has been thus from the dawn of history. Madame Scheu-Riesz, the author of the booklet and the initiator of the delightful series of little books for children called "United World Books," is enlisting the aid of eminent men in various walks of life to help put at the disposal of youth the world over the best that exists in world literature and at a price within reach. Indeed, she has already done much to make this wish a reality.

It would take a bold spirit to say that Helene Scheu-Riesz and those who have rallied to her support are laboring in vain. Who does not wish to see a united world, a world at peace, a world in which health, reason, justice, love and joy of life prevail? Even our "enemies" profess the same desire. We are all advocates of a better world, and we are all the devil's disciples. We want to change the other fellow, not ourselves; we want our children to be better than us, but do nothing to make ourselves more worthy of our children.

The moment we begin to make new plans for the young, to select their reading, for example, or their playmates, the moment we begin to reorganize life, to separate the wheat from the chaff, as it were, we are up against something more than a problem, we are up against a conundrum. To judge, to select, to discriminate, to rearrange, reapportion—can there be any end to it ever? Try to assume that you are invested with the wisdom, the mercy and the powers of the Creator. Now put the world in order! Is this not the surest way to send one to the madhouse?

America has given the world one writer, the only one I know of, who sang, in every line he wrote, of acceptance. (Let us not forget, either, that in his day he was regarded as an obscene writer, an immoral person!) This doctrine of acceptance, the most difficult yet simple of all the radical ideas man has proposed to himself, embodies the understanding that the world is made up of conflicting members in all stages of evolution and devolution, that good and evil co-exist even though the one be but the shadow of the other, and that the world, for all its ills and shortcomings, was made for our enjoyment. It does not convey the idea that life is to be enjoyed when or if we all reach the stage of perfection. The salient idea is that life may, can and should be enjoyed now, under whatever conditions. The thought is so beautifully expressed by Hermann Hesse in the book previously mentioned that I am impelled to quote.

"Listen, my friend! [Siddhartha speaking] I am a sinner and you are a sinner, but someday the sinner will be Brahma again, will someday attain Nirvana, will someday become a Buddha. Now this 'someday' is illusion; it is only a comparison. The sinner is not on the way to a Buddha-like state; he is not evolving, although our thinking cannot conceive things otherwise. No, the potential Buddha already exists in the sinner; his future is already there. The potential hidden Buddha must be recognized in him, in you, in everybody. The world, Govinda, is not imperfect or slowly evolving along a long path to perfection. No, it is perfect at every moment; every sin already carries grace within it, all small children are potential old men, all sucklings have death within them, all dying people—eternal life. It is not possible for one person to see how far another is on the way; the Buddha exists in the robber and dice player; the robber exists in the Brahmin. During deep meditation it is possible to dispel time, to see simultaneously all the past, present and future, and then everything is good, everything is perfect, everything is Brahman. Therefore, it seems to me that everything that exists is good, death as well as life, sin as well as holiness, wisdom as well as folly. Everything is necessary, everything needs only my agreement, my assent, my loving understanding; then all is well with me and nothing can harm me. I learned through my body and soul that it was necessary for me to sin, that I needed lust, that I had to strive for property and experience nausea and the depths of despair in order to learn not to resist them, in order to learn to love the world, and no longer compare it with some kind of desired imaginary world, some imaginary vision of perfection, but to leave it as it is, to love it and be glad to belong to it. . . ."

So, let us begin with "Ali Baba and the Forty Thieves"—the first title in the series of United World (Open Sesame) booklets.

Why not? It is a wonderful tale, and as a child I enjoyed it hugely. As to whether it did me harm or good, I am unable to say. I do know that some of the books which I devoured avidly, and of which I am even more uncertain (as to harm or good), will never be included in this or any other series of books for children. There are certain books which no serious "educator" would offer to the young, yet these very books opened my eyes as no "good" book could ever have done. The good books, as they are called, were usually so dull that they were incapable of doing harm or good. The point I make, if it is not already clear, is ·that no one, certainly not the parent or instructor, can possibly foresee which book or books, which sentence, which thought, which phrase sometimes it may be that will open the doors of vision for the child. We are given so much learned, pompous talk about reading for instruction, reading for inspiration, reading for a purpose, and so on. What I have discovered for myself, and I do not think my experience is unique, is that the books I enjoyed most, no matter what their specific gravity, were the ones that did the most for me . . . encouraged, inspired, instructed, awakened . . . whatever you will. What we learn, of value, we get indirectly, largely unconsciously. It is too often stressed, in my opinion, that we learn through sorrow and suffering. I do not deny this to be true, but I hold that we also learn, and perhaps more lastingly, through moments of joy, of bliss, of ecstasy. Struggle has its importance, but we tend to overrate it. Harmony, serenity, bliss do not come from struggle but from surrender.

Let us not worry too much about what our children feed on. Let them feed, forage and fend for themselves as we do, sharing our problems, nurturing our dreams, inspiring our love. Let them remain what they are, a very real part of this "one world" to which we all belong whether we know it or not, admit it or not. We can spare them nothing we do not spare ourselves. If we wish to protect them, we must first learn how to protect ourselves. But do we want to protect ourselves? Do we know what "protection" really means? Or what it involves? If we did we would long since have dropped the word from our vocabulary.

I trust that Madame Scheu-Riesz will not think that I am against her program. What I am against, if anything, is the illusion that reading the right books will make for us the right citizens. It is our destiny to live with the wrong as well as the right kind of citizens, and to learn from them, the wrong-minded ones, as much or more as from the others. If we have not yet succeeded —after how many centuries?—in eliminating from life the elements which plague us, perhaps we need to question life more closely. Perhaps our refusal to face reality is the only ill we suffer from, and all the rest but illusion and delusion.

"The Way is not difficult; but you must avoid choosing!" Or, as another ancient one put it—"The Way is near, but men seek it afar. It is in easy things, but men seek it in difficult things."

Patchen: Man of Anger and Light

The first thing one would remark on meeting Kenneth Patchen is that he is the living symbol of protest. I remember distinctly my first impression of him when we met in New York: it was that of a powerful, sensitive being who moved on velvet pads. A sort of sincere assassin, I thought to myself, as we shook hands. This impression has never left me. True or not, I feel that it would give him supreme joy to destroy with his own hands all the tyrants and sadists of this earth together with the art, the institutions and all the machinery of everyday life which sustain and glorify them. He is a fizzing human bomb ever threatening to explode in our midst. Tender and ruthless at the same time, he has the faculty of estranging the very ones who wish to help him. He is inexorable: he has no manners, no tact, no grace. He gives no quarter. Like the gangster, he follows a code of his own. He gives you the chance to put up your hands before shooting you down. Most people however, are too terrified to throw up their hands. They get mowed down.

This is the monstrous side of him, which makes him appear ruthless and rapacious. Within the snorting dragon, however, there is a gentle prince who suffers at the mention of the slightest cruelty or injustice. A tender soul, who soon learned to envelope himself in a mantle of fire in order to protect his sensitive skin. No American poet is as merciless in his invective as Patchen. There is almost an insanity to his fury and rebellion.

Like Gorky, Patchen began his career in the university of life early. The hours he sacrificed in the steel mills of Ohio, where he was born, served to fan his hatred for a society in which inequality, injustice and intolerance form the foundation of life. His years as a wanderer, during which he scattered his manuscripts like seed, corroborated the impressions gained at home, school and mill. Today he is practically an invalid, thanks to the system which puts the life of a machine above that of a human being. Suffering from arthritis of the spine, he is confined to bed most of the time. He lies on a huge bed in a doll's house near the river named after Henry Hudson, a sick giant consumed by the poisonous indifference of a world which has more use for mousetraps than for poets. He writes book after book, prose as well as poetry, never certain when "they" will come and dump him (with the bed) into the street. This has been going on now for over seven years, if I am not mistaken. If Patchen were to become well, able to use hands and feet freely, it is just possible that he would celebrate the occasion by pulling the house down about the ears of some unsuspecting victim of his scorn and contempt. He would do it slowly, deliberately, thoroughly. And in utter silence.

That is another quality of Patchen's which inspires dread on first meeting—his awesome silence. It seems to spring from his flesh, as though he had silenced the flesh. It is uncanny. Here is a man with the gift of tongues and he speaks not. Here is a man who drips words but he refuses to open his mouth. Here is a man dying to communicate, but instead of conversing with you he hands you a book or a manuscript to read. The silence which emanates from him is black. He puts one on tenterhooks. It breeds hysteria. Of course he is shy. And no matter how long he lives he will never become urbane. He is American through and through, and Americans, despite their talkiness, are fundamentally silent creatures. They talk in order to conceal their innate reticence. It is only in moments of deep intimacy that they break loose. Patchen is typical. When finally he does open his mouth it is to release a hot flood of words. His emotion tears loose in clots.

A voracious reader, he exposes himself to every influence, even the worst. Like Picasso, he makes use of everything. The innovator and initiator are strong in him. Rather than accept the collaboration of a second-rate artist, he will do the covers for a book himself, a different one for each copy. And how beautiful and original are these individual cover designs* from the hand of a writer who makes no pretense of being a painter or illustrator! How interesting, too, are the typographical arrangements which he dictates for his books! How competent he can be when he has to be his own publisher! (See *The Journal of Albion Moonlight.*) From a sickbed the poet defies and surmounts all obstacles. He has only to pick up the telephone to throw an editorial staff into a panic. He has the will of a tyrant, the persistence of a bull. "This is the way I want it done!" he bellows. And by God it gets done that way.

Let me quote a few passages from his answers to certain questions of mine:

The pain is almost a natural part of me now—only the fits of depression, common to this disease, really sap my energies and distort my native spirit. I could speak quite morbidly in this last connection. The sickness of the world probably didn't cause mine, but it certainly conditions my handling of it. Actually, the worst part is that I feel that I would be something else if I weren't rigid inside with the constant pressure of illness; I would be purer, less inclined to write, say, for the sake of being able to show my sick part that it can never become all powerful; I could experience more in other artists if I didn't have to be concerned so closely with happenings inside myself; I would have less need to be pure in the presence of the things I love, and therefore, probably, would have a more personal view of myself. . . . I think the more articulate an artist becomes the less he will know about himself to say, for usually one's greatest sense of love is inseparable from a sense of creature foreboding . . . it is hard to imagine why God should "think," yet this "thinking" is the material of the greatest art . . . we don't wish to know ourselves, we wish to be lost in knowing, as a seed in a gust of wind.

I think that if I ever got near an assured income I'd

---

* So far Patchen has done paintings for limited editions of *The Dark Kingdom* and *Sleepers Awake,* one hundred and fifty covers in all. To date he has turned a deaf ear to suggestions that these remarkable productions be exhibited—I, for one, hope he changes his mind. It would be a feather in the hat of any gallery to show these wonderful paintings!

write books along the order of great canvases, including everything in them—huge symphonies that would handle poetry and prose as they present themselves from day to day and from one aspect of my life and interests to another. But that's all over, I think. They're going to blow everything up next time—and I don't believe we have long. Always men have talked about THE END OF THE WORLD— it's nearly here. A few more straws in the wall . . . a loose brick or two replaced . . . then no stone left standing on another—and the long silence; really forever. What is there to struggle against? Nobody can put the stars back together again. There isn't much time at all. I can't say it doesn't matter; it matters more than anything—but we are helpless to stop it now.

It's very hard for me to answer your questions. Some were Rebels out of choice; I had none—I wish they'd give me just one speck of proof that this "world of theirs" couldn't have been set up and handled better by a half-dozen drugged idiots bound hand and foot at the bottom of a ten-mile well. It's always because we love that we are rebellious; it takes a great deal of love to give a damn one way or another what happens from now on: I still do. The situation for human beings is hopeless. For the while that's left, though, we can remember the Great and the gods."

The mixture of hope and despair, of love and resignation, of courage and the sense of futility, which emanates from these excerpts is revelatory. Setting himself apart from the world, as poet, as man of vision, Patchen nevertheless identifies himself with the world in the malady which has become universal. He has the humility to acknowledge that his genius, that all genius, springs from the divine source. He is also innocent enough to think that the creature world should recognize God's voice and give it its due. He has the clarity to realize that his suffering is not important, that it distorts his native spirit, as he puts it, but does he admit to himself, can he admit to himself, that the suffering of the world also distorts the world's true spirit? If he could believe in his own cure might he not believe in a universal cure? "The situation for human beings is hopeless," he says. But he is a human being himself, and he is not at all convinced that his case is hopeless. With a bit of security he imagines that he will be able to give profounder expression to his powers. The whole world now cries for security. It cries for peace, too, but makes no real effort to stop the forces which are working for war. In his agony each sincere soul doubtless refers to the world as "their world." No one in his senses wishes to admit being a voluntary part of this world, so thoroughly inhuman, so intolerable has it become. We are all, whether we admit it or not, waiting for the end of the world, as though it were not a world of our own making but a hell into which we had been thrust by a malevolent fate.

Patchen uses the language of revolt. There is no other language left to use. There is no time, when you are holding up a bank, to explain to the directors the sinister injustice of the present economic system. Explanations have been given time and again; warnings have been posted everywhere. They have gone unheeded. Time to act. "Stick up your hands! Deliver the goods!"

It is in his prose works that Patchen uses this language most effectively. With *The Journal of Albion Moonlight,* Patchen opened up a vein unique in English literature. These prose works, of which the latest to appear is *Sleepers Awake,* defy classification. Like the Wonder Books of old, every page contains some new marvel. Behind the surface chaos and madness one quickly detects the logic and the will of a daring creator. One thinks of Blake, of Lautréamont, of Picasso—and of Jakob Boehme. Strange predecessors! But one thinks also of Savonarola, of Grünewald, of John of Patmos, of Hieronymous Bosch—and of times, events and scenes recognizable only in the waiting rooms of sleep. Each new volume is an increasingly astonishing feat of legerdemain, not only in the protean variety of the text but in design, composition and format. One is no longer looking at a dead, printed book but at something alive and breathing, something which looks back at you with equal astonishment. Novelty is employed not as seduction but like the stern fist of the Zen master—to awaken and arouse the consciousness of the reader. THE WAY MEN LIVE IS A LIE!—that is the reality which screams from the pages of these books. Once again we have the revolt of the angels.

This is not the place to discuss the merits or defects of the author's work. What concerns me at the moment is the fact that, despite everything, he is a poet. I am vitally interested in the man who today has the misfortune of being an artist and a human being. By the same token I am as much interested in the maneuvers of the gangster as I am in those of the financier or the military man. They are all part and parcel of society; some are lauded for their efforts, some reviled, some persecuted and hunted like beasts. In our society the artist is not encouraged, not lauded, not rewarded, unless he makes use of a weapon more powerful than those employed by his adversaries. Such a weapon is not to be found in shops or arsenals: it has to be forged by the artist himself out of his own tissue. When he releases it he also destroys himself. It is the only method he has found to preserve his own kind. From the outset his life is mortgaged. He is a martyr whether he chooses to be or not. He no longer seeks to generate warmth, he seeks for a virus with which society must allow itself to be injected or perish. It does not matter whether he preaches love or hate, freedom or slavery; he must create room to be heard, ears that will hear. He must create, by the sacrifice of his own being, the awareness of a value and a dignity which the word *human* once connoted. This is not the time to analyze and criticize works of art. This is not the time to select the flowers of genius, differentiate between them, label and categorize. This is the time to accept what is offered and be thankful that something other than mass intolerance, mass suicide, can preoccupy the human intellect.

If through indifference and inertia we can create human as well as atomic bombs, then it seems to me that the poet has the right to explode in his own fashion at his own appointed time. If all is hopelessly given over to destruction, why should the poet not lead the way? Why should he remain amid the ruins like a crazed beast? If we deny our Maker, why should we preserve the maker of words and images? Are the forms and symbols he spins to be put above Creation itself?

When men deliberately create instruments of destruction to be used against the innocent as well as the guilty, against babes in arms as well as against the aged, the sick, the halt, the maimed,

the blind, the insane, when their targets embrace whole popula-
tions, when they are immune to every appeal, then we know that
the heart and the imagination of man are no longer capable of
being stirred. If the powerful ones of this earth are in the grip of
fear and trembling, what hope is there for the weaker ones?
What does it matter to those monsters now in control what becomes of the poet, the sculptor, the musician?

In the richest and the most powerful country in the world
there is no means of insuring an invalid poet such as Kenneth
Patchen against starvation or eviction. Neither is there a band of
loyal fellow artists who will unite to defend him against the unnecessary attacks of shallow, spiteful critics. Every day ushers
in some fresh blow, some fresh insults, some fresh punishment.
In spite of it all he continues to create. He works on two or three
books at once. He labors in a state of almost unremitting pain.
He lives in a room just about big enough to hold his carcass, a
rented coffin you might call it, and a most insecure one at that.
Would he not be better off dead? What is there for him to look
forward to—as a man, as an artist, as a member of society?

I am writing these lines for an English and a French edition
of his work. It is hardly the orthodox preface to a man's work.
But my hope is that in these distant countries Patchen (and other
now unknown American writers) will find friends, find support
and encouragement to go on living and working. America is immune to all appeals. Her people do not understand the language
of the poet. They do not wish to recognize suffering—it is too
embarrassing. They do not greet Beauty with open arms—her
presence is disturbing to heartless automatons. Their fear of
violence drives them to commit insane cruelties. They have no
reverence for form or image: they are bent on destroying whatever does not conform to their pattern, which is chaos. They are
not even concerned with their own disintegration, because they
are already putrescent. A vast congeries of rotting sepulchres,
America holds for yet a little while, awaiting the opportune moment to blow itself to smithereens.

The one thing which Patchen cannot understand, will not tolerate, indeed, is the refusal to act. In this he is adamant. Confronted with excuses and explanations, he becomes a raging lion.

It is the well-off who especially draw his ire. Now and then he
is thrown a bone. Instead of quieting him, he growls more fero-
ciously. We know, of course, what patronage means. Usually it
is hush money. "What is one to do with a man like that?" exclaim
the poor rich. Yes, a man like Patchen puts them in a dilemma.
Either he increases his demands or he uses what is given to voice
his scorn and contempt. He needs money for food and rent,
money for the doctor, money for operations, money for medi-
cines—yet he goes on turning out beautiful books. Books of
violence clothed in outward elegance. The man has uncommon
taste, no gainsaying it. But what right has he to a cultivated appetite? Tomorrow he will be asking for a seaside cottage perhaps, or for a Rouault, whose work he reveres. Perhaps for a
Capehart, since he loves music. How can one satisfy a monster
such as that?

That is the way rich people think about the starving artist.
Poor people too, sometimes. Why doesn't he get himself a job?
Why doesn't he make his wife support him? Does he have to
live in a house with two rooms? Must he have all those books
and records? When the man happens also to be an invalid, they
become even more resentful, more malicious. They will accuse
him of permitting his illness to distort his vision. "The work of
a sick man," they say, shrugging their shoulders. If he bellows,
then it is "the work of an impotent man." If he begs and entreats,
then "he has lost all sense of dignity." But if he roars? Then he
is hopelessly insane. No matter what attitude he adopts he is
condemned beforehand. When he is buried they praise him as another *"poète maudit."* What beautiful crocodile tears are shed
over our dead and accursed poets! What a galaxy of them we
have already in the short span of our history!

In 1909 Charles Péguy penned a *morceau* for his *Cahiers de
la Quinzaine* which described the then imminent debacle of the
modern world. "We are defeated," it begins. "We are defeated to
such an extent, so completely, that I doubt whether history will
ever have to record an instance of defeat such as the one we
furnish. . . . To be defeated, that is nothing. It would be nothing. On the contrary, it can be a great thing. It can be all: the
final consummation. To be defeated is nothing: [but] we have

been beaten. We have even been given a good drubbing. In a few years society, this modern society, before we have even had the time to sketch the critique of it, has fallen into a state of decomposition, into a dissolution, such, that I believe, that I am assured history had never seen anything comparable. . . . That great historical decomposition, that great dissolution, that great precedent which in a literary manner we call the decay of the Roman decadence, the dissolution of the Roman Empire, and which it suffices to call, with Sorel, the ruin of the ancient world, was nothing by comparison with the dissolution of present society, by comparison with the dissolution and degradation of this society, of the present modern society. Doubtless, at that time there were far more crimes and still more vice[s]. But there were also infinitely more resources. This putrefaction was full of seeds. People at that time did not have this sort of promise of sterility which we have today, if one may say so, if these two words can be used together."*

After two annihilating wars, in one of which Péguy gave his life, this "promise of sterility" appears anything but empty. The condition of society which was then manifest to the poet and thinker, and of course more so today (even the man in the street is aware of it), Péguy described as "a real disorder of impotence and sterility." It is well to remember these words when the hired critics of the press (both of the right and the left) direct their fulminations against the poets of the day. It is precisely the artists with the vital spark whom they set out to attack most viciously. It is the creative individual (*sic*) whom they accuse of undermining the social structure. A persecutory mania manifests itself the moment an honest word is spoken. The atmosphere of the whole modern world, from Communist Russia to capitalist America, is heavy with guilt. We are in the Time of the Assassins. The order of the day is: liquidate! The enemy, the archenemy, is the man who speaks the truth. Every realm of society is permeated with falsity and falsification. What survives, what is upheld, what is defended to the last ditch, is the lie.

"It is perhaps this condition of confusion and distress," wrote

* See *Men and Saints,* Charles Péguy, Pantheon Books, New York.

Péguy, "which, more imperiously than ever, makes it our duty
not to surrender. One must never surrender. All the less since
the position is so important and so isolated and so menaced, and
that precisely the country is in the hands of the enemy."

Those who know Kenneth Patchen will realize that I am identifying his stand with Péguy's. Perhaps there could not be two
individuals more different one from another. Perhaps there is
nothing at all in common between them except this refusal to
swallow the lie, this refusal to surrender even in the blackest
hour. I know of no American who has as vigorously insisted
that the enemy is within. If he refuses to play the game it is not
because he has been defeated; it is because he has never recognized those phantoms created out of fear and confusion which
men call "the enemy." He knows that the enemy of man is man.
He rebels out of love, not out of hate. Given his temperament,
his love of honesty, his adherence to truth, is he not justified in
saying that "he had no choice" but to rebel? Do we find him
aligned with those rebels who wish merely to depose those on
top, in order that they may hold the whip hand? No, we find him
alone, in a tiny garret, riveted to a sickbed, turning frantically
from side to side as if imprisoned in an iron cage. And it is a
very real cage indeed. He has only to open his eyes each day to
be aware of his helplessness. He could not surrender even if he
wished to: there is no one to surrender to except death. He lies
on the edge of the precipice with eyes wide open. The world
which condemns him to imprisonment is fast asleep. He is furi-
ously aware that his release does not depend on acceptance
by the multitude but on the dissolution of the world which is
strangling him.

"The situation for human beings is hopeless," did he say? In
Albion Moonlight this desperation is expressed artistically: "I
want to be a carpet in a cat-house." Thus, to use the title from
one of his own poems, "The Furious Crown Conceals Its
Throne." Thus, to paraphrase Miró, persons magnetized by the
stars may walk in comfort on the music of a furrowed landscape.
Thus we take leave of our atavistic friend, the poet, doomed to
inhabit a world that never was, never will be, the world of
"flowers born in shining wombs." For flowers will always be

born and wombs will always be radiant, particularly when the poet is accursed. For him the beast is always number, the landscape stars, the time and the place of creation now and here. He moves in a "circle of apparent fates," ruler of the dark kingdom, maligned, persecuted and forsaken in the light of day.

Once again the night approaches. And once again "the dark kingdom" will reveal to us its splendors. In the middle of this twentieth century we have all of us, none excepted, crossed a river made of human tears. We have no fathers, no mothers, no brothers, no sisters. We are returned to the creature state.

"I have put language to sleep," said Joyce. Aye, and now conscience too is being put to sleep.

The Angel Is My Watermark*

People often ask: "If you had your life to live all over again, would you do this or that?" Meaning—would you repeat the same mistakes? As for *les amours* I am not so sure. But as to water colors, yes. Because the important thing which I learned, through making water colors, was not to worry, not to care too much. We don't have to turn out a masterpiece every day. To paint is the thing, not to make masterpieces. Even the Creator, when he made this perfect universe, had to learn not to care too much. Certainly when he created Man he gave himself a prolonged headache.

And Man, when he attains fulfillment, or a state of grace, if you like, ceases to play the Creator. I mean that he no longer feels compelled to draw, paint, describe in words or music what he sees around him. He can let things be. He discovers, just by looking the world in the face, that everything is a bit of a masterpiece. Why paint? For whom? Enjoy what you see. That's quite enough. The man who can do this is an accomplished artist. The rest of us, we who must sign our names to everything we touch, are simply apprentices. Sorcerers' apprentices. For though we pretend to be instructing others how to see, hear, taste and feel, what we are really doing most of the time is to feed the ego. We refuse to remain anonymous, like the men who made the cathedrals. No, we want to see our names spelled out in neon lights. And we never refuse money for our efforts. Even when we have nothing more to say, we go on writing, painting, singing, dancing, always angling for the spotlight.

And now here I come with my water colors—and my name

* Preface to the water-color album by this title published by M. Du Mont Schanberg, Cologne, Germany, 1961.

in big letters. Another sinner. Another ego. I must confess it
gives me great pleasure. I shan't be a hypocrite and say, "I
hope it gives you pleasure also." *Pour moi, c'est un fait accompli,
c'est tout.* I waited twenty years to see these water colors gathered together in a book. Frankly, I had hoped there might be
fifty or a hundred reproduced instead of a dozen or so. However,
better half a loaf than none, as the saying goes.

The best part of it all is that I am not obliged to wait until
I die. I can view them now, *ici-bas,* with the eyes of a sinner, a
wastrel, a profligate, rather than with the eyes of an angel or a
ghost. That's something. Looking at them from another perspective, perhaps they will teach me something about true humility.

Of one thing I am certain . . . now that my dream has been
realized I will enjoy whatever I do more than ever before. I have
no ambition to become a masterful painter. I simply want to go
on painting, more and more, even though I may be committing
a crime against the Holy Ghost. The nearer I get to the grave
the more time I have to waste. Nothing is important now, in the
sense it once was. I can lean to the right or left without danger
of capsizing. I can go off the course, too, if I wish, because my
destination is no longer a fixed one. As those two delightful
bums in *Waiting for Godot* say time and again:

"*On y va?*"

"*Oui.*"

And no one budges.

I realize, of course, that these vagabond reflections and observations are hardly in the Teutonic tradition. They are not
even American, if I know my people. But doesn't it make you
feel good to read them? And, suppose it's all cockeyed, what I
say. What difference? At least you know where I stand. And
you, are you standing on solid ground? Prove it!

Long ago, when I was making merry writing *Black Spring,*
I was already reveling in the fact that the world about me was
going to pieces. From the time that I was old enough to think,
I had a hunch that this was so. Then I came upon Oswald Speng-
ler. He confirmed my inner convictions. (And what a really
good time I had reading him, reading about the "decline of the

west." It was better, honestly, than reading the Bhagavad-Gita. It bucked me up.) Nor did I have the cheek then to say as Rimbaud: *"Moi, je suis intact!"* It didn't matter to me whether I was intact or falling to pieces. I was attending a spectacle: the crumbling of our civilization. Today the disintegration is proceeding even more rapidly, thanks to our technic and efficiency. Today everybody is writing about it, even our school children. But they don't get much fun out of it, have you noticed?

What I recommend for the few remaining years that are left us is—to piss the time away enjoyably. Make water colors, for example. No need to sign your name to them, if you don't wish to. Just turn them out one after the other, good, bad, indifferent, no matter. Nero fiddled while Rome burned. Making water colors is much better. You don't harm anybody, you don't make a spectacle of yourself, you don't collaborate with the enemy. When you go to bed you will sleep soundly, not toss all night long. You may find your appetite improved too. You may even find yourself sinning with greater zest—enjoying it, I mean.

What I am trying to say in my offhand way is that in fair weather or foul the men who make the least fuss do more to save what is worth saving—and how much is worth saving, do you ever stop to think?—than those who push us about because they think they have the answer to everything. When you put your mind to such a simple, innocent thing, for example, as making a water color, you lose some of the anguish which derives from being a member of a world gone mad. Whether you paint flowers, stars, horses or angels you acquire respect and admiration for all the elements which go to make up our universe. You don't call flowers friends and stars enemies, or horses Communists and angels Fascists. You accept them for what they are and you praise God that they are what they are. You desist from improving the world or even yourself. You learn to see not what you want to see but what is. And what is is usually a thousand times better than what might be or ought to be. If we could stop tampering with the universe we might find it a far better world than we think it to be. After all, we've only occupied it a few hundred million years, which is to say that we are just beginning to get acquainted with it. And if we continue another billion years there is nothing to assure us that we will eventually know it. In the beginning as in the end it remains a mystery. And the mystery exists or thrives in every smallest part of the universe. It has nothing to do with size or distance, with grandeur or remoteness. Everything hinges upon how you look at things.

The question which emerges with every work of art that is turned out is: "Is there more to what we see than meets the eye?" And the answer is always yes. In the humblest object we can find what we seek—beauty, truth, reality, divinity. The artist does not create these attributes, he discovers them in the process of painting. When he realizes this he can go on painting without danger of sinning, because he then also knows that to paint or not to paint amounts to the same thing. One doesn't sing because he hopes one day to appear in an opera; one sings because one's lungs are full of joy. It's wonderful to listen to a great performance, but it's even more wonderful to encounter in the street a happy vagabond who can't stop singing because his heart is full of joy. Nor does your happy vagabond expect any monetary reward for his efforts. He doesn't know the meaning of effort. No one can be paid to give of his joy, it's always freely given.

An Open Letter to All and Sundry

What everyone would like to do, and the artist more than anyone, I suppose, is to make a living by doing what he enjoys doing. An artist who is noncommercial has about as much chance for survival as a sewer rat. If he remains faithful to his art he compromises in life, by begging and borrowing, by marrying rich, or by doing some stultifying work which will bring him a pittance.

Unless one is an expert at it there is a limit to what one can borrow and beg. To marry rich is an opportunity that comes once in a lifetime, if it comes at all. The usual lot is to find some kind of work which will just keep body and soul together and at the same time give one the few hours a week needed to practice one's art.

Lately it has occurred to me that I might earn the meager sum needed to keep afloat by selling the water colors which I make in my moments of recreation. I do not pretend to be a painter; I do not think my work has any value as art. But I like to paint and I like to think that whatever an artist does by way of avocation is interesting and perhaps revelatory. I know too that if upon my death I should have any fame as a writer these water colors which I have been turning out for my own amusement and the amusement of my friends will have real value. Together with notebooks and diaries they complete the picture of the writer's personality.

Actuated by real need, which is continuous and always quasi-desperate, I have decided to anticipate the moment of death and offer these post-mortem effects now. I am putting no price on these paintings, if I may call them such. I offer them with the understanding that the buyer may name his own price. (If later

I find the way to print my own books I shall do the same with them.) The primary thing is this, that whatever money is given me constitutes a mortgage on the future, *my future as a writer*. Making water colors is so much play for me; it gives me a release. In other words, it keeps me happy, enthusiastic and alive, and to be happy, enthusiastic and alive is a prerequisite for the artist.

In order to give my prospective benefactor some idea of my interest in water colors I append herewith a chapter from *Black Spring* called "The Angel Is My Watermark."* It will be seen from this that the mania took hold of me some fifteen years or so ago. Today it is stronger than ever. It is possible that before I die I shall become what is called a painter, as well as a writer. Why not? Dr. Marion Souchon of New Orleans only began to paint at the age of sixty, after performing thousands of successful operations as a surgeon.

Had I been able to afford it I would have included in this brochure a few color reproductions. As it is I can only give a few black and whites. Should anyone be interested in this phase of my activity, perhaps he will help me later in getting out a book of facsimiles. Every form of reproduction is prohibitively costly. One has to be a millionaire to gratify his whims when it comes to reproducing words or pictures in anything less than carload lots.

A word about the selection of these water colors. Today I have in my possession only the product of the last few weeks. Everything prior to this period I have given away to friends at some time or other. I am left with only a few choice "masterpieces," so to speak. No matter. I always work from scratch— and with zest. No use telling me what you would like to have: I can offer you only what I have on hand at the moment. You will have to take a chance on me. Nor can I, for practical reasons, send you a group from which to make a selection. If you ask for one I will send one, the one I think would please you. If you ask for three I will send three. If you can't stand the sight

* Impossible because of lack of funds. (The Holve-Barrows edition of *The Angel Is My Watermark* combines this Open Letter and the Black Spring chapter.)

of them on your walls you can always give them away as gifts, or use them for toilet paper. Incidentally, the toilet is an excellent place to hang water colors. I can't tell you what pleasure I get, "when I go to the bathroom," as we say in America, to see one of my masterpieces staring me in the face. Let me say in passing that I have noticed, in the homes of great collectors and connoisseurs of art, this same prepossession for the toilet. Only lately, while making pipi *chez* Walter Arensberg, the most interesting collector of modern art in America, I discovered some very unusual, very inspiring art products. So don't think, when you relegate one of my masterpieces to the water closet, that you are doing me an injury. On the contrary, I shall consider it a mark of esteem.

As to my subjects, and I suppose a word or two on this score would not be inapropos . . . Well, I am at home in all realms. I do not paint from life: I paint from the head and what's inside it. Now and then, of course, I have done a still life or a portrait or a landscape by looking at it and trying to reproduce it. The results are usually quite harrowing. Nobody, not even myself, can ever detect what is called "a resemblance." Fortunately, resemblances are no longer in vogue.

I have a limited stock of furniture which constitutes the *materiel* of my pictures. My pictorial vocabulary is limited to one tree, one house, one flower, one sky, one face; with these I render the infinite variety of trees, houses, flowers, skies and faces which exist in nature. You see, I know nothing about drawing. I couldn't even copy a drawing until the year 1926 or '27. Then, by accident one day, I discovered that I was able to make a likeness of George Grosz, whose self-portrait I had found on the cover of one of his albums. From that day I took pleasure in using pencil and brush. On good days I can draw with a cleaver. I don't go in for likenesses any more; I am satisfied with reality. Everyone has his own reality in which, if one is not too cautious, timid or frightened, one swims. This is the only reality there is. If you can get it down on paper, in words, notes, or color, so much the better. The great artists don't even bother to put it down on paper: they live with it silently, they become it.

The two men I admire most in the realm of the water color

are John Marin and Paul Klee; I would give my right hand to be able to paint like either of them. Their work seems like pure magic to me. Unfortunately, for all my admiration of their work, the influence they have had on me seems nil. I am just about where I was in 1926 or '27. I revolve in a Sargasso Sea of curiosity and delight. Everything I do looks good to me. It is always the best I know how, and if that is far from perfection, it is not so terribly far from Paradise. I make my own heavens and my own hells, and I live in them and extract all the juices. I could, as some suggest, go to an academy and learn a few things about the fundamentals of painting. *But would I be any happier?* Just as I am, good or bad, I enjoy everything I do with the brush. I have no need to prove that I am a painter, no need to make a reputation for myself. When I'm painting the world is mine!

Should this scheme which I am now broaching prove a failure I will still go on making water colors. I will paint my own grave and lie in it, and though my eyes be closed forever I shall enjoy every aspect of my demise, despite the lack of perspective, the lack of form, the lack of this and that. I will have a colorful end, perhaps not in the style of Paul Klee or John Marin (who is still alive, praise God!), but an end, my own end, the only end that anyone should aspire to.

And now, before diving into "the genesis of a masterpiece," let me suggest that you make note of my name and address, both of which are more or less permanent:

Henry Miller, Big Sur, California.

March 14, 1943

P.S. Anyone wishing to encourage the water-color mania would do well to send me paper, brushes and tubes, of which I am always in need. I would also be grateful for old clothes, shirts, socks, etc. I am 5 feet 8 inches tall, weigh 150 pounds, 15½ neck, 38 chest, 32 waist, hat and shoes both size 7 to 7½. Love corduroys.

P.P.S. This letter was mimeographed and distributed for me by a kind friend in Chicago.

First Love

In my mind's eye I can see her today just as vividly as when I first met her, which was in one of the corridors of Eastern District High School (Brooklyn) as she was going from one classroom to another. She was just a little shorter than I, well built, that is to say rather buxom, radiant, bursting with health, head high, glance at once imperious and saucy, concealing a shyness which was disconcerting. She had a warm, generous mouth filled with rather large, dazzling white teeth. But it was her hair and eyes which drew one first. Light golden hair it was, combed up stiff in the form of a conch. A natural blonde such as one seldom sees except in an opera. Her eyes, which were extremely limpid, were full and round. They were a China blue, and they matched her golden hair and her apple-blossom complexion. She was only sixteen, of course, and not very sure of herself, though she seemed to give the impression that she was. She stood out from all the other girls in the school, like someone with blue blood in her veins. Blue blood and icy, I am tempted to say.

That first glance she gave me swept me off my feet. I was not only impressed by her beauty but intimidated as well. How I ever managed to approach her and mumble a few meaningless words I can no longer recall. I know it took weeks after the first encounter to do such a brave thing. I recall vividly how she blushed each time we came within striking distance of one another. Naturally, what conversation we exchanged must have been of a telegraphic nature. She never dropped a word or a phrase that took root in my memory. As I say, these encounters always took place in the corridors, going from one classroom to another. She must have been a class or two behind me, though of the same age. For me, of course, these little nothings were filled with pregnant significance.

It was only after we had graduated from high school that we exchanged a few letters. During the summer holidays she remained at Asbury Park, New Jersey, while I continued my daily drudgery as a clerk in the offices of the Atlas Portland Cement Company. Every evening, on returning from work, I rushed to the mantelpiece over the fireplace, where the mail was always deposited, to see if there was a letter from her. If I received one or two throughout the long vacation season I was lucky. My whole impression of this strange courtship is one of utter frustration. Now and then, rarely, I met her at a dance. Twice, I think, I took her to the theater. I didn't even possess a photograph of her that I might carry in my wallet and look at secretly.

But I had no need for photographs. Her image was constantly in my mind; her absence was a perpetual torment which served to keep her image alive. I carried her inside me, as it were. Alone, I would often speak to her, either silently or aloud. Often, walking home at night, after having made a tour of her house, I would yell her name aloud, imploringly, as if to beg her to grant me the favor of an audience from on high. She was always up there somewhere, high above me, like some goddess whom I had discovered and regarded as my very own. It was I, idiot that I was, who prevented her from descending to the level of other mortals. This, to be sure, had been determined from the instant I met her: I had no choice.

The strange thing is that she never gave me any indication of being hostile or indifferent. Who knows—perhaps she for her part was pleading silently with me to show her a more human attention, to woo her like a man, to take her, forcibly if need be.

Perhaps two or three times a year we would come together at a party, one of those teen-age affairs which last until dawn with singing and dancing and silly games such as "Kiss the Pillow," or "Post Office," the game which permits one to call for the creature of one's choice and embrace her furtively in a dark room. Even then, when we might have kissed and embraced unrestrainedly, our shyness prevented us from sharing anything but the most innocent pleasure. If I danced with her I trembled from head to foot and usually stumbled over my own feet, much to her embarrassment.

All I could do was to play the piano—play and jealously watch her dance with my friends. She never came behind me to put her arms around me and whisper some silly nothing. After such evenings I would lie abed and gnash my teeth, or weep like a fool, or pray to a God I no longer believed in, beg Him to have me find favor in her eyes.

And all throughout these five or six years she remained what she had been from the first—a flaming image. I knew nothing of her mind, her hopes or dreams, her aspirations. She was a complete blank on which I fatuously inscribed what I wished. No doubt I was the same to her.

Finally there came the day I said good-by to her. The day I was leaving for the Wild West, to become a cowboy, so I thought. I went to her home and timidly rang the bell. (It was but the second or third time I had ventured to ring her doorbell.) She came to the door looking thinner, older, more careworn than ever I had seen her.

We were twenty-one now, and I had been going with "the widow" for two or three years. That was why I was running off to the Far West—to cure myself of a fatal infatuation. Instead of inviting me in, she stepped outdoors and escorted me to the gate which opened onto the sidewalk, and there we stood for perhaps fifteen or twenty minutes exchanging pointless remarks. I had, of course, warned her of my coming and related briefly my plans for the future. What I omitted to say was that I would one day send for her—and all that nonsense. Whatever I may have secretly hoped, by now I knew that the situation was irremediable. She knew that I loved her—everyone knew it—but the affair with "the widow" had put me definitely out of her pale. It was something she could not understand, much less forgive.

What a sorry figure I must have cut! Even then, had I been courageous and resolute enough, I might have won her. At least, so it seemed to me, reading the pained, lost expression in her eyes. (Yet rambling on fatuously, blindly, about the glorious Golden West.) Even though I felt it might be the last time I would see her I lacked the courage to fling my arms around her

and give her a last, passionate kiss. Instead, we shook hands politely, mumbled some awkward words of adieu, and off I walked.

Though I never once turned my head, I had the firm conviction that she was still standing at the gate, following me with her
eyes. Did she wait until I had rounded the corner before rushing
to her room, flinging herself on the bed, and sobbing fit to break
her heart? I will never know, neither in this world nor the next.

About a year later, when I had returned from the West, sadder
and wiser, to return to the arms of "the widow" from whom I had
run away, we met again by chance. The last meeting. It was on
a streetcar, and fortunately I was with an old chum who knew
her well, else I would have bolted. After a few words my friend
jokingly suggested that she invite us up to her flat. She was married now and, incredible as it may seem, was living just back
of the house in which the widow lived. We tripped up the high
stoop and entered her apartment. She took us from one room
to another, finishing with the bedroom. Then, in her embarrassment, she let slip an idiotic phrase which went through me like
a knife. "This," she said, pointing to the big double bed, "is
where we sleep." With those words it was as if an iron curtain
fell between us.

It was the end for me. And yet not an end. In all the years which
have since elapsed she remains the woman I loved and lost, the
unattainable one. In her China-blue eyes, so cold and inviting, so
round and mirror-like, I see myself forever and ever as the ridiculous man, the lonely soul, the wanderer, the rootless frustrated
artist, the man in love with love, always in search of the absolute, always seeking the unattainable. Behind the iron curtain
her image remains fresh and vivid as of yore, and nothing, it
seems, can tarnish it or cause it to fade away.

When I Reach for My Revolver

The late John Dudley, descendant of the Earl of Essex, once chalked up over my door: "When I hear the word 'Culture' I reach for my revolver." Today, when someone tries to tell me that Europe is finished, I have the same impulse—to reach for my revolver and plug him. Nobody was ever more thrilled than I to read that stupendous morphological, or phenomenological, tone-poem called *The Decline of the West*. In the days when Culture was only a bird in a gilded cage, the days—now so far off—when I was eating my heart out because I imagined I had already endured all the sorrows of Werther, no music was sweeter to my ears than this music of the end. But I have now outlived the end—Europe's end, America's end, all the ends, including the end of the Golden West. I am no longer living on clock-time or daylight-saving time or cyclical time or even sidereal time. I see that the dead are still with us, ready and willing to be summoned from the grave any time; I see that the living are one with the dead and having the devil's own time shuffling all these corpses about. I see that India and China, supposedly dead for centuries, despite the teeming millions they have been constantly spawning, are now recognized as being alive, very much alive— I might add, frighteningly alive.

I came back last August, after a seven months' stay abroad, feeling that if anything were dead and finished it might be the American view of things. Fresh from Europe, the American scene held about as much charm for me as a dead rattlesnake lying in the deep freeze. Why do we presume to think that we are the one and only people? What can possibly give us the idea that we are a vital, lusty, joyous, creative people? Compared with the European, the American strikes me as having the vivacity of a pall-bearer. He comes alive only when he is quoting facts, and for me his facts lack truth, wisdom and passion. His facts, which are sterile, and his labor-saving machines, which break his back— they seem to go together.

Every time I am challenged about Europe, whether I am in a mood to attack or a mood to defend, Wassermann's words always sing out in my head. Waremme, that astounding character which haunts the pages of *The Maurizius Case,* had been saying that only after renouncing Europe could a person of his sort begin to understand what Europe really meant. Then comes this passage: "Europe was not merely the sum total of the ties of his own individual existence, friendship and love, hatred and unhappiness, success and disappointment; it was, venerable and intangible, the existence of a unity of two thousand years, Pericles and Nostradamus, Theodoric and Voltaire, Ovid and Erasmus, Archimedes and Gauss, Calderon and Dürer, Phidias and Mozart, Petrarch and Napoleon, Galileo and Nietzsche, an immeasurable army of geniuses and an equally immeasurable army of demons. All this light driven into darkness and shining forth from it again, a sordid morass producing a golden vessel, the catastrophe and inspirations, the revolutions and periods of darkness, the moralities and the fashions, all that great common stream with its chains, its stages, and its pinnacles, making up one spirit. That was Europe, that was his Europe."

And we are supposed to believe that all is now over, because after two devastating world wars Europe, to our mind, seems listless, disinterested, cynical, skeptical, because she objects to being bullied, cajoled, threatened, bribed by our far-seeing statesmen, industrialists, bankers and warmongers? Every month some well-known American author is being translated into one of the numerous European tongues. Can anyone say that, taken as a whole, the works of our contemporary authors breathe optimism, wisdom, courage or insight? Examine the works of those American authors who won the Nobel Prize: do they reflect the spirit of a young, ardent, up-and-coming race?

In Europe, with none of that security and physical ease which Americans deem indispensable, I found men and women pursuing their vocations just as passionately as when I lived there in the thirties. The creative spirits were even more creative than before, and the old men younger than ever, and the young men older than ever. I no longer fear for the younger generation, supposedly sad and disillusioned. Nor do I fear for the old ones, because their time will soon be up. Conditions being what they are, the young have every right to be pessimistic, rebellious and thoroughly disinterested in the empty promises of their governing bodies. As for the old ones, all of them living out a glorious second youth, immune to world conditions, concerned only with the grand problems, creating with ever more freedom, daring and mastery, what have we to fear for them unless it be our failure to make use of the inspiration which their example affords us? A man is not doomed in Europe because he starts out on the wrong foot; a man is not finished in Europe when he arrives at a certain age. Go through the roster of the great names in European art; see what towering monoliths it contains. And how many of these illustrious ones only began their great works in so-called old age!

From the standpoint of quality and production alike, what monumental figures has France alone given the world in the field of literature! And continues to give the world. And what have American publishers given, in translation, of the works of contemporary French giants? How are we to know anything of the spirit which informs Europe when we know hardly anything of the works which their foremost creators are turning out? If we are mere playthings, as we undoubtedly are, in the hands of European diplomats, we are but babes in arms when it comes to grappling with European literature. The respected European writer begins on a level which our best writers seldom or never attain. Limiting one's glance to book reviews alone, the difference in tone, in reach, in judgment and in understanding, between our critics and theirs is incredible. True, occasionally one of our celebrated writers knocks out a sensational work, a shot in the dark, you might say. He himself does not know how it was done. There was no evolution preceding it and no sequel to follow. It hangs in the void, like a landscape without foreground or background. It just happened, *et c'est tout*.

What is most comforting and sustaining about the European scene is the feeling of continuity which permeates even the stones of the buildings. An artist, to survive, demands this atmosphere of continuity. Contrary to what the unthinking believe, it is tradition which nurtures change, tradition which nurtures revolution, tradition which nurtures freedom of expression. Sound the roll call of the heretics, the free-thinkers, the rebels, the pathfinders, the iconoclasts, and you will find that they are in the tradition. In her two thousand years of struggle, change and experimentation Europe has experienced well-nigh everything. Along with the flowers of culture, she has accepted, perhaps deliberately nourished, the weeds. There is still room in Europe for all manner of growths. Even the obnoxious ones, I must confess, seem less obnoxious, less dangerous, than the American variety. The European does not expect everyone to be alike and think alike. He thrives on variety and contrariety. We, on the other hand, grow panicky and hysterical when we discover that all the world does not agree with us. We behave, to the great dismay and disgust of the European, as if we were the Chosen People.

All this struggle, turmoil and confusion naturally creates a rich leaven for the European man of letters. He is not easily frightened of ideas, or paralyzed by misfortune or defeat, or silenced by bad government or misgovernment. Throughout the ages he has played a part in every kind of communal experiment. Some of the greatest figures have been, from the present standpoint, on the wrong side of the fence, have espoused the wrong cause. They remain great nonetheless. Their works are studied and talked about. What a contrast, this age-old Europe, to even that young America which Charles Dickens described over a hundred years ago! "I tremble," he writes, "for a Radical coming here, unless he is a Radical on principle, by reason and reflection, and from the sense of right. I fear that if he were anything else he would return home a Tory. . . . I say no more on that head for two months from this time, save that I do fear that the heaviest blow ever dealt at liberty will be dealt by this country, in the failure of its example on the earth."

It was my good fortune, on returning to Europe this year, to find some of my old friends still alive. Every one of them had been through hell during the Occupation. Almost every one of them had been starved, beaten, tortured, either by the enemy or by his own people. I found them all, without exception, in good spirits, working more assiduously and joyously than ever before. To be truthful, they were all younger in spirit than when I knew them before. They were not turning out black, pessimistic, nihilistic works, as one might imagine. Quite the contrary. I found none of that intolerance, bitterness, cynicism or paralysis which some of my American friends warned me to be prepared for. It is true that in order to continue their chosen work many of my old friends now found themselves obliged to do all manner of drudge work as well. One of them, a poet and playwright, confessed to me that since the end of the war he had translated some fifty full-length hooks. (It is unnecessary, I hope, for me to stress how miserably a translator is paid for his work, at home and abroad.) But perhaps because they had suffered so bitterly during the war, this additional burden, this drudgery, no longer seemed the bugaboo that it is to an American. They were all thankful to be alive, grateful, despite their situation, to be able to express their aliveness. Suffering and privation had cured them of imaginary ills and of some very real ills as well.

Certainly I do not wish to imply that war is a good thing, either for the artist or for the general run, not even for those who make it a profession. But it is undeniable that those of my friends who survived the war were strengthened by the experience. One of the strongest contrasts I can think of between my artist friends here and those abroad lies in this matter of spirit and energy. The American writer, from what I know of him through personal relations, is easily discouraged. I am baffled sometimes to know why he ever chose the pursuit of letters. He is certainly not in his calling with both feet. He is not "dedicated," perhaps that is the kindest way to put it. He is ready to renounce his calling as soon as the pressure becomes too hot. Part of the hopelessness and listlessness of the American writer is explainable by the attitude of the public, for the American public seems not only to be indifferent to the spiritual pabulum it receives, but actually prefers, if there is the slightest choice, physical or material nourishment. And even here, in this matter of physical and material comfort, the American is utterly deceived, utterly deluded. I have only to think of a day spent with any poor European artist—and how many I have known!—to realize that the American is incapable even of enjoying the little which is permitted him. . . . I mean, his physical wealth. His car may take him wherever he wishes to go, but what is he met with on arriving at his destination? If it is a restaurant, the food is usually unpalatable; if it is a theater, the spectacle bores him; if it is a resort, there is nothing to do but drink. If he remains at home with his friends, the conversation soon degenerates into a ridiculous argument, such as schoolboys enjoy, or peters out. The art of living alone, or with one's neighbor, is unknown. The American is an unsocial being who seems to find enjoyment only in the bottle or with his machines. He worships success, but on attaining it he is more miserable than ever. At the height of his powers he finds himself morally and spiritually bankrupt; a cough is enough to finish him off.

During the course of my seven months abroad I visited quite a number of writers, painters, sculptors; some were old friends, many were new ones, friends I didn't know I had until we met. Now and then I ran into an avowed enemy who usually ended up by becoming a friend. Most of these visits and encounters took place in small towns, villages and hamlets, such as Woluwe-St.-Lambert, Bruges, La Ciotat, Carcassonne, Montpellier, Périgueux, Les Eyzies, Morgeat, Lausanne, Vence, Seville, Wells (England). Corwen, Wales, will remain especially engraved in my memory. I had gone there expressly to pay a flying visit to John Cowper Powys, a man now in his eighties. Here was an Englishman (of Welsh blood) who had spent over thirty years of his life in America, "popularizing culture," as people fondly say. I had attended his lectures in New York, when I was in my early twenties; I had read a number of his books, and after a lapse of almost twenty-five years I had started up a correspondence with him. I deliberately make this digression to pay tribute once again to a great spirit. Here is a man who gave the best years of his life to America, who exerted a considerable influence over many of our contemporary writers and artists, and who some fifteen years or so ago returned to his native heath, to a tiny, remote village which none of the great world figures ever penetrate. Here, year after year, he has been turning out one profound, beautiful book after

another, most of them, I blush to say, unknown to our compatriots. In this ripe spirit I found a man of letters who is indeed an
honor to his calling, one of the few writers alive, I might add,
who can be looked upon as an example to other writers. I can
truly say of him that he is the youngest, the most alive spirit I
have ever encountered. He has evolved a philosophy of his own
—a philosophy of solitude or a philosophy of "in spite of," as he
calls it—which he practices and which keeps him literally "as
fresh as a daisy." He radiates joy and well-being. He acknowl-
edges as his sources of inspiration Homer, Dante, Rabelais,
Goethe, Shakespeare, Dostoevsky, Walt Whitman. He introduces
their names frequently in his conversations and never tires of
quoting their words. He is not only the most tolerant and gra-
cious individual I ever met but, like Whitman himself—for whom
he has the highest reverence—a man who has flowered from the
roots. Though he exudes culture and learning, he is at home with
children, nobodies and idiots. His daily routine is so simple as to
be almost primitive. It begins with a long morning prayer for the
protection of the creature world against the sadistic men of
science who torture and vivisect them. Without wants, he has become free as a bird, and what is more important, he is acutely
aware of his hard-won freedom and rejoices in it. To meet him is
an inspiration and a blessing. And this man, who has so much to
give the world, who has already given abundantly, indeed, is
hardly known, hardly ever mentioned, when the subject of letters
comes up. It ought to be written over his door, as coming from
the Lord Jehovah himself: "I am the one who fished you out of
the mud. Now you come here and listen to me!"

If I had met only John Cowper Powys my trip would have
been amply justified. But I had the great good fortune to meet
other unique individuals, all of them contributing to my enrich-
ment, enjoyment and understanding of life. Nowhere in Europe,
even in the enemy's camp, was I greeted with the silly, stupid,
pointless, and usually insulting queries which I am accustomed to
receiving from my American friends and admirers. Even the Juge
d'Instruction, before whom I was obliged to appear before leaving Paris, was more civil, tolerant and understanding of my work
than our pompous, fatuous American literary critics. It was ac-

tually a pleasure to be questioned by such a man, even though the subject was a painful one. And what shall I say of Francis Raoul, Chef du Cabinet at the Préfecture de Police in Paris, whom I had to seek out in connection with an extension of my visa? Show me his like in America! Show me the like, among police authorities, of Fernand Rude at the Sous-Préfecture in Vienne, where I spent hours looking over his library, particularly his rare collection of books dealing with Utopia, on which subject he is an authority. It was at this man's home that I met for the second time Dr. Paul-Louis Couchoud, who had once been the private physician, secretary and friend of Anatole France. Some may know him better as the author of *Le Dieu Jésus, Le Mystère de Jésus, Sages et Poètes d'Asie* and other works. I shall always remember him as the serene, gentle spirit who graced the table with his presence at the banquet offered a few intimate friends by M. et Mme Point of the Restaurant de la Pyramide in Vienne. Such a feast—for body and soul—as the Points gave that day could never have happened (for me) in any other setting. It was something that heretofore I had believed only the Romans or the Greeks capable of creating.

But how many wonderful souls I met throughout my journey! What marvelous days in the suburbs of Brussels, *chez* Pierre Lesdain; what explorations and feasts with his brother, Maurice Lambilliotte, the editor of *Synthèses;* what illuminating talks in Périgueux, Les Eyzies and Lascaux with Dr. de Fontbrune, the most brilliant of all the interpreters of Nostradamus; what serene, joyous conversations with Joseph Delteil of Montpellier, who gave us *Choléra, Sur Le Fleuve Amour, Jeanne d'Arc, La Fayette,* and the book I particularly treasured, *De Jean-Jacques Rousseau à Mistral.* How easy and natural it was to move with him from the beauty and glory of the antique world to such subjects as Jesus, Socrates and St. Francis of Assisi. And how natural again to converse, as with a long lost brother, with that amazing star of the cinema world, Michel Simon! Or shall I speak of that Saturday afternoon at the home of Blaise Cendrars, one of those giants of European literature whose name is hardly known to Americans? Who among us could "receive" in the manner of the inimitable Blaise? What a motley swarm of individuals passed in and out of his rooms that day! And with what warmth, vivacity, lucidity,

urbanity and genuine love of one's fellow man he greeted them
all!

As I write, there lies before my eyes the November issue of the
monthly bulletin put out by the Guilde du Livre in Lausanne.
What a treat for the eyes to see this little bulletin each month! Is
there a book club in America, or a publishing house large or
small, which issues anything comparable? If so, I have never
heard of it. The texts, the photos, the drawings, the reproductions, the covers, the lists of books—all are intimate, seductive,
engaging in this bulletin. I made it a point, when in Lausanne, to
call on Albert Mermoud, director of the club. I wish the directors
of American book clubs would do the same—we might have a
much needed change of diet.

I mentioned a moment ago the role of the public vis-à-vis the
writer. Certainly the European reader is a different species than
the American. He not only reads more books than the American,
he *buys* more. Everywhere I went books occupied a prominent
place in the home. And the owner knew his books, I might add. I
also had the impression that authors, living authors, play a more
important role in a man's life there. When an injustice is dealt a
writer by a court, a government, a publisher, or by another
writer, the public may be counted on to rush to the victim's defense. There are literary disputes, in European countries, which
literally rock the nation. With us only questions involving the
morals of an author seem capable of arousing public attention,
and it is then a sensational curiosity which is inflamed and not a
genuine, passionate interest. American publishers and editors
have done their utmost to destroy taste, passion and discrimination in the reading public. The situation has deteriorated to such
a point that reputable publishing houses will often urge a new
writer to permit one of their staff to rewrite his book, pretending
that such a procedure is in his own interests. A writer who is at
all different from the common run is virtually doomed. Each
house has its own idea of what is suitable or saleable. To meet
their varying demands—the most absurd, the most degrading demands—a young writer can beat his brains out and get nowhere.
The European publisher has his fixed ideas, too, I am aware; he
too is also a businessman first and foremost, and a very hard-

headed one to boot. *But,* he has a public to reckon with. He is a part of that public, in a very real sense. Besides, he is usually not just a businessman, any more than his authors are just writers. (It is only in our country, it seems to me, that a person can be "just a businessman" and not only be respected but emulated.) Though he is no angel in disguise, the European publisher has what might be called professional pride. I honestly believe the majority of them would not be content to be merely "successful."

From all this an American writer may well be inclined to ask if he would have a better chance abroad than here. My answer invariably is—Yes! Yes, even if he prove a failure. Because even as a failure he will have enjoyed contact with other writers, other kindred spirits, in an atmosphere here unknown—an atmosphere, let me hasten to add, undoubtedly more grim, more terrifying, more fecund, and ever so much more real. He will run every risk of starving to death, just as here, but he will not necessarily feel like a fish out of water, like a creature at the zoo, or like an escaped inmate of a lunatic asylum. He will not die a freak or a monstrosity, unless he possesses an unusual amount of genius. Naturally, the more genius he has the harder his lot will be. The world was not made for the genius, we know full well. It may comfort him to know, however, that if he has just the right amount of genius he will eventually be given bread instead of stones. Only in a few little countries, in this civilized world, is there any semblance of protection or encouragement given the man of talent. Russia, like America, to be sure, takes good care of those who toe the line.

When all is said and done, the greatest writers—and the most prolific ones!—are still the French. Many French writers, of course, just like many French painters, sculptors and musicians, are not French at all. It is to the honor of France that she has incorporated into her blood stream so many diverse foreign elements. It is a curious thing, on the other hand, that some of the most celebrated French writers give the illusion of being un-French. I mean by that *different,* vastly different from their compeers. Here in America, to be "different" is almost tantamount to being a traitor. Though our publishers will tell you that they are ever seeking "original" writers, nothing could be farther from the truth. What they want is more of the same, only thinly disguised. They most certainly do not want another Faulkner, another Melville, another Thoreau, another Whitman. What the *public* wants, no one knows. Not even the publishers.

In a profound sense every great artist is hastening the end. A great artist is not simply a revolutionary, in style, form or content, but a rebel against the society he is born into. What he clamors for, avowedly or unavowedly, is a new deal—in other words, *freedom*. His idea of freedom is life lived imaginatively. This is the real tradition sustaining art, this belief, this conviction, that the way of art is the way out of the wilderness. That it is, in short, *the* way of life. In no period of man's history has this type of individual ever had an easy time of it. For him the enemy is not without the gates but within. He is always the alien, the pariah, the disturber of the peace, the iconoclast and the traitor. And always "the corrupter of youth." Whenever the public loses faith in the artist, it is the artist's fault. It is his fault because it means that he has lost sight of his high role. Lost faith in himself, in other words. Who but the artist has the power to open man up, to set free the imagination? The others—priest, teacher, saint, statesman, warrior—hold us to the path of history. They keep us chained to the rock, that the vultures may eat out our hearts. It is the artist who has the courage to go against the crowd; he is the unrecognized "hero of our time"—and of all time.

We are now deep in the period (which began with the French Revolution) signalized by Nostradamus as "the vulgar advent." Everything points toward a smash-up. Again and again the leaders of the world have demonstrated that they are incapable of solving the problems which beset us. To be more accurate, we should speak of "the" problem, since it is the same age-old one of how to live together on this earth in peace and harmony. Grave and acute as the situation now may be, it is probably not unprecedented in the long, and mostly unknown, history of man. How many times the current has been shut off, how many times the light has gone out, no one knows. All we do know for a certainty is that the creative spirit is incapable of being annihilated. Man *is* capable of solving this age-old problem, and far greater ones too. The artists—I take the liberty of calling them such—who have guided and inspired the race, the great spirits who have kept the flame alive, have always made use of a language, which, because symbolic, had the flavor of the eternal. *"My kingdom is not of this earth."* That is symbolic language, from the mouth of the greatest artist that ever lived. Unless an artist accepts these words as his very own he is merely a dabbler, a maker of words and not a creator. Which explains, perhaps, why the very great have written little or nothing at all.

"What is the worst?" writes R. H. Blyth. "Sin, suffering, death. If only we can be lifted up by these waves, instead of being submerged by them, we shall be free. Free from what? Free from the illusion that we are not free. Our illusions that we are not (now) free, are our hopes. Our hopes, for a better condition than we are now in, are not only the cause of grief, but the grief itself."*

Let us face it . . . what is the worst, for an artist? To be silenced? I doubt it. One who is really a force, a mouthpiece of God, will make himself heard without opening his lips. But what a blow it would be, what a masterful stroke, if by common consent the artists all over the world would voluntarily silence themselves! It is, to be sure, an unthinkable situation. When you say artist, alas, you say ego. Nevertheless, try to think for a moment what absolute confusion, bewilderment and bedevilment would ensue as a result of such strategy. Think what it would be like to hear the roar of the mob, nothing but this voice of the mob! No doubt about it, the world would blow itself to smithereens.

The European knows the power and the fury of the mob; he has experienced it numerous times. America has never known a revolution, or a great plague. America has thus far kept the mob in hand, by deluding it into believing that it is getting what it wants. As Chesterton says somewhere: "Some beautiful ideal runs through this people, but it runs aslant." The last world war, unspeakably hideous, was not waged by barbarians; it was conducted by the foremost nations of the world, the "cultured" nations. At least, the nations engaged looked upon themselves as such. Is this, then, the be-all and end-all of culture? Does it reach

* *Zen in English Literature and Oriental Classics,* The Hokuseido Press, Tokyo, 1948.

its maximum of achievement in this unholy crusade of mutual extermination? Wherein lies the mighty role of art? Do artists also kill one another? They most certainly do. With few exceptions they too, in times of panic, go the way of the mob, often aiding and abetting the impotent puppets who unleash and direct the slaughter. Admitting this, I nevertheless firmly believe that no world order, no world harmony, is possible until the artist assumes leadership. I mean by this that the artist in man must come to the fore, over against the patriot, the warrior, the diplomat, the fanatical idealist, the misguided revolutionary. It is not against the gods man must rebel—the gods are with him, if he but knew it!—but against his own mediocre, vulgar, blighted spirit. He must free himself to look upon the world as his own divine playground and not as a battlefield of contending egos. He must lift himself by his own bootstraps, so to speak. He must throw away his crutches. Above all other men the artist has this power to free himself. More than any man he knows that what he desires is attainable, that what he imagines is true and real, the only truth, the only reality. His function is to imbue his fellow man, by whatever means he possesses, with this ineluctable view of things. Let it not be said that he lacks the means. The true artist will forge the means to make his message transparent. No matter how black the picture may look, he has everything on his side. He is the only earthly being who is truly sovereign, provided he acknowledge to himself that the source of his power and inspiration is divine, and accessible to all.

Man has proved himself a thinker; man has proved himself a maker; man has proved himself a dreamer. He has yet to prove —to himself above all—that he is completely *man*. Of what use the great religions, the great philosophies, the sciences, the arts, of what use the noble ideals—every people has had them in turn —if we cannot make way for man? Where is man? What has become of him amid his teeming creations? If God is absent from man's work, how much more so is man himself?

To travel about in Europe is a treat for an American because it is like entering a honeycomb after a long sojourn in the open desert. At every step one is made aware of the continuous, persistent, indefatigable efforts of this creature called man. It cries

out from architecture, paving blocks, monuments, landscapes,
factories, museums, libraries, schools, churches, fortresses, from
everything one looks at or touches or senses directly or indirectly. It makes itself felt even in the air one breathes. Man the
builder, man the hunter, man the warrior, man the worshipper,
man the lover, man the maker of words and of music, man the
fabricator of the most subtle and the most deadly essences, man
the keeper and the prisoner of man. Everywhere man, man, man:
his work, *his* achievements, *his* longings, *his* hopes, *his* dreams,
his failures, *his* deceptions and betrayals. Sometimes he has
worked for the glory of God, but more often for the advancement
of the devil. There he is, today as of yore, squirming and twist-
ing, elbowing his way, wriggling through knotholes, trampling
upon the dead, taking advantage of the weak, pushing on, forever pushing on, toward an invisible goal. The future. Always
the *bright* future! Not for a moment can he cease his activity,
glorious or dismal though it may be. What demon possesses him?
To what end this frightful, monstrous striving? Is he slaving to
make the world a better place? Is it for his progeny that he is
concerned or for himself? Whichever way he answers it is a lie.
He does not know why he struggles, or for what. He is caught up
in a mechanism which is beyond his understanding. He marches
on, head down, eyes closed, conditioned so from birth. *That
is man,* in the large—European man, American man, Chinese
man, Soviet man, man the world over, wherever there is culture
and civilization. And with all this "progress" he has not advanced
an inch. He stands at the same frontier he faced fifty thousand,
or a hundred thousand, years ago. He has only to make a jump
(inwardly) and he will be free of the clockwork. But he can't.
He won't. With an obstinacy unthinkable he refuses to believe
in himself, refuses to assume his full powers, refuses to raise
himself to his ordained stature. He elects for Utopia rather than
Reality. He professes to believe that things *can* be different—
by which he always means "better"—while remaining himself
the same. He has invented a complete catalogue of vile and
scabrous epithets which he is ever ready to sling at those who
think and act differently, that is, think and act as he himself
would like to, if he had the courage. He has created enemies out

of thin air. He has voluntarily enrolled in a phantom war which promises never to end. He has, moreover, deluded himself into thinking that this is the only right course to pursue. He would convince the animal world of this truth and righteousness, if he could. And wherever he appears—or erupts—he leaves a scar upon the face of the earth. Now he toys with the idea of harnessing the planets, as well as the spaces between, in order to carry on his ghastly, ghostly work of despoliation. Why does he stop at the planets? Why not ransack the entire universe? What's to hinder? Give him enough rope and, by God, he will do just this. He is now at that ripe stage of devolution wherein he is foolish enough to believe that he can take the universe apart and destroy it piece by piece—just to prove to himself that he is not impotent. He would unseat the Creator, if he had enough humility left to conceive of something greater than himself.

In his steadfast march toward utter annihilation it is conceivable that he will arrive one day at that quixotic point in time and consciousness when it will become as clear as a bell to him that he has neither created nor destroyed a blessed thing . . . not a thing . . . not even a speck, a crumb. All that he tortured, maimed, butchered, annihilated (as he thought) will then rise up before him and mock him. He will stand alone in the great void, the supreme symbol of hollowness and emptiness. And he will be seized with such a panic that the shaking of his bones will sound in his ears like the rattle of dice in a box.

And when, precisely, do you imagine all this will take place? Why, any o'clock now. Is time so important? He has already mutilated and butchered billions of his kind, to say nothing of the birds and beasts, or the microbes, or those devastating ideas which he fears even more than microbes. Let him roam the universe entire, armed with his puny inquisitional weapons. What are another million years in the face of self-discovery? Time is a hangman's rope. Let it stretch wide and taut!

And you still think Europe is a better place for the artist? Of course! Why not? Europe, Timbuctoo, Easter Island, Patagonia, Beluchistan . . . what difference does it make? *Anywhere but the place you're in.* That's present-day logic. Take your poor, weak, suffering carcass and expose it to other germs, other humiliations. Here you scratch yourself to death; there you bite yourself to death. Where here, where there? Why, *anywhere,* of course. Know, to begin with, that you are a martyr, and you will begin composing the most heavenly songs. When you burn you will be able to sing them with a will. For that is your lot, that is your destiny. Thank the good Lord that you are not as other men. Flaunt your otherness and you will earn more stripes —bloody ones, what I mean. Yours to howl and gnash the teeth. Learn to do it well and you may earn the Nobel Prize. And don't forget, when it comes your turn to address the Royal Stockholm Academy, that one of the great blessings of civilization is the electric chair.

To come back to Europe . . . Europe, when one lives it in the mind, is almost like any other place on earth. The one difference, perhaps, is that in Europe all these thoughts are familiar, all these thoughts can and do find expression, or, now and again, suppression. You can think almost *anything,* in Europe. You can *be* almost anything there. Europe is a ferment, a constant ferment. And where there is constant ferment it matters little whether you are at the bottom or the top. The important thing is to realize that it is an intangible, spiritual crucible which is in ferment and not an atomic-energy plant.

In that biographical rhapsody called *Napoleon,* in which Elie Faure gives us an awesome glimpse into the soul of Europe— its hidden fires, its frenzied struggles, its meteoric illuminations, its incorrigible anarchy—there comes a passage which goes thus:

"I do not think that Napoleon ever indicated an ideal aim to reach, an aim demanding belief in one of the entities—justice, liberty, happiness—with which it is so easy to stir the multitudes. He consistently addressed himself to their latent energy, which he developed by the most virile means, to their sense of honor, which he invoked, to their spirit of emulation, which he exalted. The social optimism of popular leaders, on the other hand, the optimism which holds before the people a metaphysical or social idol for them to capture, demands an immediate abdication of their own liberty. In order to make others believe, they, the leaders, must believe in realities situated outside themselves and accessible to all, not by means of personal risk and

personal effort but by submission to a certain number of com-
mands, to transgress which is represented as a crime. . . ."

Once again the herd is ready to stampede. Beneath all the
ferment there is an ominous silence, an attitude of lying in wait,
like a beast of prey. Europe is ready to spring into action—but
very likely in a direction which no one at present can possibly
suspect. Today, seemingly exhausted, obviously divided, without leadership and with no clear apparent goal, she seems utterly ineffectual. The error which realists are only too prone to
make is to confound the apparent with the actual. Europe is
quite capable of making a *volte-face* overnight. Even in her present state of bewilderment and anguish, with nothing to salve
her wounded pride, Europe possesses sufficient poise, sufficient
equilibrium, to make the most momentous decisions. Let us not
forget that all the striking figures in European history—and what
a galaxy they represent—have been individuals, men *and* women,
endowed with extraordinary imagination. It is a gift revealed as
much in a St. Francis as in a Napoleon, in a Dante as in a Rabelais, in a Marquis de Sade as in a Joan of Arc. The daring
which made the great saints, the great heretics, the great scientists, the great philosophers, the great artists, the great "poets
of action," is a permanent attribute of the European soul. Without it, no Europe.

If there is one thing that permeates Europe through and
through it is art. This constant communication with the spirit
pervading all life renders Europe at once potent and vulnerable.
The dilemma now facing her makes it imperative to see it through
in her own way—that is, passionately, poetically, recklessly—
or compromise and go the way of the Gadarene swine. My belief
is that she will follow the dictates of her own artistic conscience.
My conviction is that by means of the particular creative energy
which is distinctly hers she will find a solution to the dilemma, a
solution, needless to say, *bouleversante* for the rest of the world.

The day of wrath is upon us. The way has been shown us
again and again, but we have chosen to walk in darkness. When
the lights go out let us be thankful if we have left enough inner
radiance to glow like the glowworm. We have made too much—
and too little—of the dazzling light of genius. For ages we have

been content to bathe in the sputtering phosphorescence which our men of genius have given off. We have sat back and watched the spectacle instead of taking fire ourselves. And finally we have substituted a cold fire—that nothing might be harmed, nothing destroyed, by sparks of ecstasy or of madness.

> Woe to them that go down to Egypt for help; and stay on horses, and trust in chariots, because they are many; and in horsemen, because they are very strong; but they look not unto the Holy One of Israel, neither seek the Lord!

Thus singeth Isaiah—Chapter 31, Verse 1.

But I say unto you: "Even though all our creations be brought to nothingness, even though the good perish with the wicked, even though the prophets themselves be silenced, nothing will prevent the coming of Zion!"

Quest*

"What would you do if I were dead?" That is the question the author puts to the mother of his four children. It is the year 1930 in Germany, with six million people unemployed. George Dibbern is then a man of forty-one who has spent some wonderful years during his youth among the Maoris in New Zealand. Now he is on the dole and everything of value he possesses has been either hocked or sold. Everything except a thirty-two-foot boat which he had christened the *Te Rapunga*—Maori for "The Dark Sun." There is no hope for him in Germany; he is not herd-like enough to be a good Communist, or militarist enough to be a good Nazi. He has had it out with himself and he has decided he will not be a living corpse. He will take the boat and sail to New Zealand, where Mother Rangi, the Maori woman who is his spiritual mother, awaits him.

Break out or die! That is the decision we all have to make some time or other. Man does not live by bread alone. George Dibbern obeys the inner voice, leaves his wife and children whom he loves, and sets sail. It is an act of desperation, but it is an act! and he is not a man who shuns the consequences of his acts. It takes him five years to reach New Zealand and when he does Mother Rangi is dead. But in the course of this long and fruitful journey George Dibbern finds himself. "If we are in harmony with life," he discovers, "life will keep us alive." Or, as he puts it elsewhere, "The more we find ourselves—our individuality—the more we find God."

In every thought, every act, George Dibbern gives proof of his manhood. "At present," he says, "I can no longer be a member of one nation, only a member of a bigger group, humanity."

* A review of *Quest,* by George Dibbern, W. W. Norton & Co., 1941.

And when George Dibbern says a thing he means it, he acts on it. He sails the _Te Rapunga_ under a flag of his own creation; he also devises his own passport in which he declares himself to be "a citizen of the world." What would happen, I wonder, if all who preached the brotherhood of man followed suit? How long would the stupid barriers and restrictions of nationality hold?

The importance of this book, which is really the log of an inner voyage, is in the example it sets forth. Relying solely upon himself, his own inner resources, Dibbern discovers the value of dependency. Out in the middle of the ocean, sitting at the tiller in utter silence for long hours, this man thinks everything out for himself. "One needs distance and aloneness," he says. At sea few books stand the test. Everything but the Bible goes overboard. "I find that my own thoughts are quite as interesting as the thoughts in books." As a matter of fact, the reader will discover as he goes along that George Dibbern's thoughts are _more_ interesting than the thoughts of most authors. George Dibbern really thinks. And the more he thinks for himself, the more I find him in agreement with all great thinkers. But George Dibbern is greater than most thinkers in that he puts words to act. In this he approaches the religious figures. "I can find truth only through sin," he soliloquizes. "Not trying is equal to not moving, which is equal to living death. Death is the penalty of sin; therefore not moving is sin."

The long voyage is not an escape but a quest. The man is seeking for a way to be of service to the world. Toward the end he realizes what his mission in life is—"it is to be a bridge of good will." _Un homme de bonne volonté!_ He is all that, George Dibbern, and more. He is a veritable crusader. If he does nothing more than give us this book, he will have performed a great service to humanity. This is the sort of book which truly stimulates, which inspires. The physical adventures, the physical hazards, which alone would make it an exciting book, are nothing compared to the moral and spiritual struggles which he tells about. He is always truthful and revealing, and the more he strips himself the more he finds himself in harmony with his fellow man. In the wildest storms he is ecstatic, at one with the whole universe. To him the sea is like a protective mother; it is on land

Passport
George John Dibbern

Born: 26 March '89
Town: Kiel
Country: Germany
Profession: Writer
Eyes: Blue
Hair: Gray
Height: 5 ft. 9 ins.
Weight: 140 lbs.

Signature

George John Dibbern

I, George John Dibbern, through long years in different countries and sincere friendship with many people in many lands feel my place to be outside of nationality, a citizen of the world and a friend of all peoples.

I recognize the divine origin of all nations and therefore their value in being as they are, respect their laws, and feel my existence solely as a bridge of good fellowship between them.

This is why, on my own ship under my own flag, have my own passport and do not seek other protection under the goodwill of the world.

that real ugliness commences. He never fears the sea, no matter how frail the boat; it is the land which to him appears fraught with perils. At Las Palmas, Columbus' last port before he set sail for America, Dibbern visits the little church where Columbus knelt to ask a blessing for his voyage. "What went through the soul of this man, Columbus?" he asks himself. "What a destiny, what a responsibility, lie on the road of a first one. Well it is to call on the help of all good spirits, that they may unite themselves with the power of the pioneer. . . . The one who is consciously a pioneer—what courage he needs, what faith!" Reflecting thus, he finally comes to the conclusion that "our trip is only a means to an end; the adventure lies in the sail through the ocean of the spirit, to find a sea (see) way to God. No fear must I have. I must sail into the unknown, and as crew I have law-breakers, criminals—my passions, lusts, lies, laziness, and many other handicaps; but one power I have also, a heart full of warm love, love for man, for the world, for beauty, purity, truth, which we call God. Thus it is; and so let come what will. . . ."

In the Caribbean Sea ("a jewel box with the lid broken open and the gems thrown over a blood-stained deck") his mind is filled with thoughts of the Spaniards and their lust for gold, of the slave traffic, of piracy and lawlessness, of crime unending . . . all in a setting of Paradise. "Perhaps," he reflects, "a time will come when the masses on the continents will lose their freedom, to be made conscious of what freedom is. . . . How much we talk about freedom, we who are so unfree, how much we talk about Christianity, when all our nations seem to cry of service to other gods! It may be in the end as it was with me. A careless remark about going to sea in my small boat finally forced me to eat my own words, or sail. So, to justify ourselves, we may have to live Christianity yet."

Toward the end of the book he voices this same thought even more poignantly. There he is, at the end of the world, his wife and children still in Germany—and five years have elapsed. He has just said good-by to his friend Gunter, who was the mate on the _Te Rapunga,_ and a strange fellow indeed, but a great mate. Suddenly he feels lonely and unprotected, and the future stretches out in dim uncertainty. When will he see his wife and children again, he wonders. Then he says: "When a soldier gets his marching orders he just goes, he doesn't know where, or for how long, or if ever he will come back again. Nobody ever questions it, or objects, or thinks it queer; but if one follows one's God, one's own conscience, everybody objects—strange, how little man belongs to himself, how much he is yet the community's property. . . ." But by this time George Dibbern knows which flag to follow and what *is* his calling. Thoughts like the above are not relapses, merely transitory moods which assail the stoutest heart.

By the irony of fate, this man who had truly made himself free, above all free of hate, fear and prejudice, this man who had severed all ties, all claims—except to serve—was put into a concentration camp in New Zealand because of his German origin. And not for the first time. The same thing had happened to him in the same place during the First World War. His publishers do not know what has happened to him in the interim. I wrote him as soon as I had read his book. I hope that others who read him will do likewise. A man like Dibbern is entitled to know what friends he has made in the outside world through his book. It is not that he needs *us;* it is we who need *him.*

Here I had intended to stop, space being limited. But I feel I must add a few more words. . . . One of the fascinating things about this book is its leisureliness. Somewhere in the middle of the Pacific Ocean, Dibbern remarks that he has learned to sit and do nothing. A great accomplishment! Somewhere too in the midst of that long crossing, when his relations with the uncouth mate threaten to reach the breaking point, he observes that even as a boy he had always won out by giving way, by practicing jujitsu, as it were. When forced to go one mile, go two! he urges. It's that second mile that counts, that proves the man you are. "Pain is what ultimately brings home the lesson," he insists. In all these observations he reveals himself as a Taoist. One takes up the path in order to become the path.

Some might think, from reading this cursory review, that Dibbern was unadaptable, a man unfit for human society. This is not true. If anything, it is society which is unfit to accommodate itself to a man like Dibbern. In this respect he resembles our own Thoreau. These men are far ahead of society; their tragedy is that they are condemned to wait for the others to catch up. Dibbern is not a renegade or an escapist, fatuous terms, when you think of it, since the real escapist is the man who adapts himself to a world he does not suscribe to. No, it is the purity and integrity of men like Dibbern which make it difficult for them to fit into our world. Living his own life in his own way, Dibbern makes us realize _how much_ life may be enjoyed even on the fringe of society. It is not his ideal; he is striving desperately to participate, to be at one with his fellow man, but on the best terms, i.e., on the terms of his own best self. _That,_ society will not allow, it seems. It is society which rejects, not Dibbern. Dibbern merely refuses to play their rotten game. Nor will he wait to lead the ideal existence until some mythical day in the future. He will live the ideal life right now—as much as he dares and can. And that is the difference between a rebel and a man of spirit. It is a difference in Dibbern's favor.

Somewhere about the middle of the book he offers up thanks to all those who had made the trip possible. It is a very wonderful passage, for not only does he thank those who helped but those who criticized and condemned, for, as he says, "they made us think." And then he adds: "Endlessly one could thank, for one is nothing without those amongst whom one lived, from whom one learned, on whose knowledge one builds up. If only I, in my way, can some day be of use!" A man who can speak thus is the very opposite of an isolated individual; such a man is not a crank or a crackpot. He may be a dreamer, but have we not need of the dreamer most of all? "If I serve, I will be kept!" that is his motto. Serve humanity, he means, not Mammon. He seeks neither fame, nor money, nor security. He takes every risk, courts danger rather than avoids it. He concludes that "one's greatest security is to be loved." "Banks fail, love never," he says. The world, however, does not believe in this kind of security. Such talk is just mush, it pretends. But it isn't mush! It's the deepest kind of truth, and wise and good men the world over from time immemorial have testified to it. George Dibbern could never have made the great voyage if it were not true. Love is the only protection; all other kinds of protection lead to war.

If this were a world in which love prevailed, a man like George

Dibbern would never have been allowed to remain in a concentration camp. In all this wide world there could be no more innocent victim of man's stupid injustice than George Dibbern. If there were just a little love, just a little imagination, George Dibbern would be given another boat, the best boat afloat, and his flag and his passport too, and we would urge him with all our heart and soul to continue sailing the four seas in the name of freedom. Surely there ought to be room in this world for one man who wants to be nothing more, nothing less, than "a citizen of the world." Wherever he roams, George Dibbern's passport should be honored, his flag saluted. And if we had understanding as well as love, we would bow to him in passing.

Open Letter to Small Magazines

Dear George Leite: The letter "Easter Sunday 1934" to Emil Schnellock regarding Carco's *Utrillo* is one I had hoped Bern Porter would publish in *Semblance of a Devoted Past*. If he is willing to let you use it first in *Circle* I shall probably give my consent, only I would like to reread it first myself. The question of remuneration, however, I should like to clear up beforehand with *you, and all other editors of small magazines.*

You say: "A five dollar payment is all that we have at present." My dear fellow, have you any idea what an absurd sum five dollars is in a country like ours—even for an old letter? That letter appealed to you because it depicted the tragic plight of a man whose work has brought great joy to millions of art lovers. Today Utrillo is no longer in need. But Francis Carco undoubtedly is, and I, though no longer desperately in want, am still seeking a just reward for my labors.

I don't doubt you when you say that five dollars is all you can offer. But have you ever thought that there may be other ways of remunerating a writer than by giving cash? Understand, please, that I am not averse to giving things for nothing; I have contributed to many magazines without asking a penny. In Paris my friend Alfred Perlès and I ran a magazine (*The Booster*, which later became *Delta*) and it was the contributors who paid to keep the magazine going. The only American writer who could have paid, the only one of us who earned a living from his work, balked at the idea. I was also one of the contributors to a French revue called *Volontés*, where again it was we, the writers, who supported the magazine. Is there such a magazine in America, I wonder? If there were, if it were a magazine which, like the ones I mentioned, permitted the contributors to express themselves freely, I would be the first to offer my work, the best I could offer. I mention this because it might give you ideas.

When you think of paying an author for his work you ought to think generously. It is the author who makes your magazine. If you cannot pay in cold cash, why don't you write the author and ask what you could do for him? Offer to do something in the nature of a personal sacrifice, I would say. He may need to have some typing done, or some printing; he may need a table to write on, or books of reference; he may need some research work done for him. There are a thousand and one things he may need and appreciate much more than cold cash, especially when it constitutes a sum which, by American standards of living, means absolutely nothing. It costs me, for example, almost five dollars a week for postage. It costs me much more than that for the gifts of books and water colors I am obliged to make to enthusiastic admirers who are too poor to buy my work.

On the other hand, when I myself want something of a fellow artist, let us say a painting, for example, I do not write and say: "My dear Varda, or my dear Rattner, I would love to have that painting I saw at such and such a gallery. I have only five dollars to offer at the moment—will you accept it?" No, I write and say: "I am crazy about your painting. I must have it. What do you want for it? What is the top price? I can't pay for it outright, but I can give you so much a month. Would that be acceptable to you? If, while I am paying you off, someone offers you a good sum outright for it, please don't consider me . . . sell it." I do not ask to have the painting until I have paid for it in full. I am willing to wait three years, if necessary, in order to acquire it. And then, as it usually happens, I am not able to live with it after all, because I must be off somewhere and I must travel lightly.

But this, it seems to me, is the way one good artist should treat another. And you who are editors of small magazines are mostly artists yourselves, I take it. You all expect to become celebrated writers some day; you identify yourselves with the men whose work you admire and hope to publish. Well, carry out the identification to the *n*th degree, I say. Think how you would feel if, after years of labor and struggle, you are asked to accept a trivial sum. It is far, far better to say: "We have no money at all. We believe in you and your work . . . will you help us? We are willing to make any sacrifice in order to make your name known." Most authors would be touched by such an appeal; they would offer their work gladly; they would probably offer to help in other ways. I am thinking naturally of the kind of writers whom you wish to interest in your project. There can be a magnificent collaboration between author and editor, author and publisher. But you, as editor, must first begin by giving, not demanding. Give the shirt off your back, or offer to give it, and then see what sort of response you will get from the author. I have often noticed with beggars that when they ask for something and you offer them twice or ten times as much, they are so overwhelmed that they often refuse to accept anything, or else they offer to become your slave. Writers, in a way, are like beggars. They are continually begging to be heard, to be recognized. Really they are simply begging for a chance to give of their great gifts—which is the most heart-rending begging of all and a disgrace to any civilized community in which it happens. Which is to say, almost the entire civilized world.

Speaking of Carco's book, which provoked all this . . . it is too bad you cannot ferret him out and give him something. I remember so vividly the night I first saw and heard him. I was walking through that little street called the Rue Champollion in the Latin Quarter. I noticed a billboard announcing that he was to recite some of his poems that evening in this little theater. When I entered the lobby I saw a great stack of books his collected works. And he was doing a stunt that evening for a pittance, because he was in great need.

Perhaps I have recounted all this in my letter to Emil—I don't recall any more what I said in that letter. I remember only the emotion I experienced on reading his touching tribute to Utrillo. But, talking of giving, I do want to add this. When I went home that night I sat down and wrote Francis Carco a letter. I told him quite honestly that I had been moved to tears in the theater hearing him recite, knowing the agony and humiliation he must have endured in offering himself up as a spectacle. To my great surprise I received a day or two later a warm letter from Carco together with a de luxe copy of the poems he had recited that evening. He might have sent me an ordinary copy, or none at all, since his letter was more than a gift, but no, he sent me the best copy he could lay hands on. Only poverty-stricken men who are great in spirit do these things.

That's all. Good luck to you! I'm sure we understand one another.

My Life as an Echo*

One of the chief complaints leveled at me by English critics is that I never write about anything but myself. By now, it is true, I must have written several million words, scattered throughout a dozen or more so-called autobiographical romances. I am sick of hearing about myself, even from my own lips. But since I am challenged to write a few thousand more words—about myself— I must acquiesce, and with good grace, even at the risk of boring the reader. So here goes. . . .

It is usual to commence these things with a few pertinent facts —date and place of birth, education, married or divorced, and so forth. Is it necessary, I wonder? Next year I shall be seventy years old. Old enough, in other words, for even the average reader to have gleaned a few salient facts about my life. That is, if I am what rumor always purports me to be: a nine-day wonder in the realm of obscenity, farce, mysticism and obscurantism.

Though I was born in Yorkville, Manhattan, a few hours too late to be a Christmas present, and though I claim as my country the 14th Ward of Brooklyn, actually I might just as well have been born in the Himalayas or on Easter Island. American through and through, I am less at home in my own country than anywhere. I am an anomaly, a paradox and a misfit. Most of the time I live *en marge*. My ideal is to become thoroughly anonymous—a Mr. What's-his-name. Or just George, like the iceman. In short, I am at my best when nobody knows me, nobody recognizes me. When I am just another nobody, in other words.

It was about the middle of the 1930s, when I first read about Zen, that I began to perceive the delicious efficacity of being a

* Apologies to Moishe Nadir, the Yiddish writer whose title I have borrowed.

79

nobody. Not that I had ever longed to be a somebody. No, all I had ever begged of the Creator was to permit me to become a writer. Not a sensational writer, or a celebrated one, either. Just a writer. I had tried, you see, to be most everything else—without success. Even as a garbage collector, even as gravedigger, I showed no marked signs of ability. The one position I did fill with some degree of success (though unrecognized by my masters) was that of personnel director in the Western Union Telegraph Company, in New York. The four years I spent hiring and firing the miserable creatures who made up the fluctuating force of messengers of this organization were the most important years of my life, from the standpoint of my future role as writer. It was here that I was in constant touch with Heaven and Hell. It was for me what Siberia was for Dostoevsky. And it was while serving as personnel director that I made my first attempts at writing. It was high time. I was already thirty-three years old and, as the title of my trilogy indicates, it was a rosy crucifixion which I was about to experience.

To be truthful, the ordeal commenced somewhat before entering the service of the Western Union. It commenced with my first marriage and hung over into my second. (The Italian reader should bear in mind, of course, that at thirty-three an American is still somewhat of an adolescent. Few indeed, even if they live to be a hundred, ever pass beyond the stage of adolescence.) Naturally, it was not the marriages which were the cause of my suffering. Not altogether, at any rate. The cause was myself, my own cussed nature. Never satisfied with anything, never willing to compromise, never getting *adjusted*—that abominable word which the Americans have taken over and raised to apotheosis.

It was only when I got to France, where I came to grips with myself, that I realized that I alone was responsible for all the misfortunes which had befallen me. The day that truth dawned on me—and it came like a flash—the burden of guilt and suffering fell away. What a tremendous relief it was to cease blaming society, or my parents, or my country. "Guilty, Your Honor! Guilty, Your Majesty! Guilty on all points!" I could exclaim. And feel good about it.

Of course I have suffered since, many times, and undoubtedly will continue to do so . . . but in a different way. I am now like those alcoholics who, after years of abstinence, finally learn how to take a drink without fear of becoming drunk. I mean that I have made my peace with suffering. Suffering belongs, just as much as laughter, joy, treachery or what have you. When one perceives its function, its value, its usefulness, one no longer dreads it, this endless suffering which all the world is so eager to dodge. When it is regarded in the light of understanding it becomes something else. I called this process of transmutation my "rosy crucifixion." Lawrence Durrell, who was then visiting me (at Villa Seurat), expressed it in another way; he dubbed me "as of henceforth" *The Happy Rock*.

To become a writer! Little did I dream, in begging the Creator to grant me this boon, what a price I would have to pay for the privilege. Never did I dream that I would be obliged to deal with so many idiots and blunderbusses as have crossed my path these last twenty years or more. I had imagined, in writing my books, that I was addressing myself to kindred spirits. Never did I realize that I would be accepted, and for the wrong reasons, by the unthinking mob which reads with equal relish the comic strips, the sports news and the financial reports of the *Wall Street Journal*. Everyone knows, who has read my book about Big Sur (where I have been living these last fourteen years), that my life in this remote, isolated spot is that of a squirrel in a cage: perpetually on view, perpetually at the mercy of any and every curiosity seeker, every autograph hound, every tuppenny news paper reporter. Perhaps it was the premonition of just such an absurdity which led me to insert a long quotation from Papini's *Uomo Finito* in my very first book, *Tropic of Cancer*. Today, much like Einstein, I feel that if I were granted a second life I would elect to be a carpenter or fisherman, anything but a writer. The few whom one's words reach, to whom one's words make sense, give joy and comfort, will be what they are whether they read one's books or not. The whole damned business of book after book, line after line, boils down to a stroll in the park, a few doffs of the hat, and a "Good morning, Tom, how goes it?" "Just fine . . . *and you?*" Nobody is any the wiser, sadder or happier. *C'est un travail du chapeau, voilà tout!*

Then why do you continue? one may well ask. The answer is
simple. I write now because I enjoy it; it gives me pleasure. I'm
an addict, a happy addict. I no longer have any illusions about the
importance of words. Lao-Tzu put all his wisdom into a few
indestructible pages. Jesus never wrote a line. As for the Buddha,
he is remembered for the wordless sermon he gave while holding
a flower for his listeners to regard (or hear). Words, like other
waste matter, eventually drift down the drain. Acts live on. The
Acts of the Apostles, *bien entendu,* not the beehive activity which
today passes for action.

Action. Often I think of it this way: I and my body. You fling
your body around—here, there, everywhere—but *you* remain
the same. You might as well have stood still. If what must happen, what must be learned, doesn't occur in this life, it will the
next time around, or the third or the fourth time. We have all
time on our hands. What we need to discover is eternity. The
only life is the eternal life. I have no ready-made prescription
as to how to obtain it.

No doubt some of the foregoing observations are highly unpalatable, particularly to those benighted souls who long to set
the world on fire. Do they not realize, I wonder, that the world
has ever been on fire, and always will be? Aren't they aware
that the Hell we are living in is more real than the one to come—
if one deals in that nonsense? They should at least take a little
pride in the fact that they too have contributed to the making of
this Hell. Life on earth will always be a Hell; the antidote is not
a hereafter called Heaven but a new life here below—"the new
heaven and the new earth"—born of the complete acceptance
of life.

I see that I am forgetting my subject—myself. It is obvious
that there are other subjects which are more enticing to me.
Sometimes I even find theology absorbing. Believe me, it *can be,*
if one is not tempted as a result to become a theologian. Even
science can assume an interesting aspect, provided one does not
take it seriously. Any theory, any idea, any speculation can aug-
ment the zest for life so long as one does not make the mistake
of thinking that he is getting somewhere. We are getting nowhere, because (metaphysically speaking) there is nowhere to

go. We are already there, have been since eternity. All we need do is wake up to the fact.

It took me some fifty-odd years to wake up. Even now I am not thoroughly awake, else I would not be writing these extraneous words. But then, one of the things one learns as one goes along is that nonsense also has its place. The real nonsense, of course, goes under such highfalutin names as science, religion, philosophy, history, culture, civilization, and so on and so forth. The Mad Hatter is not your miserable *clochard* lying in the gutter with a bottle clasped to his bosom but His Excellency, Sir Popinjay of His Majesty's Court, he who pretends to have us believe that, armed with the right words, the right portfolio, the right top hat and spats, he can placate, tame or subdue this or that monster who is making ready to gobble up the world on behalf of The Peepul, or in the name of Christ, or whatever the song happens to be.

Frankly, if we must play with this idea of saving the world, then I say that in making an aquarelle which pleases me—*me, not you* necessarily—I am doing my share better than any cabinet minister with or without portfolio. I believe that even His Holiness, the Pope, little as I believe in him, may be doing his part too. But then, if I include him I must also include such as Al Capone and Elvis Presley. Why not? Can you prove the contrary?

As I was saying, after I quit the Messenger Employment Department, after I had been a gravedigger and a scavenger, a librarian, a bookseller, an insurance agent, a ticket chopper, a ranch hand and a hundred other equally important things (spiritually speaking), I landed in Paris, soon was down and out—would have become a pimp or a prostitute had I had the makings for it—and ended up becoming a writer. *What more would you like to know?* Between times is what I can't fill in, because I have already used up my fillers in my "autobiographical romances," which, if I have not already warned the reader, should be taken with a grain of salt. There are times when I myself no longer know whether I said and did the things I report or whether I dreamed them up. Anyway, I always dream true. If I lie a bit now and then it is mainly in the interest of truth. What I mean to say is that I try

to put together the broken parts of myself. The dreamer who
rapes or murders in his sleep is the same person who sits in the
bank all day counting somebody else's money or who officiates
as president of a republic. Or isn't he? Are all the crooks of this
world behind bars or are some of them masquerading as min-
isters of finance?

Maybe this is the moment to observe that I am at last approaching the end of my interminable autobiographical sleigh
ride. The first half of *Nexus* has recently been issued by Editions
du Chêne, Paris. The second half, which I should have written
six months ago but may not begin for another five years to come,
will bring to an end what I planned and projected in the year
1927. At that time I thought the story of my life (which is, in
truth, only the record of seven years of my life, the crucial years
before leaving for France), at that time, as I say, I thought one
huge volume would do the trick. (*The Story of My Misfortunes,*
by Henry Abélard Miller.) I would have my say, in short, and
then bury myself. It was not that simple. Nothing is simple,
except to the sage. I got caught in my own web, so to speak.
What I have now to learn is whether I can break the web or not.
"The Web and the Rock"—are they not one and the same?

Never shall I forget the impact which Otto Rank's *Art and
Artist* made upon me. Particularly that part wherein he speaks
of the type of writer who loses himself in his work: who makes
his work his tomb, in other words. And who did it most effectively, according to Rank? *Shakespeare.* I would also include
Hieronymus Bosch, of whose life we know almost as little as we
do of Shakespeare's. Where artists are concerned, we are always
desperately struggling—*itching* would be the better word—to
put our fingers on the man. As if the man called Charles Dickens, for example, were quite another entity. It is not that we
are so eager to have the complete being in our grasp as it is that
we can never quite believe that the artist and the man are one
and the same. In my own case there are friends, for example,
who know me intimately, or at least who treat me as if they did,
and who profess that they do not understand a word I have written. Or worse, who have the cheek to tell me that I invented it
all. Fortunately I have a few friends, a mere handful, who know

and accept me as a writer and as a man. Were it not so I might have grave doubts as to my true identity. To be a writer at all one must certainly have a split personality. But when it comes time to reach for your hat and take an airing, you've got to be certain that it's *your hat,* your own legs, and the name is Miller, not Mahatma Gandhi.

As for tomorrow, there just ain't any. I've lived all my yesterdays and all my tomorrows. *Pro tem* I am just treading water.

Should I write more books, books I never intended to write, I will excuse myself by calling it a stroll in the park. . . . "Good morning, Tom, how goes it?" "Fine . . . *and you?*" In other words, I now have my tail in my mouth. With your permission I'll just roll along. No need for anyone to give me a rap with a drumstick, if you get what I mean. Frankly, I don't quite get it myself, but that's the general idea, as we say in our American lingo.

The Immorality of Morality

What is moral and what is immoral? Nobody will ever answer the question satisfactorily. Not because morals are constantly changing but because the principle behind it is a factitious one. Morality is for slaves, for men without spirit. And when I say spirit, I mean the Holy Spirit.

What had Jesus, in whose name so many crimes are committed, to do with morals? The word seems never to have crossed his lips. Elie Faure refers to him as "the great immoralist." At any rate, we know this for certain, that Jesus strove to give us a way of life, not a moral code.

It goes without saying that those who strive to maintain the *status quo* are the most immoral of all. To them the great sin is to question the prevailing order. Yet every great thinker, every great artist, every great religious teacher did just that.

The subject becomes more complicated when it is admitted that these rebels or iconoclasts found a way to live in the world without being part of it. "To render unto Caesar what is Caesar's. . . ." Ambivalence? Contradictoriness? Hypocrisy? Not at all. Still less, defeatism. No, the great triumph of these original souls lay in their discovery of a solution beyond the opposites. By not resisting evil, which Jesus meant absolutely and which no one seems willing to accept, these few shining examples of light and truth evaded the pitfalls which beset the ordinary believer.

Everyone wants a better world, everyone wants to be other than he is, everyone disclaims responsibility for the evils which beset us. Everyone believes in a Paradise or a Heaven, whether here and now or in the hereafter. No one seems able to support the idea that this may be the one and only world for us. Yet, unless one does accept this unpalatable fact, there can never be a Paradise—either in the beyond or here and now.

If there ever was a period when man did not possess a soul, certainly in gaining one—or even formulating the idea of one—the whole aspect of creation has changed. As a soulful being, man is no longer a "creature" but a partner in creation—*divine* creation, for there is but one kind of creation. Realizing the significance of his own nature, man has altered the nature of prayer. No man of spirit endeavors to placate or propitiate the Creator. Fully conscious, erect, face to face with his Maker, man can but sing His praises. The only form of prayer worthy of man is a prayer of thanksgiving.

But do we remember this in our trials and tribulations? No. What we all unreasonably demand is that life be given on *our* terms. We forget the extent to which, through inertia, through silence, through abject submission, we have contributed to our own defeat. We forget that we have seldom collaborated with the Creator, which is our one and only task. Ever straying from the Source, we naïvely wonder why we find ourselves howling in the wilderness.

Every day the choice is presented to us, in a thousand different ways, to live up to the spirit which is in us or to deny it. Whenever we talk about right and wrong we are turning the light of scrutiny upon our neighbors instead of upon ourselves. We judge in order not to be judged. We uphold the law, because it is easier than to defy it.

We are all lawbreakers, all criminals, all murderers, at heart. It is not our business to get after the murderers, but to get after the murderer which exists in each and every one of us. And I mean by murder the supreme kind which consists in murdering the spirit.

There is one thing I believe to be implicit in the story of martyrdom which Jesus enacted. It is this, that we do not need to repeat the sacrifice which he made. By assuming the burden of guilt and sin for mankind Jesus meant, in my opinion, to awaken us to the real meaning of life. What is the purpose and meaning of life? To enjoy it to the utmost. We can do so only by making ourselves one with life. "The life more abundant" means simply and unequivocally "life everlasting," nothing but life.

I have an old friend whom many would characterize as an unconscionable rogue. A rogue he is, but a delicious one. A rogue
who is closer to being on the path than any righteous man I have
ever met. He does nothing for the world, and very little for himself. He simply enjoys life, taking it as he finds it. Naturally he
works as little as possible; naturally he takes no concern for the
morrow. Without making a fetish of it, he takes inordinately
good care of himself, being moderate in all things and showing
discrimination with respect to everything that demands his time
or attention. He is a connoisseur of food and wine who is never
in danger of becoming a glutton or a drunkard. He loves women
and knows how to make them happy. Though married, he does
not deprive himself of extramarital relationships. He causes no
one suffering and, if you asked him about it point-blank, he
would probably answer that he never suffered in his life. He
never thinks about suffering, either his own or other people's.
He exists as if the world were perfect and made expressly for
his own delectation. If there be a war, and if he is obliged to fight,
he will fight—no matter on which side. He doesn't worry about
whether he will be killed or not, but only about doing as little
killing as possible. When he's radiantly happy, and he's almost
always happy, he sometimes loves himself so much, is so de-
lighted with his own happiness, so to speak, that he will kiss
himself—on the hand or arm, whichever is most convenient. I
believe he would kiss his own ass, if he could, in certain moments of exaltation.

Now why would one want to call such a lovable fellow a
rogue? Obviously because he isn't playing the game as we expect
it to be played. Obviously because he is enjoying life so thoroughly. Obviously because he doesn't worry about *our* misfortunes. Obviously because he doesn't care who rules the world.
And most of all because he knows on which side his bread is
buttered.

Those who don't think of him as a rogue call him childlike.
This is meant to be even more condemnatory. That one can
freely consort with publicans, sinners, harlots, drunkards and
criminals is understandable to certain minds only if the person
in question be regarded as a nitwit. My friend often refers to

himself as a "half-wit." He does so smilingly, much as a Dostoevskian character would if he had a bit of the saint in him. Indeed, by poking fun at himself, minimizing himself, refusing to uphold or defend himself, my friend has a way of disconcerting the other fellow which is not only laughable but genuinely salutary. If he were pressed, for example, to say whether he believed in Christ or not, he is more than apt to answer: "I don't give a shit about Christ. What did he ever do for me?" He would answer that way out of annoyance, because he finds it stupid that people should ask one another such questions. But he is indubitably closer to Christ than to Satan. He is more like Christ, I wish to add, when he does those things which seem to be contrary to the way of Christ. Which is saying a great deal. Yet how can I better drive the point home? Jesus was never harsh with sinners, as we all know. He was harsh with moralists and hypocrites, with those who observed the letter of the law rather than the spirit of the law. Jesus had no social status whatever; he was fluid and flexible, until he had to do with those who were intolerant.

My friend knows very well when he is "sacrificing to the elementals," as he loves to put it. He doesn't use the word *sin*. When he gives in to the demands of the flesh he does it with the ease of a man relaxing after a hard day's work. He doesn't want to put too big a strain on himself, that is all. I'm not a hero, he means to say, or a saint, or a martyr. *I'm just me.* With such an attitude it follows that he seldom suffers from hang-overs and never from guilt complexes. He's always ready for the next issue, whether it be a feast or a spot of dirty work.

Sometimes I wonder if he'll ever die, he's so bright and fresh and new all the time. Never seems to be soiled, never gets used up. What health and vitality, what joy, radiates from his countenance! It's almost shameful to look that way in a world such as ours. And when he kisses himself all over, because the meal was good and he enjoyed it so much, he seems to be thanking the Creator in dog-like fashion. But if it be dog-like, his behavior, it is without a doubt meritorious. Would that we were all more dog-like!

If he lives on another twenty or thirty years—why not forty

or fifty years?—he will have all the attributes which the Orientals find in their "gay old dogs." Which means that he will be as wise as the serpent and as gentle as the dove. He will not be hungering for immortality because he will have enjoyed everything life offers *in the flesh*. He will not have to prove anything by dying any more than he had to prove anything in living. Asked which is best for man, this way or that, he will be able to answer: "Any old way!" Or else: *"The way you are."*

This is what I mean by morality versus immorality. Be moral and you get yourself crucified; be immoral and you ruin yourself. "There was only one Christian and He died on the cross." There is more truth in this saying of Nietzsche's than is generally suspected. Jesus did not die on the cross in order that we should follow his example. He died on the cross in order that we might have life everlasting. He did not need to die on the cross; he might have given battle to the world and triumphed over it. He might have become the Emperor of the World instead of its scapegoat. He said: "I have *overcome* the world!" That was a far greater triumph. He overcame the world so thoroughly that it has never been able to get rid of him. The world is permeated with his spirit. It seeks in vain for a solution of its ills other than the way he pointed out. If it denies him, it is none the less subject to him. "I am the light of the world," he proclaimed, and that light still shines. "The Kingdom of Heaven is within you," he announced, restoring to every man his divinity and supremacy. When he healed a man or woman, when he cast out the devil, he would say: "Go and sin no more!" He never defined sin, he never fought against it. He annihilated it by not recognizing it. That is morality and immorality.

When I was quite young I read Lecky's *History of European Morals* from cover to cover, hoping to get to the bottom of this subject. I discovered only what one would discover if he looked at anything through a kaleidoscope. After Lecky I read the theologians, and after the theologians the mystics, and after the mystics I read the Cabalists. And so on. All I seem to have discovered, of importance, is that with every expansion of consciousness a radical change in morals ensues. Or, to put it more accurately, every innovator, every individual with a fresh vision or a larger vision of life, automatically destroys the existent moral code—in favor of spirit. But his disciples soon establish a new moral code, one just as rigid as the preceding one, forgetting that the spirit will again break the vessel which contains it.

We know all too little about the great precursors—Manu, Prometheus, Zoroaster, Hammurabi and such like. But what little we do know of them permits us to believe that the great truths they handed down were simple in essence. From the earliest times man seems to have been endowed with a conscience. When we penetrate the wisdom of the truth-sayers we discover that conscience was not meant to be a burden, that it was to be used instinctively and intuitively. It is only in periods of decadence that truth becomes complicated and conscience a heavy sack of guilt.

The neurotic character of our age is not only a sign of our guiltiness, it is also an indication of hopefulness. Instead of openly expressing their rebellion against the stupid and abominable scheme of things, men are expressing it through illness and maladaptation. The sick ones in our midst, and their number is increasing by leaps and bounds, are the criminals who have yet to be found out. They are undermining the social fabric even more than the industrialists and the militarists, even more than the priests and the scientists. Unable to buck the existent code, they render themselves inoperative—by becoming mental and moral cripples. They fail to realize, most of them, that it is precisely because of their spiritual nature that they have unwittingly outlawed themselves. They are symptomatic, in a negative way.

It sounds like defeatism to say to the young of our day: "Do not rebel! Do not make victims of yourselves!" What I mean, in saying this, is that one should not fight a losing battle. The system is destroying itself; the dead are burying the dead. Why expend one's energy fighting something which is already tottering? Neither would I urge one to run away from the danger zone. The danger is everywhere: there are no safe and secure places in which to start a new life. Stay where you are and make what life you can among the impending ruins. Do not put one thing above another in importance. Do only what has to be done—

immediately. Whether the wave is ascending or descending, the ocean is always there. You are a fish in the ocean of time, you are a constant in an ocean of change, you are nothing and everything at one and the same time. Was the dinner good? Was the grass green? Did the water slake your thirst? Are the stars still in the heavens? Does the sun still shine? Can you talk, walk, sing, play? Are you still breathing?

With every breath we draw we are utilizing forces that are absolutely mysterious as well as all powerful. We are swimming in a sea of forces which demand only to be utilized and enjoyed. The problems which beset us are human problems, problems largely of our own making. The great problems remain untouched: we have not the vision as yet to recognize them. But in accepting our everyday problems, accepting them gladly and unreservedly, we may make ourselves fit to cope with the greater ones to come. The mathematician is not appalled by the problems which face him in his work, neither is the surgeon, nor anyone who engages seriously in whatever pursuit. Why then should man, as a species, be terrified of the problems which beset him? Why should he deny the monster which he has created with his own hands? If he has spawned a monster, let him devour his own monster!

The great sacrifice which we must all make, each and every one of us, is to burn away the dross. In other words, consign to the living flame that which is dead. If we put off the task, if we refuse to face the issue, the day will come when "the quick and the dead" are judged. There *is* a day of judgment, make no mistake about it. Life is continually weighing us in the balance. The Day of Judgment is not an invention of the religious-minded but a psychic or spiritual phenomenon obedient to the moving calendar of our own conscience. It is always Hades or Easter on the day of reckoning. It has been so since the beginning. And it promises to be so eternally.

This is the cross which man carries and on which he can burn with the flame of eternal life or be pilloried like a thief. There is no escape. As it says in the Avestas: "Evil exists not, only the past. The past is past; the present is a moment; the future is all."

Ionesco

1

Every now and then the theater seems to come alive. One begins to be hopeful, to realize all over again what a powerful and exhilarating medium the play is. One is amazed to see what can be done by a group of amateurs, with meager resources, who receive no reward for their efforts but the applause of the spectators. Such were my reflections on leaving the Studio Theatre in Carmel the other night after witnessing the performance of the two Ionesco plays.

When the curtain came down on *The Chairs* I was beside myself with excitement. I looked about me and was stupefied to observe that the theater was only half filled. Scanning the faces in the row behind me I was annoyed to see the same blank, impassive expressions which greet one on entering a doctor's waiting room.

What follows is pure propaganda. It is addressed to all the lonely souls whose features are ravaged with ennui whom I encounter after dark in the streets of Monterey, Pacific Grove and Carmel, or on the terrace of Nepenthe, or in the gloomy ghost-ridden bars and eating places of the Peninsula. When it gets too oppressive, the loneliness, the despair, the nausea, try The Studio on Dolores Street. Try a dose of Ionesco. He will be here for another three weeks only. After that it's Arthur Miller and his marimba band, the old one-two-three and "Waltz Me Around Again Willy."

With Ionesco you don't have to wait for the third act to see the hero die. His characters are dead from the start, many of them invisible or living in limbo. Hence exciting. Not dead alive, but alive and dead at the same time. I'm thinking of *The Chairs*

93

particularly, though *The Bald Soprano,* who never appears, is also full of tomato juice and other diuretics. The materials which Ionesco employs are altogether familiar and recognizable; so much so, in fact, that one doesn't know whether he is hearing himself think or taking a walk through Alvarado Street during Holy Week. The atmosphere has that "dry luster" which Heraclitus calls "the best and wisest condition of the spirit." All is hilarious and irredeemably tragic. No exits. When the curtain falls, start again. Nothing is ever lost because eternity is undefinable and indescribable.

So you find yourself bringing in more chairs or else waiting for someone to answer the doorbell. Meanwhile you've abandoned your aged parents, betrayed your comrades in arms, swallowed a hogshead of dialectic materialism, died at the barricades, found no cure for the piles, won the Nobel Prize and lost it, been to Agnew and back three times, joined the Church of God or Alcoholics Anonymous, remained true to your wife and all your mistresses, and signed your own death warrant with a handsome twenty-one-carat gold-pointed fountain pen, the best.

Or you may find, while dining with friends, that the woman you have been sleeping with is your wife. *Comme la vie est drôle!* It's at this point in your life that the Bald Soprano threatens to materialize. (We are never informed whether it is a male soprano or a female, only that it is bald.)

Whether it makes sense or not, this is theater. This is not what happens on Alvarado Street or in the purlieus of Pebble Beach, but what happens in the mind of a man sitting in another hemisphere, one shoe on and one shoe off. A man not listening to the radio, not watching the World's Series, not washing the baby's diapers, not putting his house in order, not asking his wife where she was all night, not thanking his boss for a raise, not counting his dividends, not worrying about satellites, not asking for another chance, and so on. A man so far out that the world and all that fills it fits like a jigsaw puzzle. All he asks is permission to take you apart and put you together again, make of you a *Massemensch* or a wild duck, for the man of the masses never existed and the wild duck can never again become a tame duck.

The theater is where the possible and the impossible meet,

where happenstance is the rule and the planets conjunct with deference to their victims. And this is exactly what occurred on the night I mentioned, and it has rarely happened to me before. I can hardly believe it happened in Carmel, though why not? since stranger things have happened there—for example, Bach losing his stainless-steel head.

But the most unbelievable thing about it all is that in a village renowned for its salubrious climate, its devotion to the arts, its wealthy widows and cracked spinsters, its curio shops and absentee landlords, nothing even remotely related to the filthy lucre accrues to the members of this theater group for whom we have such gratitude and admiration. Surely, if we can afford to destroy the natural beauty of our scenic highways at the cost of millions of dollars, we should be able to endow one group of sincere, earnest, imaginative thespians.

Let us not lay all our ills to the Communists and the Beatniks in our midst. Waiting for Godot in a comfortable seat is one thing; waiting for the Messiah in a hair shirt is another. Keep waiting and there'll be no theater left. Only the permanent open-air theater which stretches from Alvarado Street to the Nevsky Prospekt, which brings us each week the same forlorn, empty faces, the same smart uniforms of the Universal Suicide Brigade, the same nuclear-fission diet, the same hysterectomies, the same three-star Hennessys, the same sameness of the everyday, whether it's a cold war or a hot war, Easter, Christmas or Yom Kippur, whether capital punishment, euthanasia or an overdose of sleeping pills.

We particularly wish, in closing, to thank Richard Bailey for being that special kind of idiot who chooses to cast and direct plays which will be popular fifty years from now, perhaps on another planet, when His Majesty, the Emperor, comes into his own.

2

It may be interesting to the casual reader to know how I first became acquainted with Ionesco's work, that is, "The Musical Chairs," for that is how the title stuck in my crop. I was in a small French town called Die, aiding and abetting the publication of a scandalous little book called *The True Christ and His Kingdom.*

In the stationery store one day I made the acquaintance of a young professor of literature who always began and ended his strictures with Corneille, Racine, Molière. It so happened that I had just returned from a visit to Uzès, the seat of the first duchy of France, where Racine had resided for several years. I had never been enamored of Racine, but I was definitely for Uzès, which was full of ghosts, elegant ones, balustrades, esplanades, fenestrated towers and the clink of armor falling to pieces. My failure to evince the slightest interest in Racine exasperated the professor.

To mollify him I expanded on my enthusiasm for contemporary drama, beginning with a few now dead, such as Ibsen, Strindberg, Wedekind, Andreyev and that curious personage who wrote *A God of Spit,* Sologub, I believe.

In utter disdain he remarked: "And no doubt you like Ionesco too."

"Of course," I replied, never having heard the name before. "Of course! And especially his *Un Monsieur Qui Pue.* (Roughly translated—"A Gentleman Who Stinks.")

Not wishing to betray ignorance of a play which had no existence, the professor cleverly veered into a vituperative analysis of what I understood to be "The Musical Chairs." What incensed him, apparently, was not the profusion of chairs which cluttered the stage but the utter farrago created by the noncorporeal occupants of the chairs. Naturally I was utterly bewildered, but I hung on by a hair, as is recommended to all seekers of salvation.

Further bewildered by his recondite allusions to Pythagorean, Cartesian and Peloponnesian modes of approach, I somehow got the idea that the chairs not only spoke each in its own way but that they also gave forth music. A most remarkable idea, thought I to myself, and made a mental note to visit, on my return to Paris, the quaint little hole in the wall where, week after week and month after month, Ionesco was being produced.

Oddly enough, some weeks later I was back in Paris, and day after day I passed the little theater where I might have heard the music of the chairs but never did. It was difficult enough to drag my carcass home after the stupendous luncheons I was obliged to share with my publisher, who had grown rich overnight, thanks to *Lolita*. Anyway, each time I approached the Rue St. Sevérin, where my publisher had his office (as well as a restaurant, bar and *dancing*), I would stop a moment and study the poster announcing the musical chairs.

The neighborhood, first made famous by Dante and later by Elliot Paul, still retained the charm which only the truly decrepit and poverty-stricken can bequeath. Toothless hags with arms akimbo hurled coarse imprecations at one another or danced like harpies in the middle of the street; some, too drunk to know the difference, poured wine down their bosoms or squatted to make water.

Delicious décor. Just suited to the over-all philosophy of repetition exuded by the Ionesco plays. Nights the North Africans played at cutting one another's throats. Now and then a bleary-eyed tourist, usually Anglo-Saxon, was sucked into a hallway and cleaned of his superfluous wealth. The streets were so narrow that if an adding machine and a vacuum cleaner happened to meet, one or the other had to give way. Passing a second-floor restaurant it was advisable to hug the wall as the waiters frequently scraped the remnants of a meal out the window. The rats which scampered about unmolested were as large as Siamese cats and thoroughly unwholesome in appearance.

What a décor! Garbage, insanity, theft and mayhem together with shiny black olives, dates strung like cartwheels, pornographic books always wrapped in cellophane, delicious cheeses, poems to De Gaulle, not always laudatory, walls covered with graffiti, nuns hurrying stiffly along in their starched calicoes, the police with sub-machine guns, finger ever on the trigger, poets disguised as pimps and vice versa, and here it was, in the open sewer so to speak, that Dante lectured on philosophy and the art of rhetoric. Here it was, too, that Max of *The White Phagocytes* had a room on the top floor which he offered to trade with Dante, Leonardo or Joachim of Floris in exchange for a cosy hall bedroom in the Bronx.

My son Tony, whom I took occasionally to share the staggering meals which my publisher always provided, used to stand in

wonder when the old hags began to dance, scream and gesticu-
late.

"Are they crazy or are they drunk?" he once asked me.

"Both, my boy," I replied. "That's what keeps them fit."

"I don't like it," he said.

"Okay," I would say, "after lunch I'll take you over to the
Champs Elysées."

"And what'll we see there?" he wanted to know.

"Plenty," I replied. "And we'll have a *coupe* of champagne—
unless you prefer Coca-Cola."

What I meant to do, of course, was to have a quiet chat with
him, preferably at the Marignan, about the theory of instantaneous repetition. In Amsterdam the governess I had employed to
take care of the children had given him a full-course explanation
of the philosophy of Descartes. After that we had all gone to see
King Solomon's Mines, which was infinitely more exciting. That
same night, seated in the alcove of our de luxe suite, the governess (who was a young man, by the way) and I decided to put
on a one-act play for the kids. We did it impromptu and with
such éclat that the kids decided that they would do one for us.
And they did. Gosh, but we felt good that night! Think of it—we
could act! And without make-up, without rehearsals. "You lay it
down, Nazz, and we'll pick it up." That's how it went. To a *non-
sequitur* we countered with a veronica or a novena. The worst
was that none of us slept a wink all night. We were writing plays
which we would give in Oslo, Stockholm, Brussels, Paris, Berlin,
Vienna, Hong Kong, Nagasaki, Singapore, Penang. It was a little
like Pentecost, only less metaphysical.

Which brings me back to Ionesco and the delicious nougats we
ate in Montelimar on our way to the mountains of Vercors. Val,
my daughter, was talking of horses and how she missed them;
Tony was deep in one of Caryl Chessman's books, one he had already read twice. As for myself, I was conducting an imaginary
conversation with the author of *The True Christ and His Kingdom,* whom we would see in a few hours. Obeying an impulse to
water the flowers, I wandered down a winding street in search of
a picturesque urinal. Suddenly, to my amazement, I was standing
before one, the most original, the most bizarre, I have ever

stepped into. (The view to one side was of a dog and cat ceme-
tery.) As there was just room for one, I had time to study the
hieroglyphics that descended from the cupola-like dome to the
height of my head. Kilroy had been here, too, I gathered. And
not only Kilroy but Pontius Pilate, Nebuchadnezzar and Eliphas
Levi.

"Behold the work of man," it said in Sanskrit, which I happen
to read easily. The rest was in the pictorial language of Rameses
II. But the remarkable thing was that, just as I was about to make
my exit, a pigeon—a fantail, no less—settled on my shoulder.
The next instant I felt it peck at my right ear lobe. Was it a warning—or a simple endearment?

When I got back to the café where the family was devouring
the delicious nougats, I was informed that De Gaulle had just
driven by in an open barouche. "And where were *you* all this
time?" they demanded. I said I had been looking for a book.

"A *book?* What book?" they chorused.

"The Musical Chairs," I said.

"Is it funny?" asked the boy.

"You made it up," said the girl.

"I didn't either," I replied. "Yes, it's funny, and it's sad too.
All those chairs. And they make music. Can you imagine it?"

"No," said Tony flatly.

"Well I can," I said, "because I went to see it in Paris while
you were staying at Le Puy."

"What do you mean you went to see it?" said the girl. "Then
it's not a book?"

"It is and it isn't," said I. "It's a play. Or to put it more precisely—the apotheosis of a play."

"It sounds crazy," said the boy.

"Exactly," said I. "It *is* crazy, and that's why I went to see it.
There are nine acts but the curtain never falls. It opens with a
man standing on a stool to look out the window; and it ends with
him jumping out the window, his wife too. The hero, who remains invisible, is the Emperor."

Chorus: "What Emperor?"

"Any old Emperor," I replied. "He has no name. Just—*Your
Majesty.*"

"And what does he do, this Emperor?"

"Nothing. Absolutely nothing. Except to take a seat. Or, I'll put it another way. *He lends his presence.* How's that?"

I was going to add a word about the shoulder bird that had pecked at my ear, but then I thought it would only add to the confusion. So I said nothing more. I picked up Caryl Chessman, wondering if they had executed him or not.

As I say, I had intended to have a quiet chat with the boy, to explain why, as Patachou croons in her smoky voice, *'y a tant d'amour sur la terre,"* or as Ionesco puts it: "Come here, my darling, sit in my lap; you could have been this and that, if only you had had more ambition."

The whole town was drenched in the odor of nougats, a sticky, sentimental smell such as greets you when you descend to the *lavabo* of the Marignan where, for a few francs and a pat on the back, the old woman, alias Frau Emil Jannings, will give you a telephone number that will send shivers up your spine.

But the odor of nougats was too strong, and it was only six months later, seated in The Studio on Dolores Street, that it all came back to me, what I had intended to tell him—about life, about love, about the odor of sanctity . . . oh, and many other, many, many things, some sad, some profound, some utterly silly, some heart-rendingly painful, like those half-truths which women hand out when they're cutting the navel cord and saying at the same time, "But I do love you, I love you very much, I've always loved you," and so on and so on. Yes, it all came back to me between the lines, or between the chairs, as the two darlings, only in their nineties, mind you, brought back the snows of yesteryear. *"Y a tant d'amour sur la terre."* But where, darling? It was so long ago I can't remember. But he does remember, she remembers, too, we all remember. *Remember?* Remember to re-member! You handed her the violets and they slipped out of her hand; you stepped on them—you were always so awkward—and they were crushed. And she said, "It doesn't matter. . . ." She didn't add "dear," but you heard it just the same and you trembled so that when she leaned over you forgot to kiss her, but she thought you did. And then you became a general, a general nuisance, and though you were really somebody nobody took you for anybody, least of all yourself. Seventy-odd years flew by like lightning—how time flies!—and sometimes you slept in the rain on a hard bench with your pocket full of cigarette butts and sometimes you slept between silk sheets which had the faint odor of patchouli. If it wasn't your wife it was somebody else's. What difference? Love was everywhere and you were such a great soul, though nobody knew it ever, that when you laughed you were weeping and when you wept you were laughing. And from the wings there always came the same music—*Ohimé, Ohimé, Ohimé!*

Yes, my darling, it was you who told me I had a message for the world. And someday I will give it to the World! Only it wasn't she, it was the other one. He was confused. They all took care of him as if he were an infant. "Come darling, sit in my lap!" And some had begged for him, some had stolen for him, some had given their bodies. He pretended not to know, not to see. But he knew, he saw, he felt. And the message sank deeper and deeper into his bowels, so that even if he lived to be as old as Noah he would never be able to dig it out, never deliver it in person, not even with the Pope's imprimatur, never, no.

Only ninety-five, and already so feeble, so absent-minded, so childlike. The head factotum, the king stud, the chief cook and bottle washer. Such a full, rich life—and all gone down the drain. "Where are you, my darling? I can't see you." It wasn't that the light had grown dim or that love had died: he was confused, that's all. Too many memories, too much or too little ambition. Repetition. Endless repetition.

I would wait till he was a little older, then tell him. Maybe back in California, on Pico Blanco. Maybe in the Gobi Desert. I would take him with me—to Lhasa, Mecca, Timbuctoo. Suddenly it dawned on me that I had not yet visited any of those places on my imaginary itinerary: Kyoto, Kamakura, Rangoon, Samarkand, Soochow, Lesbos, Cracow, the Engadine, the Vale of Kashmir. . . . Maybe he would have to carry me on his back. Maybe he would have to apologize for my decrepitude. The Old Man of the Mountains. The Happy Rock. Maybe I would never have to tell him, he might find out everything for himself. If only he wouldn't make the same fool mistakes as his father. "Dear

Father, how are things in Big Sur? We miss you. It's time to go to school now. Thank you for the three dollars."

Always such a good boy. A regular hellion, like his dad. One little difference: he never learned the catechism. Never entered a church, as a matter of fact. Why bother, when there's television, Disneyland, good Westerns and all that. "Is there really a God, Dad?" "Of course there is!" "How do you know?"

I should have said: "Wait a while, you'll find out. Love is where the river flows, and God is when you've got your back to the wall. You'll find out, my lad. Just wait!"

Anyway, we brought in some more chairs. They were getting heavier and heavier now. Another thrombosis. Maybe it was love again. (Never wanted to.) Yeah, why didn't he ask me that— "What is love?" Always God, arithmetic problems, flying saucers, the hidden face of the moon. Or—"Do you think there'll be another war?" Love would be easier to answer. Or Truth. (Just call Khrishnamurti—Ojai 694352.) The truth is—"*Y a tant d'amour sur la terre.*" More than enough for everybody, yet it never seems to go around. Leaks and blowholes. Quagmires. Still it's true, it exists, it can even be demonstrated. Aren't children born every day? Don't the flowers come up after a rain? Peace, it's wonderful! Especially after a victorious defeat.

Oh, I could tell him so much, so much. However, I'll wait. I'll wait till he's old enough to hear the music of the chairs. Maybe Ionesco will have given us a sequel by that time. Maybe it will be a happy ending, like in Hollywood, and the Emperor will hand out nougats or Eskimo pies or, who knows? maybe he'll deliver another Sermon on the Mount and everyone will leave the theater full of love, full of truth, full of life.

"*Y a tant d'amour sur la terre.*"

3

If the reader is not already fed up with Ionesco I should like to add a few more words on the subject, this time about *The Bald Soprano,* which was only cursorily touched on in my previous letters. The reason for this imposition is that a few days ago I received from one of the readers of the *Herald* the second number of a French revue devoted to theater arts—*Spectâcles*—in which the leading article is by Ionesco himself. It is entitled "The Tragedy of Language, or how a manual for learning English became my first play."

"In 1948," he begins, "before writing my first play, 'The Bald Soprano,' I had no thought of becoming a dramatic author. I had simply an ambition to learn English. Learning English does not necessarily lead to the art of the playwright. On the contrary, it's because I failed to learn English that I became a dramatic author."

He goes on to explain that, in order to learn English he made use of a beginner's French-English conversation manual which he had bought some eight or nine years before. Conscientiously he copied the phrases given into his notebook, in order to learn them by heart.

Rereading them attentively, he learned not English but the most surprising truths—for example, that there are seven days to the week, which he already knew; that the floor is below and the ceiling above, which he knew equally well, but which he had never seriously reflected upon or had forgotten, and which now suddenly appeared to him as being astonishingly and indisputably true. From universal truths he progressed, via the manual, to more specific truths, all expressed by means of dialogue. With the third lesson two personages made their appearance, Mr. and Mrs. Smith, an English couple. (Says Ionesco: "To this day I am not sure whether they were real or invented.")

After citing a few bits of the dialogue between Mr. and Mrs. Smith, between the Smiths and the Martins, their friends, between Mr. and Mrs. Martin, all sheer nonsense torn direct from the English-French manual, he goes on to remark about the indubitable, the perfectly axiomatic character of Mr. Smith's affirmations.

At this point in his study of English he had an illumination. He no longer cared about perfecting his knowledge of English. No, his ambition had assumed greater proportions. It was nothing less than to communicate to his contemporaries the essential verities of which the conversational lessons had made him aware. He had come to the realization that these asinine conversations between the Smiths and the Martins belonged peculiarly to the theater, the theater being dialogue, as he says.

It was thus he began writing *The Bald Soprano,* a specifically "didactic" theatrical work. (He had been tempted to call the piece *English without Effort* or *The English Hour* but chose the present title precisely because no soprano, bald or hirsute, has any part in the play. Nice reasoning, what!)

He then goes on to tell how *The Bald Soprano,* which began as an English exercise and a bit of plagiarism, got out of hand. The simple, elementary truths which he had painstakingly transcribed and employed as dialogue took on a crazy quality, the language became disarticulated, the personages themselves decomposed under his hand, the language, once absurd, became empty of all content. And so on.

What was taking place, he perceived, was a disintegration of all that was real. The words themselves became like sonorous bark, denuded of all sense; the personages also, of course, were stripped of their psychology, and the world itself appeared in a most unaccustomed light, with people moving in a time without time and a space without space.

The writing of this play, which he labeled an "anti-play," that is to say, a parody of a play or a comedy of a comedy, caused him such uneasiness, such nausea, such vertigo that at times he thought the play would dissolve into nothingness and himself with it. Nevertheless, when he had finished with it he felt rather proud of himself.

"I imagined," he says, "that I had written something like 'the tragedy of language.' " When he saw it presented on the stage he was astonished, so he says, to hear the laughter of the audience —as if it were something gay! There were a few friends, however, who were not deceived, who confessed, in other words, that they had been made to feel uneasy.

In England, as well as elsewhere, the more serious critics accepted the play as a satire on bourgeois society, as well as a parody of the legitimate theater. Admitting that it might thus be regarded, Ionesco nevertheless points out that such was not his primary intention. Rather, he says, what he wished to depict was a sort of "universal petite bourgeoisie," the petit bourgeois being decidedly the man of manufactured ideas, of slogans and catch phrases—in short, the conformist par excellence in every realm. And it is precisely the language—the language of the automaton —which reveals to us this ubiquitous conformist.

The Smiths and the Martins, says Ionesco, no longer know how to think; they are unable to think because they are incapable of feeling. They are passionless. Neither do they know how *to be;* they may and can become, no matter whom, no matter what. They are of an impersonal world, always other—in short, inter-changeable.

The text concludes thus: "The tragic individual does not change, he goes to pieces; he is himself, he is real. The comic personages, the imbeciles and idiots, they have no existence."

The foregoing is an abridged transcription of Ionesco's own words. I apologize for my inadequacy in rendering the subtleties and nuances, the delicious ironic humor which pervades his candid and ever lucid text. It has that undefinable quality which the French call *"spirituel."*

It seems altogether amazing to me that in less than ten years this man whose work was ridiculed and scorned—in Paris even, in the beginning, the audience sometimes numbered only ten or twelve—should have made his own way to the top. The critics have racked their brains to categorize these "anti-plays," these "pseudo-dramas," these tragic farces.

Ionesco himself, it is said, is unable to distinguish between the tragic and the comic. Each director must choose what stance to take, for what goes on takes place on many levels, and sometimes simultaneously. But how life-like, despite all the puzzlement!

That malaise which follows so quickly upon the laughter—or tears—of the spectators, is it not the emotional constant of our sleepwalking days and our nightmarish nights? The Martins and the Smiths, whether "real or invented," are they not our friends and neighbors? This Punch and Judy language, do we not hear it on all sides? Suburbia, is it not everywhere?

The robot, does he not punch the same time clock as us? The President speaking . . . could it not be any Tom, Dick or Harry? An Einsteinian formula—is it any more difficult to swallow than a vitamin pill? Who among us has not been castrated, put in harness, depersonalized, and delivered bound and gagged to the devils of toil and bubble? We are free to express our opinions—but have we any opinions? We talk to keep from talking. The disturbing thing is not that it is nonsense—nonsense can be delicious!—but that our words are made of nothing but the current of our habitual emptiness of heart, mind and soul.

Walt Whitman

I have never understood why he should be called "the good gray poet." The color of his language, his temperament, his whole being is electric blue. I hardly think of him as poet. Bard, yes. The bard of the future.

America has never really understood Whitman, or accepted him. America has exalted Lincoln, a lesser figure.

Whitman did not address the masses. He was as far removed from the people as a saint is from the members of a church. He reviled the whole trend of American life, which he characterized as mean and vulgar. Yet only an American could have written what he did. He was not interested in culture, tradition, religion or Democracy. He was what Lawrence called "an aristocrat of the spirit."

I know of no writer whose vision is as inclusive, as all-embracing as Whitman's. It is precisely this cosmic view of things which has prevented Whitman's message from being accepted. He is all affirmation. He is completely outgoing. He recognizes no barriers of any kind, not even evil

Everyone can quote from Whitman in justification of his own point of view. No one has arisen since Whitman who can include his thought and go beyond it. The "Song of the Open Road" remains an absolute. It transcends the human view, obliges man to include the universe in his own being.

The poet in Whitman interests me far less than the seer. Perhaps the only poet with whom he can be compared is Dante. More than any other single figure, Dante symbolizes the medieval world. Whitman is the incarnation of the modern man, of whom thus far we have only had intimations. Modern life has not yet begun. Here and there men have arisen who have given us glimpses of this world to come. Whitman not only voiced the key-note of this new life in process of creation but behaved as if it already existed. The wonder is that he was not crucified. But here we touch the mystery which shrouds his seemingly open life.

Whoever has studied Whitman's life must be amazed at the skill with which he steered his bark through troubled waters. He never relinquishes his grasp of the oar, never flinches, never wavers, never compromises. From the moment of his awakening —for it was truly an awakening and not a mere development of creative talent—he marches on, calm, steady, sure of himself, certain of ultimate victory. Without effort he enlists the aid of willing disciples who serve as buffers to the blows of fate. He concentrates entirely upon the deliverance of his message. He talks little, reads little, but speculates much. It is not, however, the life of a contemplative which he leads. He is very definitely in and of the world. He is worldly through and through, yet serene, detached, the enemy of no man, the friend of all. He possesses a magic armor against wanton intrusion, against violation of his being. In many ways he reminds one of the "resurrected" Christ.

I stress this aspect of the man deliberately because Whitman himself gave expression to it most eloquently—it is one of his most revelatory utterances—in a prose work. The passage runs as follows: "A fitly born and bred race, growing up in right conditions of outdoor as much as indoor harmony, activity and development, would probably, from and in those conditions, find it enough merely *to live*—and would, in their relations to the sky, air, water, trees, etc., and to the countless common shows, and in the fact of *life* itself, discover and achieve happiness—with Being suffused night and day by wholesome ecstasy, surpassing all the pleasures that wealth, amusement, and even gratified intellect, erudition, or the sense of art, can give." This view, so utterly alien to the so-called modern world, is thoroughly Polynesian. And that is where Whitman belongs, out beyond the last frontiers of the Western world, neither of the West nor of the East but of an intermediary realm, a floating archipelago dedicated to the attainment of peace, happiness and well-being here and now.

I maintain most stoutly that Whitman's outlook is not American, any more than it is Chinese, Hindu or European. It is the unique view of an emancipated individual, expressed in the broadest American idiom, understandable to men of all languages. The flavor of his language, though altogether American, is a rare one. It has never been captured again. It probably never will. Its universality springs from its uniqueness. In this sense it has all tradition behind it. Yet, I repeat, Whitman had no respect for tradition; that he forged a new language is due entirely to the singularity of his vision, to the fact that he felt himself to be a new being. Between the early Whitman and the "awakened" Whitman there is no resemblance whatever. No one, scanning his early writings, could possibly detect the germ of the future genius. Whitman remade himself from head to foot.

I have used the word *message* several times in connection with his writings. Yes, the message is explicit as well as implicit in his work. It is the message which informs of his work. Remove the message and his poetry falls apart. Like Tolstoy, he may be said to have made of art propaganda. But is this not merely to say that unless used for life, put at the service of life, art is meaningless? Whitman is never a moralist or a religionist. His concern is to open men's vision, to lead them to the center of nowhere in order that they may find their true orientation. He does not preach, he exhorts. He is not content merely to speak his view, he sings it, shouts it triumphantly. If he looks backward it is to show that past and future are one. He sees no evil anywhere. He sees through and beyond, always.

He has been called a pantheist. Many have referred to him as the great democrat. Some have asserted that he possessed a cosmic consciousness. All attempts to label and categorize him eventually break down. Why not accept him as a pure phenomenon? Why not admit that he is without a peer? I am not attempting to divinize him. How could I, since he was so strikingly human? If I insist on the uniqueness of his being, is it not to suggest the clue which will unravel the mysterious claims of democracy?

"Make Room for Man" is the title of a poem by his faithful friend and biographer, Horace Traubel. What is it that has stood in the way of man? *Only man.* Whitman demolishes every flimsy barrier behind which man has sought to take refuge. He expresses

utter confidence in man. He is not a democrat, he is an anarchist. He has the faith born of love. He does not know the meaning
of hate, fear, envy, jealousy, rivalry. Born on Long Island, moving to Brooklyn at the commencement of his career, serving first
as carpenter and builder, later as reporter, typesetter, editor,
nursing the wounded during the bloody Civil War, he finally
settles in Camden, a most inconspicuous spot. He journeyed over
a good part of America and in his poems he has recorded his impressions, hopes and dreams.

It is a grandiose dream indeed. In his prose works he issues
warnings to his countrymen, unheeded, of course. What would he
say if he could see America today? I think his utterances would
be still more impassioned. I believe he would write a still greater
Leaves of Grass. He would see potentialities "immenser far" than
those he had originally visioned. He would see "the cradle endlessly rocking."

Since his departure we have had the "great poems of death"
which he spoke of, and they have been *living* poems of death. The
poem of life has still to be lived.

Meanwhile the cradle is endlessly rocking. . . .

Henry David Thoreau*

There are barely a half-dozen names in the history of America
which have meaning for me. Thoreau's is one of them. I think
of him as a true representative of America, a type, alas, which we
have ceased to coin. He is not a democrat at all, in the sense we
give to the word today. He is what Lawrence would call "an
aristocrat of the spirit," which is to say, that rarest thing on
earth: an individual. He is nearer to being an anarchist than a
democrat, socialist or communist. However, he was not interested in politics; he was the sort of person who, if there were
more of his kind, would soon cause governments to become non-
existent. This, to my mind, is the highest type of man a community can produce. And that is why I have an unbounded
respect and admiration for Thoreau.

The secret of his influence, which is still alive, still active, is
a very simple one. He was a man of principle whose thought and
behavior were in complete agreement. He assumed responsibility for his deeds as well as his utterances. Compromise was not
in his vocabulary. America, for all her advantages, has produced
only a handful of men of this caliber. The reason for it is obvious: men like Thoreau were never in agreement with the trend
of the times. They symbolized that America which is as far
from being born today as it was in 1776 or before. They took
the hard road instead of the easy one. They believed in themselves first and foremost, they did not worry about what their
neighbors thought of them, nor did they hesitate to defy the
government when justice was at stake. There was never any-

* Originally a Preface to *Life without Principle,* three essays by Thoreau,
hand-printed in 1946 for James Ladd Delkin.

thing supine about their acquiescence: they could be wooed or seduced but not intimidated.

The essays gathered together in this little volume were all speeches, a fact of some importance if one reflects how impossible it would be today to give public utterance to such sentiments. The very notion of "civil disobedience," for example, is now unthinkable. (Except in India, perhaps, where in his campaign of passive resistance Gandhi used this speech as a textbook.) In our country a man who dared to imitate Thoreau's behavior with regard to any crucial issue of the day would undoubtedly be sent to prison for life. Moreover, there would be none to defend him—as Thoreau once defended the name and reputation of John Brown. As always happens with bold, original utterances, these essays have now become classic. Which means that, though they still have the power to mold character, they no longer influence the men who govern our destiny. They are prescribed reading for students and a perpetual source of inspiration to the thinker and the rebel, but as for the reading public in general they carry no weight, no message any longer. The image of Thoreau has been fixed for the public by educators and "men of taste": it is that of a hermit, a crank, a nature faker. It is the caricature which has been preserved, as is usually the case with our eminent men.

The important thing about Thoreau, in my mind, is that he appeared at a time when we had, so to speak, a choice as to the direction we, the American people, would take. Like Emerson and Whitman, he pointed out the right road—the hard road, as I said before. As a people we chose differently. And we are now reaping the fruits of our choice. Thoreau, Whitman, Emerson —these men are now vindicated. In the gloom of current events these names stand out like beacons. We pay eloquent lip service to their memory, but we continue to flout their wisdom. We have become victims of the times, we look backward with longing and regret. It is too late now to change, we think. But it is not. As individuals, as *men*, it is never too late to change. That is precisely what these sturdy forerunners of ours were emphasizing all their lives.

With the creation of the atom bomb, the whole world suddenly realizes that man is faced with a dilemma whose gravity is incommensurable. In the essay called "Life without Principle," Thoreau anticipated that very possibility which shook the world when it received the news of the atom bomb. "Of what consequence," says Thoreau, "though our planet explode, if there is no character involved in the explosion? . . . I would not run around a corner to see the world blow up."

I feel certain Thoreau would have kept his word, had the planet suddenly exploded of its own accord. But I also feel certain that, had he been told of the atom bomb, of the good and bad that it was capable of producing, he would have had something memorable to say about its use. And he would have said it in defiance of the prevalent attitude. He would not have rejoiced that the secret of its manufacture was in the hands of the righteous ones. He would have asked immediately: "Who is righteous enough to employ such a diabolical instrument destructively?" He would have had no more faith in the wisdom and sanctity of this present government of the United States than he had of our government in the days of slavery. He died, let us not forget, in the midst of the Civil War, when the issue which should have been decided instantly by the conscience of every good citizen was at last being resolved in blood. No, Thoreau would have been the first to say that no government on earth is good enough or wise enough to be entrusted with such powers for good and evil. He would have predicted that we would use this new force in the same manner that we have used other natural forces, that the peace and security of the world lie not in inventions but in men's hearts, men's souls. His whole life bore testimony to the obvious fact which men are constantly overlooking, that to sustain life we need less rather than more, that to protect life we need courage and integrity, not weapons, not coalitions. In everything he said and did he was at the farthest remove from the man of today. I said earlier that his influence is still alive and active. It is, but only because truth and wisdom are incontrovertible and must eventually prevail. Consciously and unconsciously we are doing the very opposite of all that he advocated. But we are not happy about it, nor are we at all convinced that we are right. We are, in fact, more bewildered, more despairing, than we ever were in the course of our brief history. And that is most curious, most disturbing, since we are now acknowledged to be the most powerful, the most wealthy, the most secure of all the nations of the earth. We are at the top, but have we the vision to maintain this vantage point? We have a vague suspicion that we have been saddled with a responsibility which is too great for us. We know that we are not superior, in any real sense, to the other peoples of this earth. We are just waking up to the fact that morally we are far behind ourselves, so to speak. Some blissfully imagine that the threat of extinction—cosmic suicide—will rout us out of our lethargy. I am afraid that such dreams are doomed to be smashed even more effectively than the atom itself. Great things are not accomplished through fear of extinction. The deeds which move the world, which sustain life and give life, have a different motivation entirely.

The problem of power, an obsessive one with Americans, is now at the crux. Instead of *working* for peace, men ought to be urged to relax, to stop work, to take it easy, to dream and idle away their time for a change. Retire to the woods! if you can find any nearby. Think your own thoughts for a while! Examine your conscience, but only after you have thoroughly enjoyed yourself. What is your job worth, after all, if tomorrow you and yours can all be blown to smithereens by some reckless fool? Do you suppose that a government can be depended on any more than the separate individuals who compose it? Who are these individuals to whom the destiny of the planet itself now seems to be entrusted? Do you believe in them utterly, every one of them? What would *you* do if you had the control of this unheard-of power. Would you use it for the benefit of all mankind, or just for your own people, or your own little group? Do you think that men can keep such a weighty secret to themselves? Do you think it *ought* to be kept secret?

These are the sort of questions I can imagine a Thoreau firing away. They are questions which, if one has just a bit of common sense, answer themselves. But governments never seem to possess this modicum of common sense. Nor do they trust those who are in possession of it.

This American government—what is it but a tradition, though a recent one, endeavoring to transmit itself unimpaired to posterity, but each instant losing some of its integrity? It has not the vitality and force of a single living man; for a single man can bend it to his will. It is a sort of wooden gun to the people themselves. But it is not the less necessary for this, for the people must have some complicated machinery or other, and hear its din, to satisfy that idea of government which they have. Governments show thus how successfully men can be imposed on, even impose on themselves, for their own advantage. It is excellent, we must all allow. Yet this government never of itself furthered any enterprise, but by the alacrity with which it got out of its way. *It* does not keep the country free. *It* does not settle the West. *It* does not educate. The character inherent in the American people has done all that has been accomplished; and it would have done somewhat more, if the government had not sometimes got in its way. . . .

That is the way Thoreau spoke a hundred years ago. He would speak still more unflatteringly if he were alive now. In these last hundred years the State has come to be a Frankenstein. We have never had less need of the State than now when we are most tyrannized by it. The ordinary citizen everywhere has a code of ethics far above that of the government to which he owes allegiance. The fiction that the State exists for our protection has been exploded a thousand times. However, as long as men lack self-assurance and self-reliance, the State will thrive; it depends for its existence on the fear and uncertainty of its individual members.

By living his own life in his own "eccentric" way Thoreau demonstrated the futility and absurdity of the life of the (so-called) masses. It was a deep, rich life which yielded him the maximum of contentment. In the bare necessities he found adequate means for the enjoyment of life. "The opportunities of living," he pointed out, "are diminished in proportion as what are called the 'means' are increased." He was at home in Nature, where man belongs. He held communion with bird and beast,

with plant and flower, with star and stream. He was not an unsocial being, far from it. He had friends, among women as well
as men. No American has written more eloquently and truth-
fully of friendship than he. If his life seems a restricted one, it
was a thousand times wider and deeper than the life of the ordinary American today. He lost nothing by not mingling with the
crowd, by not devouring the newspapers, by not enjoying the
radio or the movies, by not having an automobile, a refrigera-
tor, a vacuum cleaner. He not only did not lose anything through
the lack of these things, but he actually enriched himself in a
way far beyond the ability of the man of today who is glutted
with these dubious comforts and conveniences. Thoreau lived,
whereas we may be said to barely exist. In power and depth his
thought not only matches that of our contemporaries, but usually surpasses it. In courage and virtue there are none among
our leading spirits today to match him. As a writer, he is among
the first three or four we can boast of. Viewed now from the
heights of our decadence, he seems almost like an early Roman.
The word *virtue* has meaning again, when connected with his
name.

It is the young people of America who may profit from his
homely wisdom, from his example even more. They need to be
reassured that what was possible then is still possible today.
America is still a vastly unpopulated country, a land abounding
in forests, streams, lakes, deserts, mountains, prairies, rivers,
where a man of good-will with a little effort and belief in his own
powers can enjoy a deep, tranquil, rich life—provided he go his
own way. He need not and should not think of making a good
living, but rather of creating a good life for himself. The wise
men always return to the soil; one has only to think of the great
men of India, China and France, their poets, sages, artists, to
realize how deep is this need in every man. I am thinking,
naturally, of creative types, for the others will gravitate to their
own unimaginative levels, never suspecting that life holds any
better promise. I think of the budding American poets, sages and
artists because they appear so appallingly helpless in this present-
day American world. They all wonder so naïvely how they will
live if they do not hire themselves out to some taskmaster; they

wonder still more how, after doing that, they will ever find time to do what they were called to do. They never think any more of going into the desert or the wilderness, of wresting a living from the soil, of doing odd jobs, of living on as little as possible. They remain in the towns and cities, flitting from one thing to another, restless, miserable, frustrated, searching in vain for a way out. They ought to be told at the outset that society, as it is now constituted, provides no way out, that the solution is in their own hands and that it can be won only by the use of their own two hands. One has to hack his way out with the ax. The real wilderness is not out there somewhere, but in the towns and cities, in that complicated web which we have made of life and which serves no purpose but to thwart, cramp and inhibit the free spirits. Let a man believe in himself and he will find a way to exist despite the barriers and traditions which hem him in. The America of Thoreau's day was just as contemptuous of, just as hostile to, his experiment as we are today to anyone who essays it. Undeveloped as the country was then, men were lured from all regions, all walks of life, by the discovery of gold in California. Thoreau stayed at home, where he cultivated his own mine. He had only to go a few miles to be deep in the heart of Nature. For most of us, no matter where we live in this great country, it is still possible to travel but a few miles and find one-self in Nature. I have traveled the length and breadth of the land, and if I was impressed by one thing it was by this—that America is empty. It is also true, to be sure, that nearly all this empty space is owned by someone or other—banks, railroads, insurance companies and so on. It is almost impossible to wander off the beaten path without "trespassing" on private property. But that nonsense would soon cease if people began to get up on their hind legs and desert the towns and cities. John Brown and a bare handful of men virtually defeated the entire popu-lation of America. It was the Abolitionists who freed the slaves, not the armies of Grant and Sherman, not Abraham Lincoln. There is no ideal condition of life to step into anywhere at any time. Everything is difficult, and everything becomes more diffi-cult still when you choose to live your own life. But, to live one's own life is still the best way of life, always was, and always

will be. The greatest snare and delusion is to postpone living
your own life until an ideal form of government is created which
will permit everyone to lead the good life. Lead the good life
now, this instant, every instant, to the best of your ability and
you will bring about indirectly and unconsciously a form of
government nearer to the ideal.

Because Thoreau laid such emphasis on conscience and on
active resistance, one is apt to think of his life as bare and grim.
One forgets that he was a man who shunned work as much as
possible, who knew how to idle his time away. Stern moralist
that he was, he had nothing in common with the professional
moralists. He was too deeply religious to have anything to do
with the Church, just as he was too much the man of action to
bother with politics. Similarly he was too rich in spirit to think
of amassing wealth, too courageous, too self-reliant, to worry
about security and protection. He found, by opening his eyes,
that life provides everything necessary for man's peace and
enjoyment—one has only to make use of what is there, ready to
hand, as it were. "Life is bountiful," he seems to be saying all
the time. "*Relax!* Life is here, all about you, not there, not over
the hill."

He found Walden. But Walden is everywhere, if the man
himself is there. Walden has become a symbol. It should become
a reality. Thoreau himself has become a symbol. But he was only
a man, let us not forget that. By making him a symbol, by raising
memorials to him, we defeat the very purpose of his life. Only
by living our own lives to the full can we honor his memory.
We should not try to imitate him but to surpass him. Each one
of us has a totally different life to lead. We should not strive to
become like Thoreau, or even like Jesus Christ, but to become
what we are in truth and in essence. That is the message of every
great individual and the whole meaning of being an individual.
To be anything less is to move nearer to nullity.

Money and How It Gets That Way

FOREWORD

About a year ago, upon reading *Tropic of Cancer,* Ezra Pound wrote me a postcard in his usual Cabalistic style, asking me if I had ever thought about money, what makes it and how it gets that way. The truth is that until Mr. Pound put the question to me I had never really thought about the subject. Since then, however, I have thought about it night and day. The result of my meditations and lucubrations I now offer to the world in the shape of this little treatise which, if it does not settle the problem once and for all, may at least *unsettle* it.

Paris, November 1, 1936

In the days of Periclean Greece money may be said to have occupied the same relation to economics as ballistics does to astral physics today. The idea of money, dimly evolved during the late Minoan culture, was sharply clarified during the dialectical dissension which occurred with the first Socratic thrust at the primacy of the State. It is not our intention, in a short treatise of this scope, to trace the biologico-economic aspects of the slave-and-master theory which underlay the then budding ideology of free finance, as it has come to be called. Professor Ernest Mac-Veagh, in a monograph entitled *The Rise of Currency,* has brilliantly depicted the nature of those oppositional forces which about the time of Pericles began to synthesize and form the elastic conception known as *money*. As Professor MacVeagh has pointed out in his trenchant little monograph, the very flexibility of the idea has permitted the survival of a *modus operandi* which would have perished of logical inanition by the time of the Renaissance, if not earlier. Indeed, as all students of the subject are aware, a most serious threat presented itself during the first epidemic of the Black Plague, due not so much to the catastrophic ravages of the plague itself as to the pernicious doctrines which grew up, ironically enough, out of the writings of Thomas Aquinas. This Cromwellian mind, attempting to reconcile the dying chattel theory with the then embyronic ideology of the super-State, almost succeeded in wrecking the very delicate structure of that money-world which had miraculously survived the disintegration of much older political vehicles. It was only toward the close of the Middle Ages that, in a secret session at Avignon, the Popes, of whom there were then six, decreed that Thomas Aquinas had been in error, thereby paving the way for that consolidation of bank and vestry which was the crowning glory of the Renaissance.

With the discovery of the New World a new and disturbing factor arose—the problem of the consubstantial relation between gold as mythos and gold as idealized metal. It was the old ethical conundrum which Socrates had essayed to solve in his *Dialectics of Logic,* a problem which has come up repeatedly in the course of history whenever a waning civilization is confronted with the danger of a barbarian invasion. For, contrary to the opinion of historians, the renewed energy created by the infusion of alien blood is more than offset by the moral disequilibrium which ensues upon the dislocation of the monetary cotter-pin. This follows inevitably because, as we have just hinted, money, or the conceptual image of it, is the residual synthesis of all the subtler life forces which are masked now by physico-economic, now by religio-aesthetic dicta.

In his quest of a new trade route to India, Columbus, unwittingly of course, created a factor of disturbance which is only now making itself manifest to a recognizable degree. Only a few years after Columbus' return to the court of Ferdinand and Isabella, the "mystic of gold," Ponce de Leon, set out to discover the Fountain of Youth. A comparative study of similar classic adventures, notably the expedition of the Argonaut, has convinced even the most cautious and conservative gold chroniclers that Ponce de Leon's exploit, far from being a wild-goose chase, was in fact a most sanguine telluric adventure undertaken to reestablish the hegemony of the rapidly disappearing yellow metal.

Those who wish to pursue the ramifications of the gold theory then in vogue will find ample corroborative evidence in the report to their Majesties, the King and Queen of Spain, drawn up by the Chancellor of the Exchequer on the eve of Ponce de Leon's departure for the New World. A most important item in this report is the crude map, drawn by the hand of the great explorer himself, which accompanied the report of the Chancellor of the Exchequer. With the most astounding accuracy this bold adventurer has traced for us the heavily charged areas of gold deposit lying south of an imaginary line extending from the tip of the Texas panhandle to the hills of Martinique. Until recently it was thought impossible to open up these lodes, owing to the vast engineering problems involved, since the most fertile region lay in the Pliocene belt which makes up the swamplands of our Southern states together with the submerged eastern shelf of the continent extending as far as the West Indies. Almost coincident, however, with the invention of the rotary bit now used in the drilling of petroleum wells, a placer miner from Alaska, named Burdock, submitted to the U.S. Patent Office the model of a portable hydraulic dredge designed to be run by a radium spark. This dredge, capable of being operated by a child, will in the course of the next ten years undoubtedly revolutionize our methods of mining gold, as well as our conceptions of the relation between gold and money. Soviet Russia is already carrying out experiments with a similar device at the base of the Urals where, it is reported from authoritative sources, there lies an incalculable supply of the precious metal.

It is in anticipation, therefore, of the dilemma which an unprecedented plethora of gold will create in financial circles—to say nothing of the political repercussions which are sure to follow in the wake of this discovery—that this little treatise on the nature of money is offered to the layman. For it is the man in the street, after all, and not the banker or the financier, to whom we shall be obliged to look for a solution of the problem. This is as true now as it was in the time of the First Pyramid when the Egyptian fellaheen, prostrated by the grandiose ideas of the mad Cheops, took the national currency into their own hands and established what is known as the "wheat ducat."

Let us put the question then as simply and nakedly as possible: *What is money and how does it get that way?* Perhaps it will be easier to grapple with this conundrum if we seize it by the tail. Whatever it may have been in the past, money has come to be what it now is only through thinking about it. Money has no life of its own except as money. It is as much a part of life as life itself; that is to say, it is both the thing itself and the process of becoming the thing itself. Or, as Dunreavy says in an early manual on coinage, "that which represents either symbolically or concretely an act of change can never be the thing exchanged." Dunreavy was of course thinking of the early Swedish economists who, because their language had grown too abstract, were responsible for a confusion of terms which has persisted down to this day. A primitive Bantu, for example, would never have made the mistake of confounding the object of barter with the act of bartering itself. On the other hand, the highly civilized Greeks of Pericles' day were often guilty of such absurd substitutions, due perhaps, we should say in all fairness, to the exaggerated role which logic played in all their forms of speculation.

To return, therefore, to the axiomatic: *Money has no life of its own except as money.* To the man in the street, unaccustomed to thinking of money in abstract terms, this obvious truism may smack of casuistry. Yet nothing could be more simple and consistent than this reduction to tautology, since money in any period whatever of man's history has, like life itself, never been found to represent the absence of money. *Money is,* and whatever form or shape it may assume it is never more nor less than *money.* To inquire, therefore, how it comes about that money has become what it now is, is as idle as to inquire what makes evolution. The Saurians in becoming extinct may have provided the Darwinians with an invaluable link in the evolutionary hypothesis, but no one would be rash enough to assert that the Saurians died out expressly to provide the disciples of Darwin with an irrefutable logic. *Pro ipso propter,* neither can it be said that money has evolved out of the primordial need of exchange in order to consolidate the highly untenable position of finance theorists in this or that part of the world. And yet a glance at any of the views now current in the upper realms of finance would tend to convince us that the sole effort of man from prehistoric times on has been to prove that money is not money at all but something which passes for something else, such as specie, for example. Even the dullest oaf can be made to understand that specie is not money, but a *form* of money. Money, then, whatever its real nature, reveals itself to us through form. Just as hydrogen and oxygen reveal their presence to us in varying forms such as water or peroxide, and yet are not themselves, either separately or combined, so money, whether in specie or counterfeit, is always something inclusive, coexistent, consubstantial and *beyond* the thing manifest. In a profound sense money may be said to resemble God Almighty. Indeed, this is neither an original thought nor a sacrilegious one, for in the century just preceding that of Thomas Aquinas there appeared in the lowlands of Scotland a monk of the Dominican order who preached the divine transvaluation of money, or to put it in everyday language, that God and Money are One. Nor did the good Fathers of the Church at that time find anything blasphemous in such preachings. It is true that toward the end of his life the monk in question was burned at the stake, but not for blasphemy. However, let us not divagate about questions of heresy in the thirteenth century. Sufficient is it to call attention to the fact that man's efforts to conceptualize the phenomenal nature of money has often led to the most abstruse vaticinations.

Undoubtedly much of the contradiction and confusion which has invested the subject of money arises from the assumption that money and gold have always existed in a symbiotic relationship. Today, when it is apparent to even the dullest banking clerk how chimerical is the role of gold, we may say without fear of contradiction that gold, while maintaining a pseudo-symbiotic relation to money, is *au fond* no more important than, or just as important as, fungus to a dead tree. To borrow an expression from the arboriculturist, we might add that gold has a tendency at times to bring about a condition of "white heart rot." That is to say that, though outwardly all may seem well, the eye of the forester can detect beneath the bark the disease which lurks in the very heart of the tree and ravages it mercilessly. White heart rot has been frequently compared to tuberculosis in the human organism; it is encountered chiefly in metropolitan areas, among city trees. In finance it is recognized as "inflation." If the disease has not completely eaten the tree away, cement may be administered to preserve what life is left. With dying currencies the treatment employed is to amass gold, or to ship it frantically from one country to another. Whenever, therefore, gold is amassed in unusual quantities, or when its movements become erratic and frenetic, the indications are that the money of the countries in question is diseased. The presence of gold, its movements and fluctuations, will, if observed with a trained eye, always reveal the symptoms of unhealthy finance. For the health of a currency is like unto physical health, in that we are unaware of it until disease manifests itself.

The evolution of the idea of money is closely associated, for reasons which must be apparent to even the most casual observer, with the development of the notions of sin and guilt. Even in the earliest periods of trade we find rudimentary principles at work such as would lead us to believe that primitive man had evolved methods of exchange which *sui generis* implied the existence of debt. It was not until Ricardo's time, however, that a formula was arrived at which expressed the relation between debtor and creditor beyond all caviling. With almost Euclidian simplicity Ricardo summed it up thus: "A debt is discharged by the delivery of money." The assumption on which Ricardo bases this well-known hypothesis is that money is not wealth. Money, as Ricardo very ably pointed out, must be first of all that which is "portable." Other factors there may be, to be sure, such as malleability, ductility, resistance to rust, high melting point, etc., but the most important factor, the one on which all modern economists are now agreed, is that *money must be portable*. As proof of the soundness of this hypothesis we have but to remind the reader of the now obsolete Swedish key money which was in vogue during the reign of Gustavus Adolphus. This monarch, more renowned in the field of war than in the economy of the State, had conceived the idea of key money through prolonged contact with the Turks, who had always steadfastly resisted the adoption of European methods of coinage. Aesthetically attractive and sound, so far as the metallic content was concerned, this innovation of Gustavus Adolphus' was nevertheless doomed owing to the difficulties which arose over the question of standardization and transportation. To the numismatist they are objects of the greatest curiosity, but to the financier or the specialist in specie they elucidate the infallibility of Ricardo's first principle, viz., that *money must be portable.*

Perhaps we should not have had to wait until Ricardo's time for a clear statement of the problem had not the English, who were always a great trading people, obscured the notion of debt and indebtedness with moral issues. Ricardo, who was of Italian descent—some say that he was a descendant of the Medici—showed a surprising and resolute courage in tackling the subject. With the usual clarity and precision of the Latin mind he promptly seized upon the most salient feature of this much mooted subject, namely, the relation of means to end. A debt, he averred, is not necessarily a question of honor among gentlemen, but rather a fiduciary problem involving liquidation, the solution of which we should devote ourselves to with the same cool objectivity that Clerk-Maxwell demonstrates in his physical experiments. Needless to say, this plain statement of fact went a long way toward lifting the fogs which had settled over this subject since the collapse of the Roman corn laws. Indeed, it is hardly too much to say that had it not been for Ricardo the men of Lombard Street would to this very day be under some modified form of vassalage to the Vatican.

As a corollary to Ricardo's maxim there followed, a century or so later, the principle laid down by Gresham. So important has this discovery of Gresham's become, in fact, that students everywhere now speak of it as Gresham's Law. It is, in brief, this—that "bad money drives out good." In reflecting upon the rugged common sense which underlies this law the reader will bear in mind, I trust, what was said a moment ago with regard to debt and indebtedness. A debt, to be discharged by the delivery of money, could quite obviously be evaded by the payment of bad money. ("Don't take any wooden money," we say in jest.) To obviate such misdealings—*"escroquerie"* it is called in French—economists such as Gresham were quick to point out that only sound money, or coin of the realm, could be used in the payment of debt. Only in this way might one acquit himself of his obligations and thus permit the free flow of gold.

For the sake of creating work, on the other hand, no such hard and fast rules were stipulated by the early nineteenth-century economists. Work and trade were kept apart in watertight compartments, although it was obvious even then, to those who had made the subject a profound study, that twist it how you will, the inevitable liaison is always there, namely *debt*. That is one of the reasons why, under the sway of the Marxian diuretic, debt is no longer regarded as a permanent element in the economic disorder, but rather as a solvent, so to speak, in the conversion of capital to labor. Countries like Germany and Italy, in as much as they refuse to adopt the Marxian diuretic, tend to increase the circuit velocity of money, in order that, as an eminent Dutch economist points out, "their currencies may drag themselves by the hair out of the quicksands of worthlessness." However salutary these tactics may be with regard to the evaporation of the national debt in the countries just mentioned, the fact is nevertheless incontestable that the gold mentality of the world remains unaffected. With money becoming ever cheaper the price of bullion naturally rises to implement the costive condition of the call market. This is the real explanation of the fact that in Pomerania, shortly after Hitler's advent to power, the turnip and swede crop fell off so markedly. For though it is undeniable that dry years have always had a definite adverse influence upon the price level, yet during the year in question the average rainfall was higher than that of the five years preceding Hitler's advent. Had this not been so we should be at a loss to account for the fact that during those five preceding years brewery shares were a feature of remarkable strength and integrity.

This leads me to make a slight digression concerning a theory which has been gaining ground of late owing to a revival of interest in meteorology. Professor Huerta, of the Institute of Technology at Madrid, made a statement before a body of physicists at Albert Hall a year or so ago to the effect that there was a very definite correlation between the cyclical recurrence of sunspots and financial crises. Unfortunately, the learned professor's remarks were slightly distorted by the newspapers. Those who have scanned the text which Professor Huerta read before the body assembled in Albert Hall will agree that the latter was not speaking in an absolute sense, but only conditionally. The professor did not assert that sunspots and financial crises were two disparate phenomena always coeval in time and mutually interactive, but that these two phenomena were known to describe similar and often parallel cycles. In the year 1907, when mortgages, bonds and debentures in the United States were singularly restricted, it did so happen that an unusual number of sunspots was observed by the Mount Wilson Observatory, but the following year there were even more sunspots and yet the depression had disappeared. What are we to conclude therefrom?

Before coming to any conclusions it would be well to pause a moment and consider the larger movement which embraces the incidence of crises, sunspots, failure of the turnip and swede crop, the advent of Hitler, Mussolini, etc. I refer to the astrologic calculations of a young Cuban who out of modesty and diffidence chooses to cling to his anonymity. Employing for practical purposes the annual report of the Finspongs Metalverks Aktiebolag, this young Cuban has achieved a brilliant synthesis of all terrestrial movements through his interpretation of the Pluto-Neptune conjunction. Using as an index the period from 1317 to 1392, a period marked by the most baffling agglomeration of diverse phenomena (including plagues, wars, miracles, fecundity of genius, etc.), he has arrived at a forecast which not only includes the date of the next war, the assassination of Hitler, Stalin, Roosevelt and other prominent figures, but gives to an eighth of an inch the figures for the annual rainfall during the next twenty years in every country of the world, as well as the fluctuation of Chinese bonds, the collapse of rubber, the quality of mangels, the lifting and clamping of potato crops, the condition of sheep and outlying cattle, the elasticity of agricultural raw materials, the activity of bunkers and washed descriptions of coal, the provisions of the oil code, the restriction of tin, etc., etc. Among other things he observes that Gresham's Law, of which we spoke a moment ago, was without a doubt known to Oresme and Copernicus. Referring to gold he remarks that research into the nature of the "halogen compounds" will lead to a revolution which will affect not only the money markets of the world, but the political and religious life of the Occidental nations of the world.

It would take us too far afield to inquire into the possible veridity of a forecast based on the unquestionably skillful manipulation of comparative tables of statistics such as this young Cuban has given evidence of. Suffice it to say in passing that the economist, particularly the specialist in money, would do well to examine the methods employed by leading astrologers who, because of their disinterestedness, often come closer to hitting the bull's eye than those who make it their business to specialize in accuracy of prediction.

And now let us get to the backbone of our subject, which is, as the reader must already have realized, *gold*. For by now it must be evident that money is not wealth, but an idea which is concretized for purposes of human intercourse in symbols, or tokens, permitting of payment by tale, and that said symbols or tokens have no value in themselves but are only the evidence, to use a Biblical expression, of things unseen. Gold, owing to the fact that it is a nondeliquescent metal, has a material and practical advantage over all other potential forms of tale, including bismuth, which though nondeliquescent is highly volatile. Ever since that day in the summer of 1203 B.C., when the expeditionary force of the Argonaut ruthlessly plundered the alluvial gold which the long-suffering and hapless people of Armenia were then washing out from the river sands with the aid of sheepskins, gold has occupied the forefront of man's consciousness to a degree unrivaled by any other telluric phenomenon. In fact, when we search for a counterpart to the role of gold in human life, we can adduce nothing to equal it in obsessive persistence unless it be man's continuous and uninterrupted preoccupation with the navel.

Though long known to the ancients, it was not until the latter part of the nineteenth century that Mendeléyev finally situated gold in the table of elements as constituting No. 79 of the series, atomic weight 197.2, specific symbol Au. We are speaking now of pure gold, which is seldom encountered in nature, though minute particles of pure gold, it has been said on good authority, may be found in ordinary sea water. So minute, however, are these particles, that even the most high-powered lens of German make is incapable of revealing their presence in the 50,000th part of a gram of water. Gold, like other precious metals, is usually to be found in alloys such as tellurium, silver, palladium, bismuth, mercury and rhodium. "Dentist gold" is one of the exceptions to the foregoing principle. Dentist gold is a perfectly pure gold found in a beaten state, what is known as a "cutch" state, or, in common parlance, golf leaf. This extreme limit of malleability is arrived at only after the most adroit manipulation with hammer and thumb, requiring usually a beating of about twenty minutes with a seventeen-pound hammer, which rebounds by the elasticity of the skin. For commercial purposes, dentist gold is about as thin and perfect as could be wished. Ductile experiments have been undertaken, nevertheless, purely for scientific reasons, which would indicate that if necessary, gold, a single gram of it, could be drawn into a wire which would reach from the easternmost point of Labrador to the city of Lhasa in Tibet. It has also been demonstrated at the University of Leipzig that gold can be beaten to a thickness, or thinness, rather, of 0.0000254. All these considerations apart, the fact to remember is that gold is permanent in air or water under all conditions of temperature. *Pure gold,* that is, and not the alloys which masquerade under the name of electrum.

Before leaving the subject of alloys, which has been a rather vexing one to weighers and minters of gold, let us make it clear that no matter what the combination, whether found with bismuth, rhodium or palladium, gold as such, all gold, that is, can be roughly divided into two main categories: "reef" gold and "alluvial" gold. The presence of no mineral can be said to constitute an infallible guide to the presence of gold, except perhaps in certain localities. Gold is almost as ubiquitous as the air we breathe and can be detected not only in the human body (usually in the neighborhood of the liver) but also in vegetation. It has been found in the Cambrian coalfields of Wyoming as well as in the lignite beds of Japan. In Yucatan, where calomel is found in abundant quantities, streaks of the yellow ore have been discovered here and there. The ore is generally invisible unless magnified, but it occurs notwithstanding in yellow splashes at Kalgoorlie and again at Kroboberg. The best indicator of gold, as all prospectors will testify, is a yellow oxide of iron known as limonite, which is usually found at the surface where the lodes are weathered. In general we might say that gold is usually extracted from quartz lodes, which are nothing but natural igneous veins brought to the surface by the denudation of river beds, called therefore "river gravels" or "bankets," or, as in the Transvaal districts, "conglomerates." In order to distinguish between the small-scale grains and the larger masses of mammilated forms the terms "gold dust" and "gold nuggets" have been popularly employed by miners. The most productive gold fields were those of ancient Egypt, where, in the deep mines, the enslaved laborers were cruelly maltreated. Legend has it that the source of Croesus's fabulous wealth was an abandoned mine in the heart of Asia Minor, where the river Pactolus now flows. We know, from examination of coins belonging to this period, that the gold which made Croesus's name legendary possessed the same physical form as the gold of Alaska, that is, the octahedra or rhombic dodecahedra. It was an "alluvial" gold, always associated at that period with magnetite or "black iron sand."

Now a strange thing about gold which has undoubtedly escaped the attention of most people is this: if a grain of gold is dissolved in aqua regia and the resulting solution freed from nitric acid by evaporation with further quantities of hydrochloric acid to near the crystallizing point, the dissolved gold compound corresponds to the formula $H_2Au\ C_{15}$, but on allowing this solution to crystallize, brownish-yellow crystals of aurichloric acid are formed, having a strongly acid reaction. This is but one of a number of examples of the way gold behaves when introduced to the Halogen Compounds, a trade name given to a family of aurichloric acids whose optimum temperature is usually 175 degrees Centigrade. Chemically speaking, gold has its bromides also. There is the well-known monobromide, which is obtained by heating the tribromide to approximately 200 degrees Centigrade. The auric bromides form what are called auribromides, and bear a great resemblance to their atomic cousins, the aurichlorides. When reduced to salt, any of these aurichloric bromides in free association are of considerable assistance in determining the atomic weight of gold.

There are two kinds of gold about which we should like to warn the reader who may be thinking of hoarding the precious metal. One of them, recognized by the laboratory worker under the sign $Au N_2 H_3 : 3H_2O$, was known to medieval alchemists as "fulminating gold." It is a black powder which is obtained by treating a solution of gold with strong ammonia. If the ammonia is weak, a precipitate known as "purple of Cassius" is formed; this substance is so saturated with tin hydroxide that it has no practical value whatever except in the preparation of ruby glass. But the black powder known as fulminating gold possesses incalculable value. If all the other materials of the earth which now go into the manufacture of high explosives should be exhausted, fulminating gold would prove its utility in chemical warfare. When dry it makes a very powerful explosive, detonating either by friction or on heating to exactly 145 degrees Centigrade. It should therefore be handled with extreme caution. Left in a subterranean vault over a period of time ordinary gold, *the ingot,* as we say, is apt to become transformed into this dangerous black powder, owing to the presence of irons found in the locks and bolts of commercial vaults. Those who have not handled their gold hoardings for some time are urgently advised to moisten the gold ingots before removing them from the vault. For this purpose ordinary tap water will do, though whenever possible the waters of the various European spas are recommended. Holy water is particularly serviceable, as the frequent fingering of it leaves precipitates of the human elements, among which phosphorus and calcium figure strongly, and as every chemist knows, phosphorus and calcium retain moisture longer than any other elements.

The other form of gold which it is equally important to know about is *Glanzgold,* so called after the name of a German explorer, Glanz. Glanz, curiously enough, was born about the same time as Schliemann, the German grocery boy who later in life discovered the ruins of Troy. They grew up in the same village, which was on the outskirts of Schleswig-Holstein. All his life

Glanz had been interested in converting gold to a liquid state. Toward the end of the year 1879, after having assisted at the siege of Paris, he returned to his native village with a formula which he had discovered in the archives of the Paris mint. With this formula he went ahead with his experiments until the day when, by treating various essential oils with small quantities of bismuth, rhodium and one of the obscure Halogen Compounds, he was successful in producing a condition which, in laboratory parlance, is referred to as "liquid gold." It must not be too readily inferred from the use of a chemical term that Glanz's gold, or *Glanzgold,* as it is now called, is necessarily a gold which runs. True, when fired to about 785 degrees Centigrade, *Glanzgold* can be poured with ease from one vessel to another. But the essential meaning of the term, the idea which fired Glanz's imagination, is that gold can be made tractable. For, in spite of all that has been said about the adaptability of gold, this precious metal has often proved to be one of the most stubborn and incalcitrant of all the metals. The ancient Greeks were early made aware of this in their attempts to inlay their funerary urns. To obtain a suitable degree of fluidity that would enable them to apply the inlay to the glazed surface of the urn, they were obliged to adulterate the native gold with various alloys of the electrum variety. It was partly out of the purely technical difficulties encountered in the art of ornamentation that Euripides wove the gold motif into the theme of *Electra.* In the Middle Ages, and again in the Renaissance, we have a recurrence of this theme in the Morality Plays and in the Mysteries. *Pilgrim's Progress* abounds in allusions to the subject. At any rate, like his fellow citizen Schliemann, Glanz realized at a fairly early age the dream of his youth, and it is probably due to his persistent and tenacious efforts that German earthenware is today the most frequently sought-after in the world markets.

And now let us devote a little attention to the Gold Coast itself, that fertile region of British Guinea where the sands of the rivers are all gold, as though touched by the hand of old King Midas. Navigation, except along the coast, is almost impossible because of the rocky headlands and the great sand bars which choke the mouths of the rivers. Great Atlantic rollers beat unceasingly upon the shore of this immensely fertile tract of land. Practically the whole of this auriferous country is traversed by the Ankobra or Snake River. Flat steam launches of the Nile variety can in the rainy season make the upper reaches of the river, but there is no regular service possible, as the river changes its course with the change of terrain. Geologically the region is extremely varied. Near the coast are found the great igneous rocks, such as granites, diorites, and dolerites; a little farther down the coast are the Cretaceous rocks, now almost hidden under superficial deposits. In the west are the "bankets" or "conglomerates," such as are found in the Transvaal, usually mixed with slate and phyllites in the highly metamorphosed gneiss rocks. Then there are the alluvial silts and gravels in which, along with the ubiquitous gold and diamonds of the river beds, is found bauxite, the miraculous green ore of the clay shales.

Though not particularly unhealthy for the European white, the climate of the Gold Coast is hot and moist. There are two rainy seasons, not clearly defined, but along toward the end of December the dry *harmattan* wind of the Sahara begins to blow and life again becomes agreeable on the Gold Coast. At Accra, which is to the leeward, the average rainfall comes to about 27 inches per annum, which is not excessive when we compare it with the upper half of Portugal, which has 28.5 inches per annum. As a result of this fairly equable, moist climate, the greater part of this highly fertile region is covered with primeval forest. The vegetation is so luxuriant that in the struggle to reach the sunlight the forest growths are almost vertical, a condition which is rare in other parts of tropical Africa. The chief trees are silk cottons, especially the bombax, a beautiful hardwood tree belonging to the same family as the ebony, mahogany, odum and camwood. The intermediate growth, or bush, is made up of the rubber vine and other creepers, some thick as hawsers, others again, like the mimosa and the bamboo, frail as orchids. West of the Prah the forest comes down to the edge of the Atlantic. Farther east, toward Accra again, the arborescent euphorbia may be found, while immediately west of the Volta one stumbles upon forests of oil palms, and grassy plains of fan palms. Here and there are little stretches of orchard-like country, cultivated no doubt by the early English settlers, where the wild plum, the shea-butter and kola trees, as well as baobabs and dwarf dates are found. Among the fruit trees are to be observed a few pawpaws and avocados, as well as the more vulgar pineapple and mango.

If the flora of this region is a perpetual delight to the florist, how much more so is the fauna to the faunographer. For here, as in the Garden of Eden, is to be found every variety of beast and fowl known to the Creator. In the predatory group are the leopard, panther, hyena, lemur, jackal, buffalo, wild hog and the chimpanzee with long, black, silky hair so much prized by the European. Of ophidians there are the python, the cobra, the horned adder and the puff adder, not to mention the various water snakes. In the rivers and lagoons are the fierce crocodiles, the manatees or sea cows, the otters and the hippopotami. In the very same rivers and lagoons one often sees lizards of brilliant hue, tortoises both soft- and hard-shelled, and snails of Gargantuan dimensions. Oysters too are plentiful, and are most frequently encountered clinging to the rocks which jut into the sea, or else tangled in the exposed roots of the mangrove trees. Naturally there are all varieties of the insect world, including beetles, ants, fireflies and jiggers. But the earthworm, strange to relate, is extremely scarce. Some have ventured to offer an explanation by pointing to the mullet that infests the mouths of the rivers, where the sand has piled up in incredible quantities. Birds, though prevalent like the winds, are also not very numerous and offer nothing unusual to the avid ornithologist ever seeking the *rara avis*. There are, of course, storks and pelicans and ospreys and spur plovers, once in a while a crossbill or a curlew, but then these specimens of the winged beast may be found in most any region of the subtemperate zone. They are, so to speak, indigenous to the belt of Capricorn.

From this rather summary account of the topography and climatic conditions prevailing on the Gold Coast one may easily see what a delicate and hazardous task must have confronted the original English gold-diggers. And yet this is not all: there was also the problem of lingual communication with the natives, all of whom are of the Negro race. Were it not for the Accra, a clever race from which spring most of the artisans and sailors of the Western coast, the problem might have been well-nigh insuperable. Luckily, the Accra tribes, whose language proper is the Ga, were also acquainted with the Krobo and Adangme dialects, of which the English had picked up a patois during their invasion of the Hottentot country opened up by Cecil B. Rhodes. The Hottentot dialects, owing to a peculiar cluck-cluck quality which gives them a strong sibilant character, are to be traced throughout all Africa. They lie at the roots of the more highly developed Hamitic tongues, which came to their climacteric in the *bled* of Morocco. Be that as it may, however, it was of inestimable advantage to the English colonists to be able to establish communication with the Accra peoples, who, unlike the Krobos around Kroboberg, were a proud and nomadic race, undoubted blood brothers to the Apollonia of the Ivory Coast. Once having mastered the Ga tongue, it was a comparatively easy matter for the English to make themselves understood in the popular language, which is called Twi or Tshi or Chi. This language has marked affinities with various Polynesian sprouts, since, like the latter, it belongs to the great prefix-prenominal group once used by the inhabitants of the lost continent of Mu. Today, thanks to the heroic and untiring activities of the Basle missionaries, books printed in Ga can be read by both the Krobo and Adangme peoples, when educated. In general it must be acknowledged that the natives of the Gold Coast show a surprisingly keen desire to be educated. Special care is taken to develop character, if possible, and also to preserve what is valuable in African culture. To this end it has been made obligatory for the teaching staffs to show an acquaintance with at least one vernacular tongue, preferably Guan or Obutu. In addition to English the natives are taught their own languages, which are Twi, Ga, Fanti, Ewe and Krobobo. "Bush" schools are discouraged and as often as not closed. On the other hand, colleges such as the Prince of Wales' College, near Accra, are encouraged. The Prince of Wales' College, costing $2,000,000 to erect, marks a great step forward in the development of native character and intelligence. The money required for this dispensation was largely contributed by the natives themselves, who, until the invasion of the ramified system of taboos which formerly took the place of statutory law, the English have drawn up a criminal and civil code which is administered in the courts of law as "native law," in so far as such law is compatible with natural justice, of which the natives are usually ignorant. Miscarriages of justice are fairly rare since the *omanhene* is jealous of his people's rights and will often travel two thousand miles to plead a trivial case before the English governor-in-chief. It is rather curious to witness one of these pilgrimages. The *omanhene* is always accompanied by the female members of the court, his stepsisters and sisters-in-law, who are even more zealous in the cause of justice than the *omanhene* himself. Usually they are borne along in palanquins covered with screaming parrots of variegated hue, to which is added the cacophonous clash of cymbals and woodwinds employed by the Kalabashi musicians in all ceremonials of the courts. The *omanhene* is veiled to the eyes, as it is considered a sacrilege, during such pilgrimages, for this high emissary of the people to be looked upon by the women of his entourage. Every morning there is a "palaver" (a word of Portuguese origin still used by the natives) outside the *omanhene's* tent. As far as can be learned there is no purpose in this palaver other than a preparation for the grand discourse which is to be delivered before the English governor-in-chief. It is a sort of oratorical exercise which, because it has been repeated so often throughout the centuries, has become a ritual. Finally, when the long journey has been accomplished and the governor lends his ear, the *omanhene* begins his speech.

Anyone who has ever had the privilege of witnessing this performance will never forget it. The *omanhene* is always a master of dialect and in fact is often chosen from other headsmen because of his superior versatility. Often as not he begins his speech in the Ewe tongue, as this is spoken by over a million of his subjects and is therefore regarded as a mark of *politesse*. But as the speech waxes in eloquence the *omanhene* switches rapidly from one tongue to another, now employing Guan, now Obutu, now Ga, now Krobobo. It is almost as though he were making rapid obeisance to each of his fellow chiefs scattered throughout the great empire of golden sands. Sometimes his voice dies down to an almost inaudible whisper, whereupon he resorts to the peculiar sibilant cluck-cluck of the Hottentots for effective punctuation; at other times he raises his voice to a shout, as though to imitate the vulgar Ashanti tribesmen who for thousands of years had oppressed his people and held them in bondage. Or he will run along like a cataract filled with boulders, employing all the dialects at once, so that even his rivals are unable to follow him. He may go on with his discourse for twenty-four hours or for twenty-four days, depending not upon the gravity of the case but rather upon his sense of exhilaration. The English, accustomed as they are to these exhibitions, adjourn at regular intervals for meals. Not the *omanhene*. If he permits himself any nourishment at all it is nothing more than the dry roots of the mango tree, or occasionally the baobab. Toward the end he lapses into English, not infrequently an Oxford English of the most distinguished sort. This he does not so much to make his case clear as to show his contempt and disdain for a foreign tongue. How the *omanhene* acquires his artful mastery of the English language no one can say. It is one of those mysteries, like telepathy, which increase our curiosity and our respect for the peoples who go to make up the Dark Continent. Stanley, in his private diary, makes reference to similar anomalies, as when for instance, upon meeting Livingstone in the heart of Africa, they both began to talk in the same unknown language. There is no explaining these incidents. We must accept them as facts that one day will be made clear to us when the men of science have found time to get around to them.

This digression, while perhaps not unprofitable, may have seemed somewhat trivial to the reader. And yet nothing is more important at the present time than a realization of the serious and tangible aspects of the gold problem. It is only in recent times—roughly, since the invention of double-entry bookkeeping—that money has come to be regarded not in terms of *pieces* of money but as an abstract symbol of wealth. In the old days a piece of gold weighing thus and so many grams avoirdupois was worth as much as a cow or a goat, according to the weight of the gold naturally. But a cow or a goat was never worth thus and so much gold, a distinction which it is imperative to get clearly. The reason for this distinction was that in the old days people were more simple-minded, or if you like, more concrete in their thinking. Even the Greeks, who were infested with logic, believed in the *quid pro quo* sort of economy which had evolved in the region of the Mediterranean littoral. It was impossible, therefore, for them to think of a cow or a goat as worth so much money. The cow or goat was worth so many grams of gold, or, by the time of Pericles, so many pieces of silver. Even during the Middle Ages goods was goods and money was silver or gold, despite all theories of transubstantiation. It is true that devaluation was common, particularly during the great plagues, but payment was always in tale and tale was always so many piasters or so many escudos or so many florins or so many dinars or so many ticals or so many bolivars. Between tale and tael there was never any confusion. But with the invention of double-entry bookkeeping, as I hinted a moment ago, the reality of money began to diminish until in our day it has almost disappeared entirely.

Now I think it is sufficiently apparent to those who have followed me thus far that there was in this new form of economic calculus a species of legerdemain which even the hardened financier found it difficult to cope with. Shakespeare himself reacted unpleasantly to this new and disturbing factor in the economic thought life of his day. In depicting Shylock as one who demanded his "pound of flesh" he was not only denouncing the Venetian usurer, but he was also emphasizing the difficulties which beset the jurisprudents of that day, attached as they were to the old methods of thinking. For if Shylock had been simply an unconscionable usurer, a *gouger,* as we say, Shakespeare would never have wasted his talent upon him. The records of that period abound in legal disputes between the yeomanry and the merchant class, then largely Scottish. No, Shakespeare would have found his material nearer home. He would have found it, for example, in a decision rendered by a Glasgow judge about the time that *As You Like It* was being staged. The decision was as follows: "Where the interest exceeds the rate of 48 per cent the court, unless the contrary is proved, shall presume that the interest charged is excessive and the transaction harsh and unconscionable." Though no overt reference was made in the records, the decision was interpreted throughout the land as a warning to the Scotch moneylenders who by this time had almost succeeded in strangulating the honest English yeomen. Other rulings by the English courts of this period tend to confirm the state of chaos into which the banking world had tumbled. There was, for instance, the utmost confusion as to the value and the price of coins. Now it is a known fact that if the coinage is perfect all coins reach the melting point at the same time. This in a general way regulates the *value* of coins. But, as one may well imagine, there are now and again imperfections in the coins thus melted. There may often be a gap, to use the language of the mint, between coinage price and melting point, not only on account of seigniorage, but possibly on account of natural imperfections. No metal on God's earth, even if intended for such an abstract usage as money, can withstand the acid test of the minter's melting pot. At any rate, it so happened that the price *at the mint* was often found to be at variance with the nominal value decreed by the exchequer. In retrospect it is easy enough to see that the question of "imperfections" had nothing to do with price and value, yet these were just the kind of vexing problems which for a while shook the very foundations of Lombard Street. The Chinese, of course, had long ago learned that payment in tale was not the same as tael itself. How could it be when usage had dictated that the two words should be spelled differently? For though the Chinese have never enjoyed the advantages of a movable alphabet, such as is employed in Western countries, nevertheless the ideogrammatists had designated certain brush strokes to mean tale and certain other brush strokes to mean tael. Tael, for the Chinaman, always signified a unit of weight. Tale, on the other hand, was something else, usually the discharge of a debt. In any case, something *portable*. Similarly in Nicaragua where, before the ratification and adoption of the North American monetary system, the cordoba meant to the average Nicaraguan not only a wooden shoe—an object of great value owing to the heavy rains—but the coin itself on which the wooden shoe, or cordoba, was stamped. In Roumania the lei never had any tangible, concrete significance for the Roumanians. It was a word which had crept into the language via the old Scythian tongue, probably in a corrupt form. Today it is worth practically nothing, not even a lei, so to speak.

Once the ability to think in terms of cows and goats or bushels of wheat or barrels of beer is lost, there is no other recourse left but to think in the nearest concrete terms, which is specie. To the Romans and Greeks wealth was always *cash on hand*. Sometimes this cash was reckoned in slaves, sometimes in acreage or jewels, or sometimes all combined. But it was always concrete, and usually *portable*. When a Caesar was thrown into exile he took his cash with him, and if he had enough of it, he could live happily for the rest of his days. But where is the Caesar today, however wealthy, who can be sure that he will not be a pauper tomorrow? Where is the cash that will make his days of exile comfortable? To the great exploiters of ancient times the budget was unknown. When they ran short of money—which happened frequently—they made a raid on a neighboring state, or else they politely assassinated their more fortunate friends who had money. It was still a fairly easy matter to confiscate the wealth of another country, or another person, because there was always "the tangible quantum of cash." And when moneylenders were scarce there was always the sacred temple, whose rates of interest were not excessive. To own slaves, in those times, was like having money in one's hand. But to own wage-slaves, as is the custom today, means practically nothing, except aggravation. It is easy to understand why. A wage-slave has no value *per se.* Often he costs more to feed, clothe and shelter than he is worth. He is certainly not worth his weight in gold, as the saying goes. And if he were, we would not be able to compute the value anyway, what with the collapse of the gold bloc. We do not know with accuracy either the *price* of gold or the *value* of gold. We know only this, that gold bears some obscure, incalculable relation to money. But gold is no longer money—not even the gold ingot which our forefathers were at such pains to amass. And this is a great pity, for gold is capable of making a greater appeal to the imagination than any other symbol known to man.

There are people in the world today who, under the suasive logic of the Marxian diurectic, pretend to believe that one day money will be eliminated from men's consciousness. Many of these people, it is plain to see, have never had money and therefore have no conception of the great sensual satisfaction which the mere handling of money means, even when said money is not one's own. How else account for the clerk in the counting house, or the Chinese prepossession for the till, or the miser, or the great financier who scarcely ever handles his own money but always other people's money? To have money in the pocket is one of the small but inestimable pleasures of life. To have money in the bank is not quite the same thing, but to take money out of the bank is indisputably a great joy. The pleasure then is in the handling, not the spending necessarily, as some economists would have us believe. It is very possible, indeed, that the coin or specie came into existence to meet this very human need, for though a man might, with sufficient patience, succeed in embracing his possessions—reckoned in slaves, cattle, jewels, wheat, hops, etc.—it is evident that to fondle one's money, or one's dough-bags, is much more convenient and even more pleasurable. For with the invention of cash it was perceived almost immediately that money *makes* money. This is a sound principle

and based on an entirely different idea from that of the late
German philosopher who tried to explain the secret of world-
economy by saying that "thinking in money generates money."
Thinking in money generates nothing but confusion. It is the
handling of money which generates wealth and hence *more
money*. It was such a simple truth as this which Christ himself,
though he was no financier, enunciated when he said: "To him
who hath shall be given and from him who hath not shall be
taken away, down to the last ducat." How clear and unmistak-
able this language as compared with the muddy and maudlin
shibboleths of the stock-exchangers: *The market was firm. . . .
The market was soft and spongy. . . . Rubber was off. . . . Tin
was volatile. . . . Bonds collapsed. . . .* Where is the sense of
reality behind these fluctuations on the big board? Can livestock
actually become soft and spongy? Does rubber collapse? Will
tin volatilize? Of course the men of the stock exchange, the great
world traders, are talking about prices. *But what are prices?* A
price is a piece of goods, a commodity as we say, expressed in
gold or any other metal that is acceptable to the public conscience, without the necessity of being weighed on the spot.
Price has value only to the extent that there is a mobile cash
quantum to back it up. Anything which can inflate today and
collapse tomorrow has neither weight, substance nor value. It is
not even gas, because gas, after all, answers to all three of these
descriptions. This is to my mind the best proof of what thinking
in money leads to, which is the collapse of thinking, or, as Sir
Isaac Newton expressed it, "a vacuum in extenso."

It took our forefathers a great many centuries to realize that
mere weight does not create value. For a coin, be it understood,
can only be said to become a piece of money when it is accepted
without weighing. Of course, it should have, and really must
have, been weighed beforehand; otherwise it would be specious
and spurious. At any rate, it was not until the invention of scales
that weight took the place of a particular shape, such as the bells,
knives, keys and skirts of the ancient Chinese currency or the
tripods, axes and basins of Homer's day. One of the advantages
of the weighed coin, for the Romans at least, was the elimination
of fines in cattle, a practice which had persisted down to the
fifth century B.C. The abolition of this primitive method of hand-

ing out fines gave rise to the word *pecuniary,* always associated with *difficulties.* (The Latin word *pecunia,* which means money, came from the older word *pecus,* meaning a head of cattle.) In any case, all these peoples who made up the great civilizations of the past had a real sense of money, whether expressed in cows and goats, bushels of wheat, hops, barley, human slaves, trinkets or specie. There were no negative numbers to indicate debit. The wealth of a nation, or of an individual, was reckoned in money and expressed in money or its equivalents. There were debts, but no debits! Men thought positively and concretely, which incidentally did not lessen their sorrows. Today, on the other hand, there are people and nations whose immense wealth can be expressed only negatively, in debits. They are the people who think about money, what makes it and how it gets that way. They live in an atmosphere of perpetual bankruptcy and thrive on it. In the textbooks there is an axiom which explains this paradox. It is known as the law of diminishing returns and is stated thus: "The poorer a man the greater his burden of taxation." For, as Confucius long ago pointed out, it is the poor who make the rich, and not *vice versa.* Unless we can have an ever-increasing number of "free paupers" we shall be obliged to return to the ancient mode of thinking which was, as we have already indicated, the idea of a "mobile quantum of cash on hand." Indeed, there is evidence to believe that our grandchildren will yet live to see the day when the solid-gold "talent" of the *Iliad* is restored. For never in the numismatic history of this precious metal have we seen such a consecration to the altar of gold. Like the Nibelungen family of old we are again burying it in the bowels of the earth, covering it with artificial lakes, laying up untold stores of pemmican and ammunition and high explosives in defense of it. Yet all the while this same gold is being shuffled back and forth from one country to another, almost as the communion loaf is passed around in church. Despite deflation, devaluation, debunking, its efficacy seems never to be totally lost. Gold is gold and as long as men live there will never be enough of it. It is the most pleasant thing in the world to handle and at the same time the source of our most delightful reveries. Why then should we abandon it? *Can we abandon it?*

Taking a backward glance at the history of money we are at

once impressed by the fact that gold was the great currency of
Asia. I am thinking now not of the "white gold" of the Greeks,
but of the bright yellow gold which Croesus extracted from the
bowels of the earth in Lydia. I am thinking of the "talent" of
Homer's day, of the dinars of the early Caliphs. What a contrast
to the aluminum of our postwar currency, to the cheap decep-
tive nickel of the United States, whose purchasing power is no
longer reckoned even in cigars. What a difference between this
auriferous Asiatic currency and the filthy iron lucre of the Spar-
tans, or the rude lead discs of the Dravidians and the Malays!
Silver there was, to be sure, since it is always found in the alloy
electrum. Throughout the great fifth century there was the famous
free-silver currency of Cyzicus, the predecessor of William Jen-
nings Bryan. But Cyzicus had the sense to call things by their
right name. He pronounced the currency of his kingdom *electrum,* and he saw to it that the coins of the realm contained so
much gold and so much silver. It was not "free-silver," but a
heavenly marriage of the two precious metals, and it is for this
reason that to this very day the name of Cyzicus is honored by
his people. . . . After a time silver won out; it became the ex-
clusive currency of the Parthians and, we might say, on the whole
that of the Sassanians. Somewhat later bronze, or copper, came
into vogue but, with the exception of the Chinese, it was generally used only to make small change. The French sou with a
hole in it is an exception to the rule, since not only is its composition dubious but nobody can make change with it, not even
the French themselves. Its origin is reminiscent of that of the
obeliskos of Homer's time. The obol, as it is now called, was an
iron spit of such infinitesimal value that it was used by the wily
Greeks only for donations. We have another example of this kind
of money later, in Biblical times, in the form of "the widow's
mite." It is the sort of money used the world over by miserly individuals, and is the last pretense of generosity.

Coins have always borne some sort of inscription, some
stamped replica of the animal or vegetable world. The Jewish
shekel, for example, was always stamped with a sprig of wild
parsley which, because of the three little balls of the parsley, came
eventually to be the abstract symbol of the usurer, or pawn-
broker. Historians have endeavored to ascribe the origin of this

unique emblem to the escutcheon of a Jewish baron of the Middle Ages, but there is no truth whatever in these assertions. The Jewish shekel was stamped with a sprig of wild parsley because parsley was the commonest product of Judea, the source of her early riches. It was the same with Egypt, with the "wheat ducat" of Cheops' time. And again with Nicaragua, her cordoba, which everyone was familiar with because everyone was obliged to wear the cordoba when it rained. Apart from the human figure, or bust, which came later, there were other types of inscriptions for coins, notably the "agonistic," so called because they were struck in commemoration of games and festivals. These are coming into vogue again with the advent of Hitler and Mussolini. The reader may very likely fall into the error of assuming that the term "agonistic" is here used in the Miltonian sense—*Samson Agonistes*—but in truth it has a much more prosaic and practical origin. The fact is that the ancient tyrants had enormous difficulties in raising the money to defray the expense of these great games and festivals. To finance the Olympic Games, for example, was an agonizing experience. Many a Greek moneyer went on the rocks in the attempt. Finally one of the more astute promoters of this great spectacle hit upon the happy idea of making new money for the games and thus the coins which were struck off in honor of the occasion came to be known as "agonistic" coins. They always featured a wrestler or a discus thrower—of pure Aryan blood. In time they became worthless, but then they had served their purpose and so nobody complained very much. For a long time only mythological figures were represented on the coins, figures such as Hercules or Castor and Pollux, "the Heavenly Twins," who had fought so well for Rome. As time went on the representations became more abstract, so that there was scarcely anything detectable except the family pride of the moneyer. The same tendency may be observed in the American silver pieces, particularly the dollar and the half dollar, whereon is inscribed with the utmost naïveté—"In God We Trust." Yet God knows, there is no more practical-minded, hard-headed species on earth than the American Yankee. These instances are cited merely to illustrate the natural evolution which governs the aesthetics of numismatics.

The history of Roman currency and coinage tactics is the most interesting of all owing to the whimsical ideas of the mad Caesars. The antoniniani of the disgraceful third century tell the whole story. They had been so debased that even the solid copper coin, which was the mainstay of the poor freedmen, fell into the background. It was not until about a century before the collapse of the Roman Empire that Aurelian, "the restorer of the world," put the Roman currency on its feet. It was then too late, of course, as the Empire was already on the toboggan. The great problem for the Romans was to strike a coin which would divide evenly into so many asses. Under Augustus an attempt to solve the dilemma was made by striking the copper "as" which was a quadran of the brass sestertius. The denarius, which was the coin of the realm, was equal in value to ten asses, while its half, the quinarius, equaled five asses. The next denomination was the brass sestertius which, being a fourth of the quinarius, was equal to one and a quarter asses. Finally came the copper "as" itself, which being a fourth of the sestertius was therefore less than an ass in value and hence equivalent to small change or pocket money. Eventually the currency became so complicated that the Romans wisely abandoned all ideas of equating money to asses. In the anarchy of the third century, as I hinted previously, the little copper "as" fell entirely into the background and ultimately passed over into the famous besant of the Byzantine Empire. Throughout the reign of the Caesars the cost of living was constantly high and remained so even after the edict of Diocletian in A.D. 301, which had for its aim the fixing of maximum prices. The sad experience of the Roman Emperors has taught us one thing at least—that there is no *maximum price* for a commodity. It also reveals another aspect of economic life—that when the Caesars appear money goes to the dogs. For the Caesars, in this respect, are very much like the Russians: they have no understanding of money whatever. They like to play God, and in their simple, whimsical fashion they allow themselves to believe that everything can be regulated by fiat or ukase or edict. Human beings may perhaps be, and often are, controlled in this manner, but money never. Money obeys its own laws which, if not divine, are at least beyond man's control.

In Europe it was not until the time of the great Swabian, Conrad III, that a coinage worthy of the name was established. Throughout the Middle Ages almost all the gold of Europe was in the hands of the alchemists, with the result that silver began to take precedence over gold as currency. For a time gold was so scarce that it became "anonymous." In France, Pepin the Short issued an edict abolishing the gold coin. Louis le Debonnaire consequently was the last Carolingian to strike gold. When the Popes, under Urban V, began to strike their own coinage, confusion became rampant. The kings, who had been reduced to mere puppets by the feudal lords, were finally too weak to issue coins in their own name and thus it came about that the Counts of Schlick, who were all Swabians, hit upon the silver thaler, which eventually gave rise to the much respected crowns, ecus and scudos of Central Europe. With the advent of Frederick the Great the gold coinage of the Fatimids was restored; they were struck in Latin and were known as ducats. On one side was a bust of Caesar Augustus and on the other side the German Imperial Eagle later adopted by the Hohenzollerns. Florence and Venice continued to strike their own coins, the florin and the sequin, the former depicting Christ standing, the latter depicting Christ seated. Now and then the Virgin Mary was depicted standing on the fifth wall of the City of God mentioned in Revelation. From the time of Louis the Child until the reign of Maria Theresa there was no standard currency worth mentioning unless it was that of the Bans of Bosnia, who ruled for about a century. There were, to be sure, the phenomenal Christian monies of the Balkan states, of great morphological interest, but of no great value as fisc. Eric of Pomerania is perhaps an exception; after uniting Norway and Denmark he set about to reform the currency of Scandinavia. Traces of his great influence are still to be discovered in the small thin pennies which once flooded Europe. If one examines them under the microscope one may still read the letters of the Runic alphabet which were used for the inscriptions on these pennies. In Morocco there was an extremely degenerate currency which was only improved during the last century by the mints of Berlin and Birmingham. Under the Moguls, India turned out a series of the most beautiful zodiacal coins, said to have been inspired by the wife of one of

the grand Moguls. Verses from the *Rubaiyat* often made a striking epigraphic adornment of these coins.

China, as always, had her own ideas about money. For eight
solid centuries she maintained the five-chu piece which was originally struck by the Emperor Wu Ti. Then followed a relapse to
the more archaic form of the *pu*-and-knife currency, which came
to a scandalous climax with the brazen introduction by the government of its own clever forgerers and counterfeiters. From
about the ninth century on, paper money—the first to be seen
anywhere in the world—was used almost exclusively. It is described at some length by Marco Polo, who was personally conducted through the great mint by the Mongol Emperor Kublai
Khan. But for over two thousand years the celebrated "copper
cash" of China held its own, a record which has been unequaled
by the currency of any other country. Finally the "copper cash"
became too monotonous even for such a placid people as the
Chinese, and so the Emperor Wen Teh invented the lead coin
in the shape of a boat, on the bottom of which he scratched a
fingernail mark. It is from this time on—roughly about the
middle of the twelfth century—that the Chinese have assiduously
and fastidiously cultivated long nails.

Before leaving this fascinating subject of coinage I think that
a brief mention of some of the more bizarre currencies of the
world would be in order. One of the most unusual is without
doubt the silver tical of Siam, which was made in the shape of a
bread pellet or ball. This morphological sport came into existence, it is said, because of a passion which one of the child emperors displayed for throwing money to the poor. When he came
of age he racked his undernourished brain to discover a means
of prolonging the scrimmage which usually ensued when he appeared in public dispensing his regal bounty. And so one day
there came to the court a company of Chinese jugglers and one
of them, being rather fond of the addlepated emperor, suggested
the idea of the tical, which was immediately adopted because it
tickled the emperor's fancy. Traveling onward, through the
Malay states, we find other anomalies, such as the spear and
canoe money of the crinivorous Nagas, the willow-leaf money
of the Shan tribes, the exotic snail shells of the Burmese indi-

genes, and so on. Finally there comes the most curious money of all, the "hat money" of Pahang. The coin, which follows the form of the Pahang hat, is based on the hollow square studded with truncated pyramids. It is the only atavistic coin known to numismatists. Beyond all question of doubt it owes its origin to the celebrated "wheat ducat" of the Egyptian fellaheen who, having risen in revolt against the cruel Cheops, insisted upon perpetuating the stigma of their degradation by stamping the hated pyramids on their "wheat ducats." How this stigmatic device came to be employed by the men of Pahang is an open mystery, since all communication with Egypt had been severed centuries ago. It is said, however, that one of the emperors of Pahang, just before running amok, had been visited by a strange dream in which he saw his people again cruelly maltreated and, since he could not conceive of anyone capable of inflicting such maltreatment upon his subjects except himself, he went mad and ran amok. And so, in memory of his extraordinary benevolence, his subjects clamored for the recrudescence of the ancient pyramids and finally prevailed upon the Chancellor of the Exchequer to embody their gratitude toward the late monarch by incorporating the pyramids with the hat of Pahang in the form of a coin.

Traveling over the ridge of the submerged Atlantis we come upon another curious coin, the bolivar of Venezuela. As everybody of course knows, the bolivar owes its name to the national hero, Patsy Bolívar. It was Bolívar who liberated the small South American countries from the oppressive yoke of the Spaniards. Ever since the days of Montezuma the natives of South America had been under the heel of the conquistadores. What currencies they had had, under the socialist regimes of the Incas and the Aztecs, had been well-nigh ruined by the greed of the Spaniards who, like other conquering nations, cared nothing for the currency itself but only for the gold which went into the making of the various pieces of tale. The story of Spanish greed and plunder is similar, in many ways, to that of Persia under the Sassoons. So thorough was the vandalism of the Spaniards and the Sassoons that not a coin of either of these great dynasties remains. Today, in the little gold bolivar, we see the dove of peace which has at last united the scattered South American republics. It is no larger than a fingernail but the workmanship is perfect and the gold content remains unvaried. The dove, of course, is very minute, but it is there and it will remain there in honor of the national hero.

In our own beloved States there was the wampum of the red Indians, which was manufactured in the wigwams. It is the oldest form of currency known to man and is the direct offspring of the shell money used in prehistoric times by the men of the kitchen middens. Proof of this astounding fact may be had any day by a visit to the eastern coast of Denmark, where the most important prehistoric dumps are located. There, in addition to the remains of the Neolithic cockle, mussel and periwinkle, then of "full ocean size," may be found this old medium of exchange in the form of tusk shells. How enormous these shells must have been one can gather from the fact that twenty-five of them strung together end to end measured exactly a fathom. They had a value, up until the gold bloc collapsed, of about two hundred dollars. Among the ancient Dravidians it was good legal tender until the time of the Mogul invasion, when devaluation set in and brought this old shell money down to about thirty-nine hundred to the rupee. After that the harassed natives fell back upon the shell of the land snail, which was extremely rare in those parts and consequently more valuable.

The wampum of the North American Indians consisted of beads which were manufactured from old sea shells, chiefly the hard-shell clam, or quahog, as it was popularly called. This was the dark wampum, or gold, of the Indians. The white wampum, which was equivalent to the copper cash of the Chinese, was made of the shell of whelks and had little value. The Indians of Virginia, somewhat spoiled by the succulent bivalves which abound in the mud flats of that region, referred to the white wampum contemptuously as *roenoke*. Wampum, strange to say, is the only currency we have record of whose value was determined by color. This may be due to the fact that the Indians, like their descendants in the southern hemisphere, were notoriously poor at figures. We know from the rope-and-quoit system of notation used by the Incas that number and tale amounted to the same thing. By the same token we also know that they must have been a very old race, since the etymology of the word *tale* always includes the notion of number, which the Chinese, who are again a very old people, have preserved in their word *tael*. It goes to show, if we pursue the question far enough, that in the long run men will always prefer payment in kind, which is tale. All other considerations apart, the fact remains—and it is a distinction in the long and complicated history of money—that our red Indians not only used money (their wampum) as a medium of exchange but also as an alphabet. To the white man who had long been accustomed to books the Indians were at first regarded as an analphabetic people, but later, when men like William Penn and Davy Crockett and Daniel Boone came along, men who re-respected the Indians and took the pains to study their ways, it was discovered that the Indians could read, only they read from beads instead of books. This bead language, in fact, was highly subtle and intricate. A belt of wampum such as the proud Iroquois chief often wore about his waist could tell as much as, sometimes even more than, the hieroglyphic inscriptions on an obelisk. Often it recounted the exploits of a battle, giving the date, place, and number of killed and wounded. Sometimes it was just a mythological narrative depicting the life of a departed hero in the happy hunting grounds. In any event it was always money, and, whether it was the account of a famous battle or just a mythological tale, it could always be exchanged for food or weapons—or, as happened later on, for rum.

We have seen from the foregoing what makes money. Let us now examine the reasons why it has come to be what it is today, which is pretty sad.

There can be no understanding of the present deplorable condition of money unless we understand first of all what is meant by a depression, as the history of money in our time is nothing but one series of depressions after another. We find at the very outset that, in order to avoid using such a gloomy word as depression, the economist makes use of the phrase "business cycle." What he means by this is that business has its ups and downs. Sometimes these cyclical fluctuations, as they are called, are rhythmical, sometimes they are only quasi-rhythmical. But in any case the law is that whatever goes up must come down again. This is such a natural phenomenon, so simple to grasp, that it has always been a source of amazement to the writer that men should rack their brains trying to find a way to eliminate these cycles, or to smooth them out. It is almost like expecting the heart to beat without going through the rigmarole of systole and diastole. Money, as we have said before, is as much a part of life as life itself, and it obeys its own laws.

When a country is prosperous it must pay for its prosperity by getting ill. If it is rich enough to afford a good doctor it may recover, but that is not to say that it will remain healthy and prosperous forever. No, one day it must go the way of all flesh and die. The money may live on, just as the cells of the body live on after death, undergoing mysterious transformations and eventually creating new forms of life. But men of affairs, practical and hard-headed though they may appear to be, are often loath to admit these facts. The wealthier ones display a tendency to run up idle bank balances, as though to prolong their private prosperity by identifying themselves with their wealth. But just as we know that even in sleep time runs on and with time nature takes her course, so we ought to realize that money never rests idle, even though it be locked in a vault. Money is always active, either constructively or destructively. When it is destructively active we have depressions. Usually we have more depressions than prosperity, which is only natural when we reflect that man himself has always been more destructive than constructive. Man would like to shift the burden of his guilt and make money the root of all evil, but as the Pope himself has said—*money is not the source of evil!* Money is the evidence of wealth, and wealth is temporal, evanescent and highly fluctuating. That is the most we can say against money.

There is, of course, an unequal distribution of wealth. Some aver that all our ills are directly traceable to this lamentable fact. There are some who would destroy wealth altogether in order that we may be equally miserable before the Lord. For this point of view there is this to be said—that it would at least develop our sympathies, which are now at a notoriously low ebb. Money, however, is only theoretically related to wealth. In the realm of theory it is true that "action and reaction are equal and opposite," but money is more than a theory, and wealth, even if it is not money, is at any rate something real. What is needed above everything is a clear conception of *money*.

The dilemma in which we find ourselves today is that no matter how much we increase the purchasing power of the wage earner he never has enough. If he has enough money to own a Ford he wants a Packard; if he has a Packard he wants a Rolls Royce, and if he has a Rolls Royce he wants an aeroplane. To have this or that—the object of one's desire, as we say—one must have money. Where is the money to come from? Not from the sky, certainly. Money must be made, as all other things are made. For that a certain kind of intelligence is required, which fortunately most men are lacking in. Men imagine that they need money, that if they had it they could satisfy their desires, cure their ills, insure their old age, and so on. Nothing could be farther from the truth. For if it were so that money could accomplish all these miracles, then the happiest man on earth would be the millionaire, which is obviously an untruth. Naturally those who have neither enough to eat nor a place to sleep are just as miserable as the millionaire, perhaps even more miserable, though it is difficult at times to say with certainty. As always, the golden mean obtains. He is sure to be more happy who has eaten well and slept well and has besides a little money in his jeans. Such men are rare to find for the simple reason that most men are incapable of appreciating the wisdom of such a simple truth. The worker thinks he would be better off if he were running the factory; the owner of the factory thinks he would be better off if he were a financier; and the financier *knows* he would be better off if he were clean out of the bloody mess and living the simple life. Clearly, as the Pope has said, money is *not* the root of all evil! The evil is in us, in our dissatisfaction with the condition of life we find ourselves in.

Is there a remedy? No, none whatever. The man who has money will lie awake nights thinking about his money—how to hold on to it, or how to increase it. The man who has none will also lie awake, thinking how to get it and what he will do with it when he gets it. If it were not money which kept men on tenterhooks, it would be something else. It has been said that all wars are economic wars, which is true if for no other reason than that man has had little time to think of anything else but the necessities of life. To suppose that there will come a time when we shall have economic peace and security, or any other kind of peace and security, is the delusion of idealists. The man who has a full belly and a comfortable place to sleep would like to believe that this soothing condition will last forever. But nothing lasts forever, whether we are active about it or inactive about it. Whether a man has talent or wealth, he creates envy and dissatisfaction in those who have not, and thus a polarity is established which keeps men perpetually at loggerheads.

Yesterday we were on the gold standard. Today we are off it. Has the situation improved? Not visibly. The error which financiers as well as other people make is to suppose that every problem has its solution. In geometry yes, because it is a closed system and purely abstract. But finance, especially high finance, is identified with life—and life admits of no solutions. The best that we may hope for is that our minds shall be diverted and our activities stimulated. When a war breaks out those who are not killed or engaged in killing are kept busy feeding, clothing and arming those who are fighting. When the slaughter is concluded a general state of bankruptcy is declared. In olden times wars were conducted for booty. To rape and plunder: that was the motivating idea. In any case, it was worth a man's while to go to war. In addition to death and mutilation modern warfare means bankruptcy, revolution, Spanish influenza, cooties, syphilis, and iron medals or ribbons of no intrinsic value. There are no victors and no vanquished; both sides are usually demoralized. Even the peoples who do not participate often become demoralized, because they are geared up to such a frenzy of activity that when peace is declared they are unable to apply the brakes. They go on overproducing, as we say, until finally there is a panic which is always followed by a severe depression. When all the obvious reasons for explaining the depression have been exhausted, there usually arises a professor of economics who proves beyond peradventure of a doubt that the planet Venus or the planet Uranus was the cause of it all. Meanwhile the people, who have had a bellyful of explanations, overthrow their governments and set up new governments. The new government is always said to be run in the interests of the people. But new governments soon become old governments and the people are usually where they were before, which is in the ditch. Often with the appearance of the new government a new currency is established, and then everybody is happy for a while because the new money is presumed to possess magic properties. And while the faith lasts the new money does seem to have magic power—but faith dies as does everything else. Soon there is poverty again, and injustice, and then war or revolution or both. And then death and mutilation and bankruptcy and cooties and Spanish influenza.

Money is one of the insoluble problems of life. Men of theory will tell you that it is unnecessary, but men of theory are generally very ignorant fellows. Often they have never had any money, and if they had it they wouldn't know what to do with it. The last thing in the world to occur to their minds would be to *spend* it. And yet that is the chief satisfaction which money affords. Whoever has money, let him put it in circulation! When money circulates freely it attains a velocity. Economists call it a "circuit velocity," meaning thereby that it always reverts to the spender, usually doubled or tripled. It blesseth him that giveth and him that receiveth. This principle of spending, which is often referred to as the "boomerang" principle, is what made the Caesars distinguished and is why their names will remain forever illustrious. They knew the value, psychologically, of keeping money in circulation. Our own General Grant likewise understood the value of this principle. Was it not just before the decisive battle of Antietam that he ordered President Lincoln to get busy and have the men of the Treasury Department turn out more scrip? "Better scrip," he said, "than no money at all." And he was right, so far as winning the Civil War goes. In private life he appears to have managed his money less well. Some even say he died a pauper. But that is neither here nor there, as Shakespeare says. The important thing for every man to learn is that money is not to be despised. If a man be fortunate enough to have a little gold in his possession, let him put a value on it. The value of gold is not thirty-six dollars to the fine ounce, or whatever it may be, nor the number of asses that it can be equated to;

the value of gold resides in its mystic presence, in the pleasure it evokes when handled. To give heed to edicts, mandates, ukases or papal bulls and injunctions is the height of folly. Gold should be kept about the house where it may be seen and felt. If gold is unobtainable, then money, money in whatever form. For when all the theories of economists are exploded, those who had the good sense to keep a "mobile quantum of cash" on hand will be the least cruelly deceived.

To Read or Not to Read

After writing a work (*The Books in My Life*) which the critics find too long and too disorderly, I find it somewhat difficult to say in a few words what I was unable to say in a single volume. Perhaps the best would be to restate a few salient observations which apparently failed to hit the mark.

First of all, I tried to make it clear that, as a result of indiscriminate reading over a period of sixty years, my desire now is to read less and less. (A difficult thing to accomplish!) With every mail there comes an unsolicited batch of books, most of which I never look at. If I had been wise enough to follow the example set me by the friend of my youth, Robert Hamilton Challacombe, I would today probably have better eyesight, better physique, and a keener intellect. I believe it was in the *Tropic of Capricorn* that I explained how this friend instructed me, all unwittingly, in the art of reading. Up until the age of thirty he him self had not read more than three or four books. (Whitman, Thoreau, Emerson.) I have never again met anyone who could get so much from a book, or one who had so little need to refer to books. To squeeze every drop of juice out of a book is an art, almost as great an art as writing itself. When one learns it, one book does the work of a hundred.

It is not the so-called bad books whose influence I deplore as much as the mediocre ones. A bad book may often exert as stimulating an effect upon the reader as a so-called good book. I say "so-called" because I honestly believe that no man can tell another what may be a good or bad book—*for him*. The mediocre work, on the other hand, which is the daily fare for most of us, I regard as harmful because it is produced by automatons for automatons. And it is the automatons among us who are more of a hazard to society than the evil ones. If it is our fate to be destroyed by a bomb, it is the sleepwalker who is most apt to do the trick.

In my book I stressed a point which seems to have been completely ignored or overlooked. I said that one ought to begin (his reading) with his own time, with his contemporaries. Our educational system the world over is built on the fallacy that the young should first know everything that has led up to the present, and then begin. I can think of nothing more absurd, more futile, or more reprehensible. Small wonder that adults, so-called, have little originality, even less imagination, and virtually no flexibility. The wonder is that we are not all lunatics by the time we come of age.

When I think of what it means merely to know the literature of one's own country I am flabbergasted. To say nothing about acquiring a smattering of art, science, religion and philosophy. How well I remember the day I quit college! (I was there only three months when I walked out.) It was Spenser's *Faerie Queene* which decided the issue for me. To think that this huge epic is still considered indispensable reading in any college curriculum! Only the other day I dipped into it again, to reassure myself that I had not made a grave error of judgment. Let me confess that today it seems even more insane to me than when I was a lad of eighteen. I am talking, be it understood, of "the poets' poet," as the English call him. What a poor second to Pindar!

No, I am not ashamed to repeat that from my comrades of the gutter I learned more, gained a greater appreciation of literature, than ever I did from the pedagogues who clutter our halls of learning. School never provided us with an open forum where we could discuss passionately and freely the books and authors we found to our liking. It all serves to remind me of our so-called democratic system of voting. We vote only for the figures who are nominated—men who, need I say, are scarcely the sort an intelligent person would like to see in office.

But perhaps the point which was supremely overlooked by the critics is the nonliterary character of my escapades in the realm of books. All the jumble and confusion which so irritates the critics is really the heart of my tale. Of what use books if they lead us not back to life, if they fail to make us drink more avidly of life? The very search for a book, as some of us know, is sometimes more rewarding than the reading of the book.

What I wish to say, briefly, is that a book, like anything else, often serves as a pretext for that which we really seek. Books recommended to us by our mentors may, if they happen to reach us at the right moment, produce the desired result, but how on earth can such happy coincidences be predicated? On the other hand, if these books—and I am referring to the treasures of literature, not the trash!—happen to fall into our hands before we are ready for them, or when we are sated or jaded, or if they are thrust upon us against the grain, the results can be disastrous. If "the open road" is the way to take in journeying through life, surely the same applies to reading. Let it be an adventure! Let it *happen*! Enough buttons are being pushed every day to make this world increasingly unfit to live in!

What we all hope, in reaching for a book, is to meet a man after our own heart, to experience tragedies and delights which we ourselves lack the courage to invite, to dream dreams which will render life more hallucinating, perhaps also to discover a philosophy of life which will make us more adequate in meeting the trials and ordeals which beset us. To merely add to our store of knowledge or improve our culture—whatever that may mean— seems worthless to me. I would rather see a man moved to crime, if he cannot be otherwise moved, than to see him grow more and more bookish.

But perhaps the greatest thing to be gained from the reading of books is the desire to truly communicate with one's fellow man. To read a book properly is to wake up and live, to acquire a renewed interest in one's neighbors, more especially those who are alien to us in every way. Never has there been such a plethora of books and never has there been such an abysmal indifference to the plight of our fellow man. Or such little ability to think and act for oneself.

On the whole, I must say, I have found better men—better in every sense of the word—among the uncultured than among the cultured ones of this world. The most monstrous crimes against humanity are being committed every day by those who have had all the advantages of learning. By making people more literate, more book conscious, we can hardly say that we are thereby making better citizens of them.

A book is no better than, and usually not as good as, a rock, a tree, a creature of the wild, a wisp of cloud, a wave, or a shadow on the wall. We who make books are indebted not to books but to the things which impel men to write books: earth, air, fire and water. If there were not a common source from which author and reader alike draw, there would be no books. Would it be such a calamity, a world without books? Could we not still communicate our joys, our discoveries, by word of mouth? Falling back on the tongue there would be no need to destroy whole forests, mar the landscape, befoul the air, or dull the minds and bodies of those who toil to provide us with mental and spiritual fodder in the form of books.

Lime Twigs and Treachery

(Chapter One)

"Ah, hapless birdie, thou wilt fly no more!"

We bring them into the world, we remark on their purity and innocence, and then we abandon them to their cruel fate.

Who are the children and who are the adults?

From the moment they enter our world they are the victims of ignorance, superstition, cruelty, hypocrisy, tyranny and neglect. What chance have they to defend themselves? If they are angels they will be crucified; if individuals, maimed and tortured. And if they are born "bent," where is the hand that will straighten them?

They are doomed, as we who brought them into the world are doomed. The "savage" has a chance, if he remains in his milieu; over untold millennia he has demonstrated that he can adjust, withstand, endure and abide. With us, every day that passes hastens our destruction. But must we murder our off-spring as well?

No! Don't! Stop it! It begins with the cradle.

Discipline. As if *we* knew what was good for them. "Theirs not to ask the reason why . . ." Do it, take it, eat it! We say so. *We know.*

Now then, are you going to be a good little boy or a bad little boy? The culprit doesn't know what to answer. He has been tried, judged, condemned before he can open his mouth.

He will be a bad little boy—it's more natural.

Whatever adults do, say or teach I find questionable. What have they thought out for themselves? Wherein have they proved their freedom, their understanding, their right to command, to judge, to punish, to thwart?

161

It would be more seemly, considering what a mess each and every one of us has made of his life, to not play God twenty-four hours of the day. To say sometimes, in answer to a question: "I don't know. What is your opinion?" We know so very little, any of us, about anything.

Though the child does not expect such an answer he is only too well aware of how little we know, how bigoted and narrow-minded we are, how insensitive, unimaginative, impatient and intolerant. He also knows how cowardly we are. He never sits with hands folded while the Supreme Court makes its labored, tardy decision; he protests energetically, he proclaims the injustice he senses. For which he gets it in the neck.

And when he asks why *we* don't do something—about this evil or that—can you answer him honestly? Can you explain clearly and meaningfully why men are left to rot in prison, why they are tortured for believing other than they should, why this, why that? Can you tell him what civilization is? Do you know? Or will you be content to tell him what was told you?

Are you certain that the earth revolves around the sun? Can you define motion? Can you swear that the composition of a distant planet is such and such? Are you even sure that the sun is a ball of fire?

The men from whom you get your answers are not so cocksure. There are no absolutes any more. There is theory and there is speculation. And experimentation. All kinds of proofs, too. Proofs! How we love that word!

Yet everything is a flux, everything is contestable and disputable, subject to perpetual proof and disproof. Even God. Where the child is concerned, nothing must be left in doubt. He must be given the answer, even if we have to ram it down his throat. When it comes to truth, that is something else. With regard to certain matters he is not to hear the truth until he is able to swallow it. And then it is already too late. He has already discovered some distorted, disillusioning kind of truth which turns everything sour. Not the truth that shall make ye free! This truth he will never learn—unless he rebels, unless he renounces your authority, unless he disowns you.

You write books which you force him to read—history, science, religion, philosophy—and in these books you lie, you distort, you pretend, you assume divine omniscience. You never tell the truth about your country, your gods, your heroes, your discoveries and inventions. You would have him believe that the sun rises and sets in his mother's arse.

Whatever lies outside your field of touch or vision is perverted. "Love thy fellow man!" you exclaim, but you don't trust your fellow man, you don't respect him, you don't take counsel with him, you don't tolerate his deviations. We are what we are. *Dixit.* And what exactly are you, you creepers, crawlers, cringers, malingerers? One hundred per cent what? Pure *merde,* that's what. Fall in, forward! Forward March! That's *you.* Wherever you stand, creep or crawl there's a flag protecting you. Or are you protecting *it*? Answer that, if you can.

The plagues which were visited upon the Egyptians were many and sore to bear. The plagues *you* have unloosed are uncountable and unnamable. No God of wrath visited them upon you; you invented every one of your unthinkable scourges. Whereas the Almighty Jehovah claimed only the first-born, including the beasts of the field, you spare none, not even the grass, not even the air we breathe. Woe unto you, proud parents, you are rendering the earth desolate.

> You placed us at Shamoking and Wyoming. You have sold that land. I sit like a bird upon a bough. I look around and know not where I may take my rest. Let me come down and make that land my own, that I may have a home forever.*

What a race we are, we adults, forever breaking treaties, forever preying upon the unfortunate, forever dictating to others how to live, and know not how ourselves. Each day that we go forth to earn our bread we come home shamefaced, detesting the work of our hands, reviling ourselves for being the lickspittles we are. Pretending that we are supporting our loved ones, we rob, cheat, prevaricate, punish, maim, torture, wound and kill

* The words of Teedyuscung, Chief of the Delawares, at a treaty conference in Easton, Pennsylvania, 1756.

our fellow men. Each one passes the buck: thus no one is responsible. This we call civilization.

Is the child to be proud of his distinguished father, the Generalissimo, by whose orders thousands met their death and countless others were maimed and crippled for life? Is the child to be proud of his august father, the Judge, who every day of his life sentences men and women to rot in prison for the rest of their lives? Is the child to be proud of his honorable father, the Legislator, who passed so many laws that he cannot remember even a tenth of them? Is he to be proud of his devoted father, the Scientist, who spends his days cutting up helpless creatures in the pursuit of magic cures? Or butchers cows, sheep, pigs until he runs amok? Can he respect a father who is a bank teller, a department-store clerk, a chain-belt mechanic, an insurance salesman, a vote getter, an F.B.I. agent, an adding-machine operator, a labor-union leader, a steel or iron magnate? Is this the work of the world? Is this what makes the world go round? How low one must fall to earn that crust of bread!

Parents are always demanding the child's respect and obedience. They demand it, but they do not know how to command it. How can one obey and respect these crippled slaves who return from work each evening frustrated, defeated, ashamed of themselves? No wonder they reach for the bottle or sit like mutes before the television screen!

"Je sais l'avenir par coeur," wrote Paul Valéry.

The child too knows the future by heart. He knows the poor wretches who daily commit every sin in the calendar—in his name. Soon he will be doing likewise. Like father, like son. *Soit.* Only tomorrow will be even more like yesterday.

Poor dad! He never had a chance. Once he might have stood up on his two hind feet, once he might have protested that he was a man, once he might have sworn to die rather than endure such degradation—but that was before he took unto himself a mate. Once in harness he can only bend the back.

He might have dreamed, poor man, that in taking a helpmate he would have moral support, that two could face a problem better than one. But that was a pipe dream. Once in harness, to revolt is treason. Even to dream constitutes sabotage. Mothers no longer urge the breadwinner to free himself of his chains. The modern mother, indeed, is not only a mother but a bread- winner too. She worries even less about the chains than Dad. She wants to be free to be a slave, she wants the right to vote for the wrong man, she wants to get drunk when she pleases and sleep with whom she pleases, she wants the clothes, the trinkets, the hundred and one things which her husband is never able to give her despite the fabulous wages he earns.

Thus the children are left to their fate: to the nurse, the teacher, the empty home, the television set, the rowdies in the vacant lot. They learn fast. They learn that life is a reform school, that the only way to escape is to break out. Break out or die. Most of them die. They die on their feet: they become cadavers, sepulchral facsimilies of Mom and Dad, content to bide their time until their number is called.

"In the twentieth century," said Victor Hugo, "war will be dead, the scaffold will be dead, frontier boundaries will be dead, dogmas will be dead; man will live. He will possess something higher than all these—a great country, the whole earth, and a great hope, the whole heaven."

Was this the utterance of a visionary? Was it the prophet speaking through the poet? Was it sheer vital exuberance which inspired such a mad promise? For Victor Hugo, as every one knows, was one of the most vital men that ever lived.

Who are we to believe—the men of vision or the realists who know nothing of reality?

The very name *Jesus*, it is said, means "that which is lib- erated," or "the nature of reality is to set free."

Know the truth and the truth shall make ye free!

Whose truth? The truth which every master of reality has proclaimed, the truth of God in man—or the bogus truths of the scientist, the preacher, the teacher, the legislator, the poli- tician, the statesman, the diplomat, the warrior, the business- man, the labor leader, the financier, the newspaper editor?

When your child asks for the truth, what do you give him? Do you even think about the truth? Is there even a shred of it in you?

"I do my best," I hear you say. What a comforting delusion!

A child wants much more than your best. He wants your all, your very utmost. What do you expect of him—that he is to make excuses for *you*, for your shortcomings, your lack of will, lack of guts, lack of imagination, for your confusion, your despair, your boredom, your perpetual state of frustration? Or will you beg *his* forgiveness? Beg it with a full heart, every day of your life?

He gives you so much trouble, doesn't he? He simply will not understand, will not co-operate, will not see it your way. And your way, is it really *your* way? Can you honestly say that you have a way of life?

What, moreover, can you truly call your own? The house you live in, the food you swallow, the clothes you wear—you neither built the house nor raised the food nor made the clothes. You made the money—and how!—to buy these necessities. Someone else made them for you.

The same goes for your ideas. You moved into them readymade. Someone else thought them up for you. As for yourself, you haven't the time to think, or the energy, or even the desire.

And you want obedience and respect, you who are nothing in yourself, you who never do anything of vital import, either with your two hands or with your brain or with your heart. You want a free world, leisure in which to dream and create, a harmonious home life, children who love and adore you, and all the material comforts which your heart craves, together with peace, security and unending happiness.

You can't have all that sweet jazz, and you know it. But that's your ticket, and that's what you vote for. Yet you never lift a finger to obtain it. And your children, who also want all this instinctively, they are to have none of it unless you can have it first. Isn't it the truth? If you are unhappy they will be unhappy too; if you know neither love nor adoration, neither truth, loyalty nor devotion, how can they? If you crave freedom and leisure, so do they. Are they not of the same blood and substance? If you cannot stop quarreling and bickering, why should they? Do you address them with love and understanding, with tolerance and patience? Step forth, ye paragons of virtue, that I may see you better! To me you all look very much alike, whether you call yourself judge, stool pigeon, priest, knuckle pusher, pimp, Salvation Army Nell, prostitute or pickpocket. As husbands and wives, as parents and begetters, as preachers and teachers, as workers and criminals, as patriots and deliverers, as tyrants and slave drivers, as fawns and lickspittles, as traitors and perverts, there is nothing to distinguish one from the other. You are still tarred with the same brush: you worship the same god, you repeat the same errors, you mouth identical inanities, offer the same outworn excuses, commit the same follies, the same crimes, the same sins.

Why then should your child be different? How can he help be the same as you, as ignorant as you, as intolerant as you? Where will he find proper instruction, worthy models of behavior, inspiring exemplars? What hope is he to nourish, when you yourself have none? Who will give him courage if you yourself have abdicated?

Lord save little children! They abide. The wind blows and the rain is cold. Yet they abide.*

* From *The Night of the Hunter,* by Davis Grubb, Harper & Bros., New York, 1953.

Let Us Be Content with
Three Little Newborn Elephants

"Everything was working towards its destiny: the trees, the plants, the sharks. All—except the Creator!" Thus sings Lautréamont in the third canto wherein the Omnipotent is made to assume the role of He Who Gets Slapped. But that was all long ago, as Isidore himself says, only to add quickly, "but I think he knows where I am now." (I wonder.) And then, in one of the most revelatory passages of the entire work, he continues: "He avoids my place and we both live like two neighboring monarchs who are aware of one another's respective powers, cannot overcome one another, and are weary of the useless battles of the past."

Like two neighboring monarchs! Or, The Ego and his Own. . . .

*Maldoror** deals almost exclusively with God the Omnipotent One. God in man, man in God, and the Devil take the hindmost. But always God. This is important to stress, because should it become overnight a best seller (due to those by-products so hungrily sought after by Anglo-Saxons, viz., lust, cruelty, vice, hate, vindictiveness, rage, violence, despair, ennui, rape, etc.), God may be forgotten and only the ferocious little Isidore Ducasse, alias the Comte de Lautréamont, remembered. God had a hand in the creation of this book, as he did in the creation of *A Season in Hell, Flowers of Evil* and other so-called disturbing works, which are disturbing only because we are loath to recognize the shadow as well as the majesty of the Almighty. It is most important to emphasize this because, unless the miracle happens

* *Maldoror,* by Lautréamont, translated by Guy Wernham, New Directions.

168

or Chance be defeated, some obscure and innocent printer will, like Etienne Dolet, take the rap and go to the gibbet. Almost seventy-five years after the appearance of this infamous work (which, incidentally, failed to establish a precedent for the Hundred and Twenty Days) an eminent American lawyer, elated over the decision rendered by Judge Woolsey (James Joyce *vs.* America), raves publicly in a Foreword to a cheap edition of Ulysses about the body-blow then (1933, year of forgotten miracles) delivered the censors. "The necessity," says he, "for hypocrisy and circumlocution in literature has been eliminated. Writers need no longer seek refuge in euphemisms. They may now describe basic human functions without fear of the law." This is precisely what the young Isidore did. He asked no quarter and he gave none. His predecessor was Jonathan Swift and his chief executor was the Marquis de Sade, who spent most of his life in jail. Isidore escaped with a whole skin by dying young. In time he came to be for André Breton and his group what Rimbaud was for Claudel and the unknown galaxy to follow.

Baudelaire was a rain of frogs, Rimbaud a nova (which still blazes), and Lautréamont a black messenger heralding the death of illusion and the nightmare of impotence to follow. Had there been only these three sinister luminaries in the whole of the nineteenth century that century would have claim to being one of the most illustrious in all literature. But there were others— Blake, Nietzsche, Whitman, Kierkegaard, Dostoevsky, to cite just a few. In the middle of this amazing century a border line was crossed, and there will be no returning. Almost every European nation, and even America, contributed to this *Putsch:* it was the century of great gangsters in every walk of life, in every realm, including the celestial.

The three great bandits were Baudelaire, Rimbaud and Lautréamont. And now they have become sanctified. Now we see that they were angels in disguise. Seventy-five years behind time, like a derailed train which finds its own way, even through Pontine marshes, cemeteries and the crooked deals of financiers, Lautréamont arrives in America. (He arrived at least once before, if I am not mistaken, but passed unnoticed. Just as Breton moves along Third Avenue, New York, looking into junk-shop windows, entirely unnoticed.)

"I go on existing, like basalt! In the middle as in the beginning of life, angels resemble themselves: how long it has been since I ceased to resemble myself!" Thus he laments in the fourth canto, which opens: "It is a man or a stone or a tree about to begin the fourth canto." It is. It is like nothing ever before invented, not even the Fourth Eclogue of Vergil. But so indeed are the other cantos. They do not even resemble one another: they are angel-lamps. Sometimes they "bellow like vast flocks of buffaloes from the pampas." Or they spout sperm, like the sperm whale. Or they impersonate themselves, like "The Hair" which the Creator left behind in the brothel, to his great embarrassment. To get the true flavor of them one has to visualize this young Montevidean (who "probably died of some respectable bourgeois disease induced by his unhealthy and Bohemian habits of life") pounding the piano as he composed them. They are French only in the language chosen. There is something Aztec, something Patagonian, in all of them. Something too of Tierra del Fuego, which lies buried like a dislocated toe in the chill waters that wrap it round. And perhaps, too, something of Easter Island. Not perhaps—certainly, most certainly.

What I wonder is not how the Anglo-Saxon will take this book, but how the Oriental will. Tamerlane could not have inspired in his own people the feelings he awakened in the peoples he slaughtered. Similarly, Ramakrishna has become for the Westerner a sort of "monster" of ecstasy. Lautréamont, following his own example exclusively, took the European gong (which had been sounding its own death knell for centuries) and literally kicked the gong around. This does not make him in the least like Cab Calloway, or Minnie the Moocher. It makes him more and more like Lautréamont, which (to us) is insufferable.

It might be called a new Bible, written from a new Sinai, expressly for "the boa of absent morality and the monstrous snail of idiocy." The mysterious brothers are implicated, as well as the neighboring monarchs—and the angel-lamp. Nor can we ignore his first cruel love, the shark, with all her fins. Marvelous. Marvelous throughout, and not like the ink spots—just here and there. Pluto rising, God and man sealed in one death. Enter now the Janizaries of Satan and his *camelot* the machine. Enter the weird birds and beasts from North America. Enter Broken Blossom and Broken Brow, followed in strict sequence by that movie which we are still making, called *The Slaughter of the Innocents.*

Rimbaud was doomed at birth—he hadn't the ghost of a chance. Yet no one had noticed, prior to his coming, that the sun was burned out. Now, do you hear it plainly?—piteous moans smothered in sea wrack. Frabjous caterwauls, since the snails (shorn of their temples) are out in force. Oh yes, there will be more delightful little works of fantasy—that man all in black, Lewis Carroll, for instance—but the horse has been definitely disemboweled. Look no more for drunken boats, or Armageddons where dragon and eagle fight it out. Don't look for doubt's duck with the vermilion lips because we are all out of that flavor.

Suddenly, as if a volcano had erupted under the floor of a boudoir, just when France is about to receive her first mortal blow, comes a burst of passion black as pitch. Passion, I say, and not lukewarm piss from a printer's soiled bladder. All personal feuds have passion, even if the feud is only with the Creator. Isidore had one feud, one passion. He was alone. But alone, mind you, and that in a world where even to take a walk, as one French genius put it laconically, costs money. There was no sadder world than the world of the nineteenth century—for those who had wings. What does one do in such periods? One takes wing. One flees. One sails aloft with the albatross. But whither? That we are just beginning to discover. Wing it first, that's the moral of the nineteenth century. And leave the world of snails and boas to sink like a diseased cork.

It is the habit of critics to deal with style and such things. There is no style here to talk about. It was out of style even before it was written. Understand, please, that we are dealing with a Bedouin in a button factory. We have, if you insist, the ode, the litany, the apostrophe, the invective, the jeremiad, the bromide, the round dance, the refrain, the revolver shot, the death and the resurrection, the apocrypha, the curse and the maul, to-

gether with the vocabulary of a diamond cutter pickled in malm-
sey—all in full glory like a six-masted schooner. There is also
the foam on the beer, even the louse, if you are itchy. You will
learn nothing from analyzing these ingredients and scaffoldings.
Someone crucified himself: that's all that matters. And he had
an evil name, worse than it sounds. (But it always rings like a
tocsin, no matter what the language!) You will also find tender-
ness in these cantos, and abysmal humility. And if you have never
traveled to the nadir, then here is the opportunity.

When Isidore took himself to Paris the whole world was roll-
ing down hill. A veritable toboggan slide, but taking place in the
Unconscious, as we imagine. A right jolly *dégringolade* it was.
So jolly that some, like Wordsworth, Tennyson and other in-
fatuates, were sticking their toes through Heaven's bangled tam-
bourine. Then began a series of the most unethical assassinations,
now taking on the proportions of a pogrom. (We're still at the
threshold . . . livelier things are in store, don't fret.) When the
split could no longer be concealed, a fusion took place, a piece
of expert welding, and dream and reality—like two boxers in the
arena—shook hands. The man who had sawed the two realms
apart folded up like a jackknife. It was as if he had sawed the
Virgin Mary in two on a busy street, fired a revolver to summon
the police, waited calmly for the next bus, and then at some
unpredicted *carrefour* transferred to a vehicle more to his liking.
Ordinarily, were such a man apprehended, he would be put in
a straitjacket. Not Isidore. He lives beyond apprehension. He
writes those advertisements in the sky which when read backward always spell Maldoror. A golden roar of pure spite, malice,
vituperation. In it is the roar of gold—pure gold, not gleit-gold.
And in it too is pure evil, not the counterfeit of spinsters and
clericals. (How little genuine evil is in the world! And how much
gold! And what do all these black crucifixes mean?)

"NOW WE ARE IN THE MIDST OF REALITY, INSOFAR AS THE
TARANTULA IS CONCERNED."

The style, the effect, the intent, everything about this black
bible is monstrous. So is the image of Kali. So is mathematics,
if only you would think about it. So are the good deeds of little
men. So are the legends of heroes. And so finally and inevitably

is the Creator, seen from here below. Otherwise would it not be too simple, like a beautiful dream, say, that had turned sour? And why not monsters now and then, in a world packed with fools and angels? In the evil tongue of Maldoror—"I shall advise them to suck the penis of crime, since another has already done it." Not the language of the court, to be sure, but then we are not dealing with a charlatan.

So, in the middle of the nineteenth century, just when the Minnesingers seemed to have a clear field, a time bomb went off. It was like a most horrendous fart. It splattered too. And that is how almost a century later—how swift is progress!—we have a beautiful mauve edition of an infernal machine which, in exploding the caul, blew up the embryo as well. That is why we all resemble one another so disgustingly, even when we are not beautiful and maimed. That is why we are so many BB bullets hitting the same target and always the bull's-eye. The bull doesn't even blink. Nobody blinks or winks. It's a shambles, with the bull's-eye remaining wide open, staring ceaselessly and remorselessly. What happened never occurred, because it was a bad dream. It hangs like a flitch of bacon and rots. It points the azimuth. In the end it will make that most delightful of all mathematical figures, the asymptote. And there approximately you have it in a nutshell.

Anderson the Storyteller

I must say, to begin with, that I hardly knew Sherwood Anderson the man, having met him only in the last year of his life and then only two or three times. I had always lived in the hope of meeting him one day because I was extremely curious to observe whether he could tell a story as well as he could write one. My admiration for his tales has always been and always will be unbounded. Only a couple of months before our accidental meeting, in the lobby of his hotel, I had made an impromptu speech about him before a group of Greek friends in Constitutional Square, Athens. I remember well how pleased he was when I requested him to affix his signature to a few of his volumes which I was sending to my Greek friends shortly after my return to America. I was even more pleased than he, because the volume which I prized most—*Many Marriages*—was being dispatched to one of the greatest storytellers I have ever met, George Katsimbalis of Amaroussion, whom I have written about in *The Colossus of Maroussi*.

The good fortune I have had to know a few remarkable storytellers is due, I suppose, to the fact that I am what is called "the perfect listener." The ones I admire most, not forgetting the great Katsimbalis, are Hans Reichel, the painter; Blaise Cendrars, a French author known only slightly to English and American readers, more's the pity; and Conrad Moricand of Paris, an astrologer and occultist. Had I become better acquainted with Anderson there is no telling where I might place him in the rank of fascinating raconteurs. But I have only the memory of several all too brief meetings, and these in the presence of other persons.

I suppose the remark he made upon the occasion of our very

first meeting is one that all his friends are familiar with. I had
the feeling that he must have said it over and over again. It was
a sort of apology to the effect that he had really stolen his material from other men—not from other writers, to be sure, but
from simple, unsuspecting people who had no realization of the
artistic possibilities hidden in their crude, faltering tales, the
tales he listened to so patiently and reverently. The way he put
it rather surprised me, for I had always been of the opinion
that the writer looked to life for his material and not to his own
empty little head. But Anderson, stressing it the way he did,
laughing a bit sheepishly as he spoke, was either suffering from
a guilt which was absurd or else revealing his abnormal sense
of honesty. Perhaps too, there was something artful about his
naïveté, a desire possibly to disguise the amount of labor he put
into the telling of his artless tales. All the superb writers of
stories, those especially who have a weakness for simplicity,
slave like convicts over their manuscripts. Integrity and respect
for one's métier are not the only explanations of this passionate,
self-imposed toil. Writers of this genre get their material directly
from life. Being artists, they are not content with the imperfections of life, but seek to refine the crude ore to bare, abstract
quintessentials. They strive to make life more lifelike, as it were.
It is a dilemma which will never be straddled by craftsmanship.
The better their stories become, the worse for art. Art and life
are separate, and the only link between them is the artist himself
who, as he reveals himself more and more, realizes that union
between the two which is entirely a matter of creation. Entirely
a question of daring, I might say, for what is creation but imagination made manifest? The scrupulousness and meticulousness
of the simplifier is a sign of fear. The nature or content of the
story is nothing; the approach, the handling of it is everything.
Saroyan is today the most daring of all our storytellers, and yet
I feel that he is timid. He is timid, I mean, judged by his own
criteria. His evolution is not in the direction one would imagine.
He took a big hurdle in the beginning, but he refuses to go on
hurdling. He is running now, and his stride is pleasant and easy,
but we had expected him to be a chamois and not a yearling.

Of the storytellers I have known, the best are those who tell them. In the case of those who do both I prefer the man, the natural storyteller, to the writer. In saying this I feel I am paying these men a greater tribute than if it were the other way round. A story, to achieve its full effect, must be told; there must be gestures, pauses, false starts, confusion, raveling and unraveling, entanglement and disentanglement. There ought to be a certain amount of self-consciousness and embarrassment followed by a complete forgetfulness of self, followed by ecstasy and abandon and delirium. A story should be written in the air, consigned to the four winds, forgotten the moment it is told. In itself it is nothing—an act of creation of which there are millions taking place constantly. The only important thing about a story is that a man felt like telling it. To preserve it between cloth covers and study it as if it were a dead insect, to try and imitate it or rival it or surpass it, all this is lost motion and kills creation. The storyteller is an actor who enriches and enhances the sense of life. The writer of short stories is more often than not a pest. If he is not doing it to keep a wife and child from starvation, he is doing it because he was defeated in his original aims, whatever they may have been. The writers of short stories, as a rule, do not go about their work joyously, recklessly, defiantly; they go at it grumblingly, grudgingly, with the most silly, painstaking effort, one eye on the clock and the other on the imaginary and often invisible pay check. They give their life blood to make it easy for uncreative dolts to pass the time away. The reward, when or if it comes, only serves to embitter them. They do not have an audience—they have "customers" who desert them like rats the moment a more tempting piece of cheese is dangled before their eyes.

What impressed me about Anderson was his genius for seizing on the trivial and making it important and universal. A story like "The Triumph of the Egg" is a classic. (In one of his latest books, *Kit Brandon,* there is another magnificent achievement, a little story in itself about the man who became a horse, who got down on all fours and was a horse for ten or fifteen minutes— such a horse as was never seen on land or sea or in the sky or in the myth.) I was extremely happy to be able to tell Anderson how much I enjoyed the book *The Triumph of the Egg.* It fell into my hands at a time when, in complete despair over my inability to say what I wanted to say, I was about to give up. That book encouraged me. All Anderson's books did. (Up to *Dark Laughter,* when I practically ceased reading American authors.) He seemed to have the real, the authentic American voice. The style was as free and natural, I thought then, as the glass of ice water which stands on every table in every home and restaurant. Later I learned that it was not so free and natural, that it had been acquired through long apprenticeship.

In Anderson, when all is said and done, it is the strong human quality which draws one to him and leads one to prefer him sometimes to those who are undeniably superior to him as artists. This quality I felt immediately when I met him. Dos Passos, whom I had also just met for the first time, was with us. We repaired to a bar nearby, just the three of us. "Now talk!" I said to myself. "Prove to me that you are the born storyteller I have always believed you to be!" And he did. That quality which I adore so much, that mania for trivia (which Cendrars has to an even greater degree) came immediately to the fore. I clung to every word he dropped, as though they were little round nuggets of gold. His way of stringing the words together, of breaking off, of fumbling and faltering, of searching and stumbling, all this was exactly as I had experienced it in his writing.

This talk of his, so natural, so easy-flowing, so gentle and good-humored, welled out of a man who was in love with the world. There was no malice, no chagrin, no meanness or pettiness about his language. At the worst there was a quiet melancholy—never a feeling of disillusionment. He had an unbounded faith in the little man. I think myself he made too much of him, but that is rather in Anderson's favor. One can't make too much of the nonentities; they are the hope of the future.

Others writers whom I have met were very much like their books. Anderson was more than his books. He was all his stories plus the man who wrote them—plus the man who listened to them! You could tell from the way he told a story about some character he had met, some trivial incident which had stuck in his crop, that he had reverence for his material which was almost religious. He didn't try to dominate or control or direct his sub-

ject matter. He always let his man speak for himself. He had
the patience not just of the artist but of the religious man: he
knew that there was bright shining ore beneath the scabby crust.
He knew that fundamentally everything is of equal value, that
manure is just as vital and inspiring as stars and planets. He
knew his own limitations too. He didn't write about the common
man as though he were some rare bird just discovered by the
sociologist or his caricature the social worker; he wrote about
the common man because he was one himself, and because he
could only write about men and women he knew and understood.

I was told by one of his friends that when Anderson arrived
in Paris and saw for the first time the Louvre, the Seine, the Jar-
din des Tuileries, he broke down and wept. The story has an
authentic ring. Anderson had the gift of surrender. He was hum-
ble and reverent. He could become ecstatic about a knife and
fork. He also recognized and admitted his own weaknesses—
could make fun of them when it suited him to do so. He didn't
try to crowd his fellow artists off the map; all he asked was that
they make a little space for him, permit him to be one of them,
one of the least among them. Sterling qualities and so rare now-
adays.

Stressing the storyteller, as I do, I want to make a distinction,
a very vital one, between him and the professional storytellers
with whom America is infested. The professional storyteller
bores me to tears. His yarns are sterile, saddening and madden-
ing. What one misses in them is creation. All that they seem to
accomplish, all indeed that they aim to accomplish obviously,
is to postpone that moment which the American dreads most,
the moment when he will be alone with himself and know that
he is empty.

The other kind of storyteller, such as Anderson, is never trying to stave off a vacuum. If he tells a story it is to create a mood,
an atmosphere, in which all may participate. He isn't seeking to
hold the floor or put himself in the spotlight. He isn't worried
about awkward silences or whether the evening will be a success or not. It's an exchange, a communion through words, by
means of which the unique experiences of the others present
may be melted into the common fund of human experience and

make of a simple gathering a feast of real brotherliness. I liked
the very way in which Anderson sat down to the table on the
several occasions we were together. He plunked himself down
to stay, secure in the knowledge that if nobody else had anything to contribute he did, because he never came without his
instrument. I mean that instrument which he had made of himself. He brought himself along, that's how I want to put it. And
he gave himself! What a relief to encounter such a man! Naturally his stories were good. They were like ripe fruit dropping
from an overladen tree. You wouldn't want a man like that to
argue with you, as Americans seem determined to do whenever
they come together. You wanted to listen, to dream, to wander
off in your own mind, just as he wandered off in his. You felt
that you had his silent consent to do as you pleased. He wasn't
fastening you down with a beady eye or expecting you to smile
at the right moment or applaud him when he got through. He
didn't pretend to be the Almighty telling the story of Creation.
He was just an interpreter, a mouthpiece, an actor doing his part.
You felt easy and rested when he had finished his story. You
knew that another was coming if you'd just give him time to
finish his drink or wipe his mouth. He made you feel that there
was all the time in the world, that there was nothing better to do
than just what you were doing. Part of him wasn't off somewhere
trying to catch a train or organize a strike. He was all there and
giving of himself in his easy, steady way ("easy does it!"), giving what was ripe and ready to fall to the ground, not straining,
not pumping it up, not wondering if it were just the right quality
or not.

And that's how I like to think of him now that he's gone. I
like to think of him as a quiet, easy spirit seated at a round table
under a shady tree holding converse with other departed spirits.
Probably talking about celestial trivia, the stuff that wings are
made of, or some such thing. Drinking celestial ambrosia and
comparing it with the earthly imitations. Feeling the ethereal
grass or stroking the astral cows. "A beautiful place!" I can hear
him saying. "Rather like I imagined it would be. Not so different from down below either." Yes, I can follow him as he strolls
leisurely about looking for a bridge perhaps where there might

be a contented fisherman, wondering to himself what the man's story might be. Thanking his stars, no doubt, that here at least he will not be expected to put it down on paper. An eternity in which to wander about, touching things, smelling things, and swapping stories with old and new comers.

Most people think of Heaven as a boring place, but that's because they are themselves bores. I'm sure Anderson isn't finding it boring. Heaven was just made for him. And when we get there some day and meet again, what heavenly stories he'll have to beguile us with!

I don't feel the least bad about his passing. I envy him. I know he's at peace there, as he was here.

The Novels of Albert Cossery

Albert Cossery is a young Egyptian, born in Cairo, who spent a number of years in Paris and writes his books in French. He is rapidly gaining recognition not only in the French-speaking world but in England and soon, we expect, in America, where his first book (*Men God Forgot*) is now being published in English. He has just finished a third book, a long novel, called *Les Faineants dans la Vallée Fertile,* which will be published at the end of this year [1945]. All his books have been translated into Arabic and are creating a stir in the Near and Middle East. They are destined, in my opinion, to be translated into many tongues, for their appeal is universal. He writes exclusively about the unalleviated misery of the masses, about the little men, the forgotten men—men, women and children, I should say—forgotten of God. No living writer that I know of describes more poignantly and implacably the lives of the vast submerged multitude of mankind. He touches depths of despair, degradation and resignation which neither Gorky nor Dostoevsky has registered. He is dealing, of course, with his own people, whose misery began before Western civilization was dreamed of. Despite the seemingly unrelieved gloom and futility in which his figures move, the author nevertheless expresses in every work his indomitable faith in the power of the people to throw off the yoke. Usually this hope is voiced by one of the characters apparently without hope. It is not a shout which is given forth but a quiet, determined affirmation—like the sudden appearance of a bud in the darkest hour of the night.

In *Men God Forgot* we have five rather short vignettes which give a foretaste of Cossery's bite and fervor. To me the book was a complete surprise, the first of its kind that I have seen since the work of the great Russian writers of the past. It is the sort of book that precedes revolutions, and begets revolution, if the tongue of man possesses any power whatever. Cossery here gives tongues to the speechless ones. Naturally, they do not speak like the professional agitators indoctrinated with Marxism. Their language is childlike, simple to the point of foolishness, but pregnant with a meaning which, when understood by those in power, will cause them to tremble and shudder. Often they express themselves in fantasy, a dream language which, in their case, demands no psychoanalytical interpretation. It is as clear as the handwriting on the wall. In effect, this is precisely what Cossery is doing—writing his message on the wall! Only, he is not speaking for himself but for the multitude. He does not revel in the horrors of misery, as might be imagined from a cursory glance; he is heralding the coming of a new dawn, a mighty dawn from the Near, the Middle and the Far East.

His books are saturated with a mordant, savage humor which makes one laugh and weep at the same time. There is no separation between the author and the pitiable figures he depicts. He is not only for them, he is of them too. In expressing their vagaries, one feels that Albert Cossery is also just learning to use his voice, to use it in a new way, a way that will never be forgotten. To a Westerner, especially an American, his types will probably seem outlandish and ridiculous, almost incredible. We have forgotten that men can sink so low; we know nothing of this abysmal level of existence, not even in our most backward regions. But I am assured by those who know that there is nothing the least incredible, the least fantastic, about Cossery's creatures or their situation. He has given us a reality all too real, incredible only that in such an "enlightened" era such things can be.

The House of Certain Death, his second book, could well be taken as symbolic. We are all living in that house, whether we realize it or not. The huge crack in the wall is patent to every eye, except that of the landlord. The question is, whither shall we go and how? For the vast multitude seeking a bare means of subsistence every house is doomed. The solution, as one of the characters in the book sees it, is not to pay rent any longer. They have tried every means in their power to bring attention

to their ominous plight, but unsuccessfully. They have even
written a letter to the Government, about which there is a grave
question—does the Government know how to read? This letter,
incidentally, is a masterpiece. It was written for the tenants by
Ahmed Safa, formerly a tramway motorman, now a vendor of
stolen cats and a confirmed hashish smoker. In it Ahmed Safa
expresses the pious hope that the Government will come to look
at the house, in order to see for itself. If not, he adds, we will
bring it to you, which amounts to the same. (!) There is one
tenant, however, who seems not to care whether the house
crumbles or not. That is Bayoumi, the man who keeps trained
monkeys. "Why not live in the streets?" he tells one of the other
tenants. "The streets are made for everybody. No one will ask
you for rent then."

Abdel Al is of another mind. He is the one who has been
urging the others to cease paying rent. It is he who finally inspires fear and dread in the heartless owner, Si Khalil. Toward
the end of the book they meet one day in a park. Si Khalil pretends that they ought to understand one another, get together in
some way. "You and I will never reach an understanding," replies Abdel Al. "We have nothing in common." Nevertheless Si
Khalil persists. He is terrified of what may happen should all
the witless tenants of all his crumbling houses think like Abdel Al.

Says Abdel Al: "What gives you fear is not me but the whole
multitude of men hidden behind me, don't you see them?"

Si Khalil tries to tell him that sorrow has touched him. "On
life's highways sorrows are without number."

"On life's highway," retorts Abdel Al, "one sometimes encounters vengeance."

Si Khalil registers skepticism and disdain. "There's no sense
to your words," he keeps saying.

"You'll know differently one day," says Abdel Al.

"You'll be dead well before that," Si Khalil replies.

"The house will cave in on us all," says Abdel Al. "But we
are numberless. It will not kill all of us. The people will live
and they will know how to avenge themselves."

With this they take leave of one another. We wait now for
the house to collapse.

Stand Still Like the Hummingbird

It was on the jet from New York to San Francisco, at an altitude of thirty to forty thousand feet and never so much as a tremor, that all unwittingly I moved a few centimeters into the future. We were making the flight in five and a half hours. It was a daytime flight and, despite the altitude, the earth below (and man's transformation of it) was clearly recognizable. What a geometer, man! Whole counties laid out in squares and rectangles: counties traversed in the wink of an eye. All very much like Walt Disney's graphic Pythagorean demonstrations in "Mathemagic Land."

It was the comfort, the motionless motion, the unaccustomed perspective which doubtless threw me. Together with the copies of *Life* and *Time,* now more than ever superannuated, which floated from hand to hand like the wreckage from some exploded planet. They belonged to such a distant past, it seemed. A past far more remote than that of Altamira or Lascaux. They belonged to the world of things, and we had left the world of things far behind. We were of the airs now, and they were filled with secret vibrations, with rays invisible and of power unimaginable. Yes, though only a few inches from the ground, so to speak, we were already verging on the *carrefours* of uncharted lanes of force, mysterious, magical force destined to alter not only our concepts of life but our very being. A little more effort, another push, and who knows? we might make it. Make it to Vega, Betelgeuse, farther even. Out of our limitless universe and into the blue—the blue of the poet and dreamer, the blue of the mystics. Perhaps into the "upper partials" of some divine musical space.

Like a refrain I kept repeating to myself: "Today five and a half hours; tomorrow two; the day after just a few minutes, perhaps. And then—for what's to stop us?—a speed which will render speed meaningless.

We speak so glibly of the speed of light. What reality has it for us, this speed of light? Man's struggle, ever since he ceased to grovel like the worm, has been to equate imagination with deed. For this the poets and the saviors were crucified. This was the nature of their heresy, that they dared to reach out, touch finger tips with the Creator, complete the circle.

Nothing too startling will ever be accomplished by means of technic. The universe has no armature, no weight, no substance. No purpose even. Neither is it dream and illusion. *It is*. The highest thought can neither add to it nor subtract from it. It grows, changes, responds to every need, every demand. It can exist with God or without. It is like a Mind which asks and answers its own questions.

Our needs . . . What is it that we need? Certainly the more liberated one feels the less one needs. The sage demonstrates it daily, and the idiot too. Just to breathe, to know that you are alive, isn't it marvelous? Looking down from a height of forty thousand feet upon the activity of this geometer of an ant called man, one is struck by the utter senselessness of sweat and struggle, toil and bubble. For all that he has achieved—merely to sustain life, mind you—he has merely scratched the surface of the planet. Does all this effort constitute an advance? The birds wing their way above the din and hubbub, content to ride the wind. They leave no monuments in space, no writings in the sky. Every creature of the wild is a demonstration of faith and joy. Man alone, the Lord of Creation, suffers. Suffers not from want but from an unnamable deprivation.

The world of things is fast drawing to a close. It is inevitable. For the labor of man, his cunning and inventiveness, have been in vain. The mind of man is beginning to look not merely into space and the mysteries concealed therein but to some greater level of being. His thoughts already move in new dimensions. More and more he seeks to live imaginatively, daringly, in accord with his own divine nature. He is thoroughly sick of machines, of therapies which offer no balm, of religions and philosophies which have no rapport with the magical existence he is about to lead. He has come to perceive that life is everywhere, in all things, at the edges of the universe as well as the center, and that nowhere is it absent, even in death. Why cling to it then with such stubbornness? What can be gained that is not already lost? Surrender! whispers the still small voice. Overboard with the baggage!

It seems impossible that in our present state of being we can hope to find out there anything vastly different than we already know, than we already have right here. We seek only that which we are ready and prepared to find. But it could happen that, struggling to perfect ways and means of assaulting the unknown, we may stumble on shattering verities which have ever been right under our nose. We may discover that in our own mysterious mind and heart there exists all that is necessary to satisfy our longings, our maddest dreams. It may prove not only dangerous and absurd to go on breaking down resistant nothingnesses, such as the atom, but futile as well. Are we not miraculous in our very being? Why not think miraculously, act miraculously, live miraculously? Fumbling with the lock—man's immemorial pastime!—the door may suddenly open of itself. The door to reality, I mean. Was it ever locked?

The greatest miracle is the discovery that all is miraculous. And the nature of the miraculous is—utter simplicity. Nothing has been gained by sweat and struggle, by taking thought, by devotion, prayer, perseverance, patience, fortitude—or by sloth, need it be added. Imagine the planets pausing to decide the direction of their orbits! Imagine them struggling to change their fiery courses! *Thinking*—what a vice! *Struggling*—what absurdity! To *know* is so easy, so painless. The ground for any kind of growth and cultivation is prepared by lying fallow.

How then is the break to be made? It is man himself who must break. Up to now he has only been splintered, like the glass he uses for his windshields. He has collided only with heavier bodies, never with a shattering, devastating idea. Craving a foolproof world, he refuses to submit himself to the slaughter which the mind can wreak. Even when he goes insane the thought machine still functions. No matter if the cogs be jammed

—man is that peculiar breed of animal that can function in a world completely mad. It would still be *his* world.

And is it not an insane world which we have come to inhabit? What valid meaning is there to any of our acts, plans, thoughts? Whatever we create only adds to our distress and confusion, our eventual annihilation. Nothing our sick brains invent can add an ounce of joy to this thoroughly empty existence. The more we discover, the more we invent, the more crippled and frustrated we become. And this drunken mechanic, this push-button maniac, thinks to explore the outer universe. What a joke!

No, *Homo sapiens* will never make it. He is in the last stage of devolution. His world of things, thingamajig that it is, will vanish in the twinkle of an eye. The pity is that he could have come so close, and missed. Wherein did he fail? In refusing to recognize the wondrous nature of his own being. He asked for power instead of mastery, for efficiency rather than glory. In time to come it may be said of him that never did life spawn a more efficient misfit.

There may be such a thing as evolution, with all the incredible tedium which the notion implies. But from seed to bud to flower is another thing. There is such a thing as growth—and there is endless transmogrification. One can rearrange the pieces ad infinitum, giving check and check again, but never mate. Or one can take the leap into the blue. For the visionary, the act is all. Nirvana, in the sense of awakening. The awakening being the fulfillment.

Is the future, like speed and motion, destined to become a meaningless term? Have not the men of the future been with us from the very beginning? What is the universe but a state of mind? Grappling with the problem of speed—or is it the riddle of light?—it becomes more and more evident that there is no such thing as motion, or gravity, or heat, or light. Any more than there are atoms, molecules, protons, electrons. Only gods and devils, birth and death, ignorance and bliss. Nothing out there can possibly be more mysterious, more enigmatic, than here within our own breasts. The corporeal is the phantasmal, the shadow realm. Mind *is* all, and its realm is reality. What is, defies knowing. With regard to the tiniest, the most insignificant morsel of this unsubstantial universe, thought wears itself out. The mind can only toy with what food or substance is presented to it; it can never know in any ultimate, absolute sense.

Without intention, though not without reason, we grow each day more metaphysical-minded. The dream of mastery over the forces of nature has finally led us to ask—what *is* mastery? At what point, for example, in the development of speed will it be possible to say that we have mastered the situation? When we are able to attain the speed of light? When we can transport ourselves instantaneously from any point in the universe to any other point? Is there any reason to attain such awesome speed? The only point in pursuing such miraculous ends, it seems to me, would be that in the doing we ourselves would become transformed. Perhaps only through the achievement of such freedom will we begin to question the nature and purpose of all our activity. If mind alone is capable of making these incredible leaps, why drag the body along? Or, if mind and body are one, as we tend more and more to believe now, would we not be there, in body, soul and spirit, wherever we wished whenever we wished?

From various quarters and from earliest times we have had testimony relating to superhuman feats on the part of certain beings. However skeptical we may be with regard to such statements, we are all nevertheless capable of being excited by the prospect of visits from other worlds. It has even been asserted that these visitors from outer space are at present walking about among us here on earth. Some indeed claim to have spoken with them. True or not, the point is that if they *are* here it did not take them a million years to make the journey. Nor, I venture to add, did it take them aeons to learn to speak our language, or any language used by earth men. And if they are capable of speaking in any tongue, what is to prevent us from assuming that they could speak to all men in all tongues simultaneously? Or, in Pentecostal fashion, give the illusion of doing so? Language at best is but a poor means of communication; it is the soul speaking to the soul, the spirit informing speech, which gives words meaning.

This is what I meant when I referred a moment ago to our growing metaphysical cast of mind. The problems which have plagued us for so many millennia tend to change face as we approach their seeming solution. What, for instance, will speed mean when one can travel faster than light, as some sober-minded men of science now predict is within the realm of possibility? What sense is there in developing radar or other techniques of communication when it has already been proved that men can communicate telepathically at any distance apart? (And would it be any more difficult, do you suppose, to communicate telepathically from one planet to another, one universe to another?) And if, as has also been demonstrated again and again over countless years, men have been healed (even brought back from death) by a word or a touch of the hand, sometimes by their own powers of suggestion, why go on turning out medicine men who make not the least effort to understand or investigate such phenomena?

At a certain point in his life Gautama the Buddha sat himself beneath a bo tree and resolved not to move from the spot until he had pierced the secret of human suffering. Jesus disappeared for seventeen years, to return to his native land steeped in a wisdom of life which sets at nought all our knowledge.

We are so accustomed to thinking in terms of death. Yet death promises nothing, solves nothing. Life does not begin in some remote, ideal world, some paradisiacal hereafter; it begins and ends here, wherever we are, in whatever circumstances. Three-dimensional beings that we are, we are nevertheless capable of living in multiple dimensions. That is the meaning of life, that it is infinitely variable, inexhaustible, inextinguishable.

The current desire to conquer space and time is premature, to say the least. It is only another, more spectacular, manifestation of our itch to free ourselves from the problems we have created for ourselves. Never has any real attention been paid to the words of the elect; in every domain, from jurisprudence to astrophysics, the quack still dominates. We make no effort to rid ourselves of our ills, our vices, our shortcomings; we beg for the impossible— to sin without paying the price. Refusing to admit that we ourselves are as mysterious and indestructible as the universe itself, we regard the outer universe as a kind of game reserve to be exploited for our televised entertainment and prolonged stultification. It is the familiar pattern of exploration, spoliation, exploitation, nullification.

What makes it all the more ironical is that our problems here on earth are as yet so ridiculously petty. Hardly have we begun to use our minds when we find ourselves dying. We grow old before we have matured. Worse, for the better part of our lives we are diseased, crippled, frustrated. In short, we are used up almost from the start.

There is one comforting truth which is inescapable. Each time we run away from ourselves we are driven home again with greater force. Every effort to break out only pushes us further back into ourselves. It *may* be possible for man to reach the outer edges of the universe, but the importance of it will lie not in the getting there but in knowing more about ourselves. If we could pick up a stone in the field and truly grasp its nature, its essence, its being, so to speak, we would understand and know and appreciate the whole outer universe. We would not need to fling our bodies around like comets gone wild. Being fully here and of the moment, we would also be there, anywhere, and of all moments.

Much too simple, doubtless. But such is the nature of the real. Why change the world? *Change worlds!* Quite a difference.

Thus I mused as we lumbered along at five hundred miles an hour. Tomorrow, a thousand an hour; the day after, five thousand. Multiply it by a zillion . . . what difference? Are we getting somewhere? *Where?* Is the body and mind of twentieth-century man geared to cope with all this abstract jazz? Ought we not first learn to fly backward too, or stand still in the air like a hummingbird? *And what about the honey?* Before we can get ahead of ourselves we must get behind ourselves. Licking space we lick time too. What time will it be then? And what vector would we then regard as ours?

Buddha gave us the eight-fold path. Jesus showed us the perfect life. Lao-tzu rode off on a water buffalo, having condensed his vast and joyous wisdom into a few imperishable words. What they tried to convey to us, these luminaries, was that there is no need for all these laws of ours, these codes and conventions, these books of learning, these armies and navies, these rockets and spaceships, these thousand and one impedimenta which weigh us down, keep us apart, and bring us sickness and death. We need only to behave as brothers and sisters, follow our hearts not our minds, play not work, create and not add invention upon invention. Though we realize it not, they demolished the props which sustain our world of make-believe. True, the world still stands or spins, but the meaning has gone out of it. It is more dead, this illusory, everyday world, than if it had been shattered by a million atom bombs. We live as ghosts amid a world in ruins. All is senseless repetition. "There am I, and there I always am," as Rimbaud said. Neither Lao-tzu, nor the Enlightened One, nor the Prince of Peace made any excursions into outer space, unless in their astral bodies. They changed worlds, yes. They traveled far. But standing still. Let us not forget that the road inward toward the source stretches as far and as deep as the road outward.

Among other bizzare thoughts which invaded me as we hummed along up there a few inches above the skin of the earth was this one about Milarepa, the Tibetan saint. According to his biographers, he had ascended to heaven not in the dead of night but in broad daylight, and in full view of his beloved followers. He had left his raiment behind, in a little pile, and even as he was ascending heavenward he warned his disciples not to quarrel about his belongings, few that they were. But lo and behold, his feet had hardly left the earth when they fell to, snatched the beloved's garments from one another's hands, and in their greed to possess tore them to shreds. This drama so familiar, so oft repeated, served to remind me that the disciple is ever the betrayer, the believer ever the murderer.

From this I fell to thinking of a book which had greatly intrigued me, *Star of the Unborn.** It concerns a Utopia which comes about some five hundred thousand years hence. A monumental reach of the imagination, this work. How did it come about, the great change in man's outlook? How did it happen that from the senseless savage such as man now is he became a man of peace, a space traveler, an immortal, if he chose to be? By pure happenstance. By the fact of the stars moving in a little closer, overwhelming men by their radiance. Preposterous as the

* By Franz Werfel, Viking Press, New York.

device may seem, it should not be overlooked that for all our skillful reading of the movements of the celestial bodies, no one can say with certainty that tomorrow or the next day new planets, new stars, even more resplendent worlds may not heave into view, traveling from some corner of the universe (or multi-verse) we have overlooked, traveling at a speed greater than any we have been able to imagine, much less calculate.

That things may simply *happen*—let us reckon with that always. Marvelous geometers that we are, drunken mathematicians that we are, nevertheless we are always a few light years behind in our reckoning. We deal only with what is given, not with what is about to be or may be. No, we have yet to come face to face with the supreme Mathematician, the faceless mind of Mind itself. Plot, plan, calculate or postulate as we may, there will always be surprises in store for us. Count on it!

"Up, Josephine, in our flying machine . . . and away we go!" Up we have been going, for fifty years or more now. Yet we do not know, can not say, which way is up or down, backward or forward, outward or inward. One thing is certain: if parallel lines can meet in infinity then machines can run without fuel and men fly without machines and thought travel faster than light and neither bend nor refract.

The machine is only the substance of a thought. Think harder, think faster, my lads! These awesome rockets are just so many firecrackers and pinwheels. Bounce your radar signals back and forth from galaxy to galaxy—it's fun. But why play badminton when there are beings out there, lesser or greater than ourselves, who knows? waiting for us men of earth to really say something? Are you working on the message you will send when you finally make contact with our celestial neighbors? Will you be able to describe in code the array of new-found lethal weapons we have created? And if they are bored, will you bully them into listening?

If at only forty thousand feet above sea level such queries sound ridiculous, how must they sound twelve million light years distant on some unspotted planet to minds which no longer think as primates, bipeds and quadrupeds?

(A suggestion: don't fail to inquire as early as possible whether there are Communists out there in space or not. You might also ask the titles of their favorite banned books. And if they use flush toilets or simply plain 'loos.)

If evolution is a fact, and why not, since there are slow facts and fast facts, just as there are cold wars and hot wars, then it is safe to predict that in less than a light year we shall be able to do all the fool things we now dream of, perhaps more. If in a slow-moving jet at an altitude of only forty thousand feet one can still hear the music of a departed Beethoven, the lullabies of a Crosby, the sugared messages of an Eisenhower or the ravings of a Khrushchev, what's to hinder our listening eventually to that music of the spheres which, according to the men of old, is forever going on, without scores, conductors or instruments? Perhaps in Einsteinian fashion that modest saint Milarepa, seated on a comet's horn, holds converse even now with that delicious rogue Lao-tzu, as they make their merry way from planet to planet, universe to universe. Perhaps they have long ceased to discuss the impossibility of transmitting from one level to another, unless asymptotically, the elixir of wisdom, the truth of love, the bliss of perfect understanding.

Ah yes, musing thus I sometimes wonder if one of the great surprises in store for our bold space explorers may not be the collision with murdered saints and saviors, their bodies fully restored and glowing with health as they move along in the etheric currents, sportive as dolphins, free as the birds, cured of all such follies as doing good, healing the sick, raising the dead, instructing the ignorant.

We are only, alas, what we imagine ourselves to be. But in that "only" vast universes of being are capable of taking form and shape. If only we knew that we can be all that we imagine! That we already are what we wish to be.

Even a peek into the future can give the illusion that the hideous clamor has ceased. Is it because the necessity, or compulsion, to make and destroy is done for? I could not help thinking what this continent of ours was like before the white man took it over. It seemed to me that silence was a great factor in the world of the Indian, that he made no unnecessary stir, that he took the long way about rather than the short cut. Perhaps his mind was at rest. Certainly he had no need of stock exchanges, iron foundries, sheet and roller mills, Krupp works, laboratories, newspapers, mints, ammunition dumps. He had need of nothing, it would seem, which to us is so indispensable. Not that his world was a Paradise. But it was never a senseless world. It had beauty, depth, great interludes of silence, and it vibrated with feeling.

From the clouds all that appeared to be left of this ancient world was the great barren stretch which begins with the Far West. The most beautiful, the most exciting part of the five-hour spectacle. Deserted though it was, an air of peace pervaded it. The remainder of the continent appeared to be criss-crossed by the tracks of a maniac, a monster of a chess master who had forgotten the rules of the game.

So transitory, the maniacal labor of the geometer! Above, all was smooth, co-ordinated, effortless; below, babel and confusion, struggle and ineptitude. For a brief moment I had the impression that I was riding out of it, leaving it all behind, permanently. But the voices coming over the air belied the thought. They were the voices of earth men, and whether they crooned or rocked and rolled, whether they threatened imminent war or babbled of lasting peace, they had the ring of dolts, blunderers, misfits. No escaping them, even up there in the blue. The machine was theirs and would come home to roost. It would engender more machines, more intricate machines, more amazing machines, more machine-like machines, until the world and all its man-made parts became one vast interlocking machine of a machine.

New Directions Paperbooks—A Partial Listing

For a complete listing request free catalog from New Directions, 80 Eighth Avenue,
New York 10011; or visit our website, www.ndpublishing.com

†Bilingual

Miroslav Krleža, *On the Edge of Reason*. NDP810.
Shimpei Kusano, *Asking Myself/Answering Myself*. NDP566.
Davide Lajolo, *An Absurd Vice*. NDP545.
P. Lal, ed., *Great Sanskrit Plays*. NDP142.
Tommaso Landolfi, *Gogol's Wife*. NDP155.
James Laughlin, *The Love Poems*, NDP865.
  Poems New and Selected. NDP857.
Comte de Lautréamont, *Maldoror*. NDP207.
D.H. Lawrence, *Quetzalcoatl*. NDP864.
Irving Layton, *Selected Poems*. NDP431.
Christine Lehner, *Expecting*. NDP572.
Siegfried Lenz, *The German Lesson*. NDP618.
Denise Levertov, *The Life Around Us*. NDP843.
  Selected Poems. NDP968.
  The Stream and the Sapphire. NDP844.
  This Great Unknowing. NDP910.
Li Ch'ing-Chao, *Complete Poems*. NDP492.
Li Po, *The Selected Poems*. NDP823.
Enrique Lihn, *The Dark Room*.† NDP452.
Clarice Lispector, *The Hour of the Star*. NDP733.
  Near to the Wild Heart. NDP698.
  Soulstorm. NDP671.
Luljeta Lleshanaku, *Fresco*. NDP941.
Federico García Lorca, *The Cricket Sings*.† NDP506.
  Five Plays. NDP506.
  In Search of Duende.† NDP858.
  Selected Letters. NDP557.
  Selected Poems.† NDP114.
Xavier de Maistre,*Voyage Around My Room*. NDP791.
Stéphane Mallarmé, *Mallarmé in Prose*. NDP904.
  Selected Poetry and Prose.† NDP529.
Oscar Mandel, *The Book of Elaborations*. NDP643.
Abby Mann, *Judgment at Nuremberg*. NDP950.
Javier Marías, *All Souls*. NDP905.
  A Heart So White. NDP937.
  Tomorrow in the Battle Think On Me. NDP923.
Bernadette Mayer, *A Bernadette Mayer Reader*. NDP739.
Michael McClure, *Rain Mirror*. NDP887.
Carson McCullers, *The Member of the Wedding*. NDP394.
Thomas Merton, *Bread in the Wilderness*. NDP840.
  Gandhi on Non-Violence. NDP197.
  New Seeds of Contemplation. NDP337.
  Thoughts on the East. NDP802.
Henri Michaux, *Ideograms in China*. NDP929.
  Selected Writings.† NDP263.
Henry Miller, *The Air-Conditioned Nightmare*. NDP587.
  The Henry Miller Reader. NDP269.
  Into the Heart of Life. NDP728.
Yukio Mishima, *Confessions of a Mask*. NDP253.
  Death in Midsummer. NDP215.
Frédéric Mistral, *The Memoirs*. NDP632.
Eugenio Montale, *Selected Poems*.† NDP193.
Paul Morand, *Fancy Goods* (tr. by Ezra Pound). NDP567.
Vladimir Nabokov, *Laughter in the Dark*. NDP729.
  Nikolai Gogol. NDP78.
  The Real Life of Sebastian Knight. NDP432.
Pablo Neruda, *The Captain's Verses*.† NDP345.
  Residence on Earth,† NDP340.
Robert Nichols, *Arrival*. NDP437.
Charles Olson, *Selected Writings*. NDP231.
Toby Olson, *Human Nature*. NDP897.
George Oppen, *Selected Poems*. NDP970.
Wilfred Owen, *Collected Poems*. NDP210.
José Pacheco, *Battles in the Desert*. NDP637.
Michael Palmer, *Codes Appearing*. NDP914.
  The Promises of Glass. NDP922.
Nicanor Parra, *Antipoems: New and Selected*. NDP603.
Boris Pasternak, *Safe Conduct*. NDP77.
Kenneth Patchen, *Memoirs of a Shy Pornographer*. NDP879.
Octavio Paz, *The Collected Poems*.† NDP719.
  Sunstone.† NDP735.
  A Tale of Two Gardens: Poems from India. NDP841.
Victor Pelevin, *Omon Ra*. NDP851.
  A Werewolf Problem in Central Russia. NDP959.
  The Yellow Arrow. NDP845.
Saint-John Perse, *Selected Poems*.† NDP547.
Po Chü-i, *The Selected Poems*. NDP880.
Ezra Pound, *ABC of Reading*. NDP89.
  Confucius.† NDP285.
  Confucius to Cummings. NDP126.

A Draft of XXX Cantos. NDP690.
  The Pisan Cantos. NDP977.
Caradog Prichard, *One Moonlit Night*. NDP835.
Qian Zhongshu, *Fortress Besieged*. NDP966.
Raymond Queneau, *The Blue Flowers*. NDP595.
  Exercises in Style. NDP513.
Margaret Randall, *Part of the Solution*. NDP350.
Raja Rao, *Kanthapura*. NDP224.
Herbert Read, *The Green Child*. NDP208.
Kenneth Rexroth, *Classics Revisited*. NDP621.
  100 Poems from the Chinese. NDP192.
  Selected Poems. NDP581.
Rainer Maria Rilke, *Poems from the Book of Hours*.† NDP408.
  Possibility of Being. NDP436.
  Where Silence Reigns. NDP464.
Arthur Rimbaud, *Illuminations*.† NDP56.
  A Season in Hell & The Drunken Boat.† NDP97.
Edouard Roditi, *The Delights of Turkey*. NDP487.
Rodrigo Rey Rosa, *The Good Cripple*. NDP979.
Jerome Rothenberg, *A Book of Witness*. NDP955.
Ralf Rothmann, *Knife Edge*. NDP744.
Nayantara Sahgal, *Mistaken Identity*. NDP742.
Ihara Saikaku, *The Life of an Amorous Woman*. NDP270.
St. John of the Cross. *The Poems of St. John ...* † NDP341.
William Saroyan. *The Daring Young Man ...* NDP852.
Jean-Paul Sartre. *Nausea*. NDP82.
  The Wall (Intimacy). NDP272.
Delmore Schwartz, *In Dreams Begin Responsibilities*. NDP454.
  Screeno: Stories and Poems. NDP985.
Peter Dale Scott, *Coming to Jakarta*, NDP672.
W.G. Sebald, *The Emigrants*. NDP853.
  The Rings of Saturn. NDP881.
  Vertigo. NDP925.
Aharon Shabtai, *J'Accuse*. NDP957.
Hasan Shah, *The Dancing Girl*. NDP777.
Merchant-Prince Shattan, *Manimekhalaï*. NDP674.
Kazuko Shiraishi, *Let Those Who Appear*. NDP940.
C.H. Sisson, *Selected Poems*. NDP826.
Stevie Smith, *Collected Poems*. NDP562.
  Novel on Yellow Paper. NDP778.
Gary Snyder, *Look Out*. NDP949.
  Turtle Island. NDP306.
Gustaf Sobin, *Breaths' Burials*. NDP781.
Muriel Spark, *All the Stories of Muriel Spark*. NDP933.
  The Ghost Stories of Muriel Spark. NDP963.
  Memento Mori. NDP895.
Enid Starkie, *Arthur Rimbaud*. NDP254.
Stendhal, *Three Italian Chronicles*. NDP704.
Antonio Tabucchi, *Pereira Declares*. NDP848.
  Requiem: A Hallucination. NDP944.
Nathaniel Tarn, *Lyrics for the Bride of God*. NDP391.
Emma Tennant, *Strangers: A Family Romance*. NDP960.
Dylan Thomas, *A Child's Christmas in Wales*. NDP972.
  Selected Poems 1934-1952. NDP958.
Tian Wen: *A Chinese Book of Origins*.† NDP624.
Uwe Timm, *The Invention of Curried Sausage*. NDP854.
Charles Tomlinson, *Selected Poems*. NDP855.
Federico Tozzi, *Love in Vain*. NDP921.
Yuko Tsushima, *The Shooting Gallery*. NDP846.
Leonid Tsypkin, *Summer in Baden-Baden*. NDP962.
Tu Fu, *The Selected Poems*. NDP675.
Niccolò Tucci, *The Rain Came Last*. NDP688.
Dubravka Ugrešić, *The Museum of Unconditional ...* NDP932.
Paul Valéry, *Selected Writings*.† NDP184.
Elio Vittorini, *Conversations in Sicily*. NDP907.
Rosmarie Waldrop, *Blindsight*. NDP971.
Robert Penn Warren, *At Heaven's Gate*. NDP588.
Eliot Weinberger, *Karmic Traces*. NDP908.
Nathanael West, *Miss Lonelyhearts*. NDP125.
Tennessee Williams, *Cat on a Hot Tin Roof*. NDP398.
  The Glass Menagerie. NDP874.
  A Streetcar Named Desire. NDP501.
William Carlos Williams, *Asphodel ...* NDP794.
  Collected Poems: Volumes I & II. NDP730 & NDP731.
  Paterson: Revised Edition, NDP806.
Wisdom Books:
  St. Francis. NDP477.
  Taoists. NDP509.
  *The Wisdom of the Desert (*Edited by Merton). NDP295.
  Zen Masters. NDP415.

For a complete listing request free catalog from New Directions, 80 Eighth Avenue
New York 10011; or go visit our website, www.ndpublishing.com